Waverly Lake

MARY SHOTWELL

CITY OWL
PRESS

WAVERLY LAKE
Waverly Lake, Book 1

CITY OWL PRESS
www.cityowlpress.com

Cover Design by MiblArt. All stock photos licensed appropriately.

Edited by Tee Tate.

For information on subsidiary rights, please contact the publisher at info@cityowlpress.com.

Print Edition ISBN: 978-1-64898-176-0

Digital Edition ISBN: 978-1-64898-177-7

Printed in the United States of America

To my high school classmates

Chapter One

SOMEWHERE AMONG THE BUSTLE OF THE MORNING pedestrians lining the sidewalks of Manhattan, Kara Carter strolled with a bounce in her step. Her energy could be blamed on the high-octane caffeinated coffee she guarded with her bony elbows, or the three packets of sugar she had poured in it. Perhaps it was the fact that the horns honking, sirens blaring, and neighbors shouting through the pane of her one-bedroom apartment window had become soothing for her, lulling her to sleep in an ironic security blanket. But anyone who knew Kara, or at least knew Kara as she was in New York City, knew that today was an important day.

She had awakened nowhere near refreshed, the anticipation too much to allow rest through the night. The meeting had been marked on her calendar for a week, after her return from photographing elephants in Namibia for an ivory trade piece. There was no hint to the meeting's topic, but she knew what it was about. She could feel it in her gut. Her photographs helped win *International Ecologic* the reputed Carroll Award for Excellence in Environmental Reporting. It was time for her to call the shots—literally. The stories she wanted to cover. The art she wanted to capture and create.

Her phone buzzed in her purse pocket, the one kept closest to her chest for such an occasion.

"Hey, babe." Marcus Goodwin's soothing deep voice greeted her. "I just wanted to talk to you before you arrived and say happy anniversary."

"Happy anniversary to you. To us," she said. Two years. They had met at the magazine—she the junior-level photographer, he the new assistant executive editor. They had kept their dating low-key. Society said it was tricky dating a colleague, but they were the exception.

"I didn't want to make a scene at work."

"I know." She stopped at a crosswalk, the crowd growing in all directions. "You hate PDA, especially at work."

It was effortless with Marcus. Work together yet separately, dinner together, weekend together. Repeat. Sure, it was routine, but it was reliable. Two years of reliability.

They had technically celebrated their anniversary last night. Marcus had insisted on taking her to Maître D', the newest eatery in the Village, but he couldn't get a reservation for Friday night, so they settled for Thursday.

"You're radiant," he had said, lifting his glass of champagne. The candlelight and instrumental music added to the surreal movie feel of it all. "No matter what tomorrow brings, know I love you and believe in you."

He had done it. Two years in the making, and he had gotten on one knee and opened the box, adding, "Enough to want you as my wife."

Just thinking about last night, rolling the diamond around her finger, nearly brought back tears of joy. She couldn't have planned it better. College, internship, job, dating, marriage. And now—crossing fingers—promotion. It was all working out.

"I'll see you in a few, fiancée?"

The word tickled her ears. "Yes, Mr. Goodwin. Crossing over to the building now." She slid the phone into her purse.

"Good morning, Miss Kara," said Barkley, the doorman to the

First American Bank building in Midtown. His beyond six-foot stature dwarfed her five-and-a-half-foot frame. He glanced at his watch and smirked. "Is it possible you're here early this morning?"

"You'd better believe it. Today is my day."

"Well, you go and grab it then, Miss Kara."

His morning pep always put a smile on her face. She headed to the elevator, a gaggle of men in suits already waiting for the doors to open.

She rode the elevator up to the eleventh floor. The elevator opened as Suzie walked by the front doors of *International Ecologic*, the green leaf logo etched on the glass.

"Morning, Kara." Suzie, one of the office assistants and, quite frankly, one of her best friends in town outside of Marcus, held the office door open, eyeing the elevator.

"Morning."

"That was quite the crowd in the elevator with you."

Kara shook her head. "They say New York has a shortage of men, but I have yet to see it in the corporate world."

"Amen to that. Maybe I should move to corporate." Suzie chuckled, a high-pitched genuine laugh. "Care to join me?"

"No, thank you. You know I'm taken." Kara briefly flashed the ring on her hand. They had agreed not to make it a big deal in the office today. But what was the harm in telling Suzie?

"Are you kidding me?" She hugged Kara. "Here I thought I'd try to introduce a little fun in your life, and you've gone and nailed that coffin."

Kara gave her *the* look—the one she gave whenever Suzie took a backhanded stab at Marcus. *That* was the harm in telling Suzie. Ever since his arrival, she had put up her guard and wanted Kara to do the same. To Suzie, Marcus was either a liar or, in fact, as boring as he seemed.

Kara embraced his sense of order. What was wrong with structure, with knowing what to expect? Heck, her first love, Danny Bennett, had given her a taste of unpredictability and unreliability and all the other negative "uns." He had toyed with her heart, and she learned her lesson. No more Danny Bennetts.

Marcus walked into her office as Kara organized the top layer of her desk. He always made sure his shirts were crisp and ties perfectly knotted. Kara especially liked his choice for her special day—a perfectly fitted charcoal suit with a splash of blush on his tie. It brought a flash of color to his fair complexion. And made her feel underdressed in her navy pants and white high-collared shirt. "Why would I need to cross over to corporate to find a man when I have the perfect one right here?"

Kara rested her head on his shoulder and kept her eyes locked on Suzie.

"Ugh. You guys are depressing."

"Kara, come on now." Marcus slipped away, straightening his jacket.

"It's just Suzie. Lighten up. We're all friends." She rolled her eyes. "See you in the meeting, Suzie?" Surely, Suzie would be there at least to record the meeting's minutes.

"I wouldn't miss it. Considering it's my job and all." She walked off down the hall.

Kara patted Marcus's arm, thin yet solid under his firm-fitting suit jacket. "Come on. We have to get going."

He scratched his neck beneath the shirt collar. "Well, just remember. Whatever happens in there, I'm here for you."

Kara raised her right eyebrow. The rogue eyebrow had a mind of its own when she was confused. No *Good luck*? No *I'm proud of you*? What did *I'm here for you* mean?

"You coming, Kara?" Jamie, the newest addition to the administrative team, stopped in her doorway.

"Yep. Be right there," Kara said.

"See you later then?" Marcus said.

"Later? Are you not coming?"

"Afraid not." He adjusted his perfect tie.

"But I thought—"

"Hey." He placed his hands over hers. "You'll be fine. You're a great photographer. Have some confidence in yourself. Okay?"

Kara nodded. "Okay."

"Good," he said. "Now get."

She grabbed a notebook and pen. Marcus held his arm out for Kara to leave the room first. She turned out of the office and walked down the hallway, smoothing down the flyaways back into her sleek ponytail. The only privacy the conference room afforded was one of sound, with a glass wall separating the room from the general office space. The long table was occupied by five coworkers.

Kara checked her watch. Even though she had arrived at the building early, she made it to the meeting room at nine o'clock on the dot.

"You're all here." Editor-in-chief Rick Simon clapped his hands upon entering. "Let's get this going. I don't want to waste your time."

Rick's bluntness was also reliable—and very much appreciated.

"Many of you already know of the success stories *International Ecologic* has had in the past few weeks," he said. "Mainly, the Carroll Award for Excellence, for which we would be remiss to not acknowledge Kara Carter, who is with us here today." He gestured to the distant end of the table at Kara. She nodded in recognition. Suzie clapped and the others joined, reluctantly, based on their lack of enthusiasm behind it.

"That achievement is the good news," he said. Kara's heart sank. What was happening?

"Unfortunately, the bad news is, well, bad."

Her mouth turned dry, and she swallowed hard. Her hands grew sweaty.

"Subscriptions have declined the last six quarters, this last quarter being the worst. It's been my opinion, as well as that of our sister company, that it's time to go completely digital."

Kara sighed, releasing the tension built up in her body. Going digital wasn't bad news at all. In fact, she had been awaiting the transition for over a year. It was long overdue to keep up with the times, let alone the competition. She didn't need to see the numbers to know the sales of physical copies weren't worth the print costs.

"It may take some time, but we believe the magazine will endure the transition and eventually rebuild its fan base. We have already procured a new generation of readers in the online environment with the little we've done with it so far. All around, we will become more efficient and cost-effective."

"Sounds good to me," Meredith, a junior writer, said.

"Yeah..." Rick stared at the table. "It is good. Unfortunately, in our efforts to streamline, we will have to make some cuts. That means employees."

"How many are we talking here?" Calvin, an art designer, squirmed in his seat.

Rick held up his hand. "We've looked it over, many times. Crunched the numbers. We tried to find alternatives. But we're going to have to let six of you go."

"Six!" Meredith shook her head. "When will this happen? Does everyone else know?"

Kara looked at her coworkers. All five of them. Suzie met her gaze, a look of dread on her face. Kara cleared her throat and found the strength to speak. "You've already decided, haven't you? It's the six of us."

Her colleagues looked each other over, back and forth, like tourists crossing Seventh Avenue for the first time.

"I'm terribly sorry," Rick said. "I wish there was a better way. Of course, once we get our footing back, you may be able to reapply for your positions when announced."

"Reapply?" Calvin said. "I've worked here for six years."

And Kara the last four. But not as long as at least two other photographers.

Marcus stood outside the room, leaning on Vince's desk and chatting. Kara locked eyes with him briefly before he turned away.

"I'm sorry we couldn't do more," Rick said. "We've organized a severance package for each of you. I know it's not much, but I'd be happy to serve as a reference for your next endeavor."

His assistant, Giles handed out sealed manila envelopes. Poor Suzie had to sit there with her competition, who was keeping his job.

No one bothered to open their packets. The newly unemployed huffed out of the room, the air sucked out of their lungs and joy sapped from their faces. Kara took a breath, stood tall, and approached Marcus at Vince's desk.

"You knew about this, didn't you?" She slapped his arm with the envelope. It was painful to believe it, but it was obviously true. "You knew and you didn't tell me."

"Kara—"

"How could you not tell me?"

He couldn't manage to look her in the eyes, opting for the floor.

She sighed and put her fist on her waist. "Everything I've built here. It's over." She turned away and stormed off to her desk. Or her former desk.

"Kara! Come on." Marcus trailed behind her. "What do you want me to say?"

Giles interrupted, delivering an empty box on her desk. It sat there, awaiting the contents of her life, her goals, her dreams in its four cardboard walls.

"Nothing." Kara stacked her papers and camera equipment into the box. "Say nothing, Marcus."

"What are you going to do? Where are you going to go?"

She paused to look him in the eyes. "I don't know."

"You can find something else. I'll help you. We can look together."

She picked up the weighted box, struggling to keep her fingers underneath to support it. "Together? You should've thought about together when you decided not to tell me I was going to lose my job."

"Come on, Kara. It's our two-year anniversary. Let's talk about this tonight and we can celebrate our engagement. You know how you overreact. Don't make a decision in the heat of emotions."

"I don't—I can't even look at you right now. You made a very bad decision by not telling me. But as much as I hate to say it, you're right. I don't want to make a bad decision in reaction to it." This certainly was a curveball. Her gut told her to leave him in the dust, but her head forced her to weigh two years of history. Not to mention they were planning to marry sometime in the near future.

"I think I'm going to need time to process this and plan what's next. Time to think. Which is what I have an absurd abundance of now."

She brushed past Marcus and refused to look back. "Please open," she mumbled, pushing the elevator button. "Please, please, please." If Marcus was coming after her, she didn't want to argue. Not now, after her livelihood had been pulled out from under her.

The elevator doors separated, welcoming her into their cold, steel arms. As the elevator descended, her emotions rose. She fought back the tears. It wasn't worth it. "Just a job," she whispered.

She arrived on the ground floor and rushed out.

"Got the good news already?" Barkley said from behind the reception desk.

She walked by, unable to say a word. She exited the First American Bank building onto Seventh Avenue, the brake screeches and vehicle rumblings hitting her at the same time as the smell of dirt and meat vendors and sweat. Half an hour ago, she was an award-winning photographer with a promising career and a fiancé, and everything had flipped upside down. She made the journey to her apartment building but didn't quite make it up the stairs before she let the tears roll freely.

Chapter Two

Danny Bennett crouched low on his knees, stretching over the inboard diesel engine of *Permanent Vacay*. The thirty-foot cutter held itself well with the mild churning of the waters of Waverly Lake. "Go ahead and start her!"

He moved his face just before a puff of dirty smoke blew out. "Stop! Cut it!"

"You okay?" The high-pitched twangy voice of Carly Fletcher sharply echoed its way down the hull.

"I'm fine." He stood up and wiped his wet hands on his slate-gray work pants. The August temperatures in Waverly Lake reached the upper nineties, with a heat index of swamp fire. But he had one too many a scar from working in shorts during his marine tech certification training days to risk another one.

He climbed to the deck and squinted from the sunlight, the sun still above the peaks of the Appalachian Mountains to the northwest.

"What isn't fine is your fuel port pipe." He wiped his brow with the sleeve of his white T-shirt. Well, oil-stained, used-to-be-white T-shirt.

"Is it serious? Will we be able to race in the regatta?"

"Mrs. Fletcher—"

"Danny, how many times must I tell you? The name is Carly."

"Okay, Carly." It felt weird. She was his daughter's hairdresser and at least a generation, if not two, older than his twenty-eight years. His parents had taught him proper addressing—Mister, Missus, Miss, Sir, and Ma'am. He disagreed with many things his parents believed, but old-fashioned manners were unshakeable.

"You'll be able to race in the regatta regardless of your engine, because it's a sailing race."

"Just how do you expect us to get to the starting line? A tugboat?"

Admittedly, he had little idea how sailing worked. At least he knew motors.

"Okay. I can work on it. But it'll take a few days to get that part in. The regatta isn't for another week or two, so as long as the part comes, it'll be ready."

"Super. What would Waverly Lake do without you?"

"Hm. *Sail* their sailboats?"

"You're terrible."

He laughed.

She threw a towel at him. "Clean yourself up. You're a mess."

"No sense in cleaning up now. I've got one more to look at before the end of the day."

"Well, you never know who might see you like that. How do you expect to find a nice lady?"

"Who said I want to?" He ran the towel through his hair, as dark as the marine engine oil that stained his pants.

"I'm just saying." She handed him a bottle of water, and he took a sip. "You know, word is Kara Carter is returning to town."

He coughed, the water burning in his throat. Kara Carter. The name flustered him as if the ordeal ten years ago had happened yesterday. "Yeah? Where'd you hear that from?"

"Oh, people. Gossip travels faster than the wind here. You haven't spoken to her at all since—"

His phone's ringtone blasted, vibrating it across the dash of the boat. "Excuse me." Perfect timing. The last thing he needed right now was a counseling session over his past with the queen bee of town gossip.

"Hello?"

"Hi Danny. I'm sorry to do this to you." He heard his seven-year-old daughter, Hannah, humming behind Mrs. Warren's regret. "I need to get back to Francis."

It was the second time this week the nanny had backed out of her normal hours watching Hannah. In the past two years she had never called off or shown up late. But recently her husband, Francis, had been in and out of the hospital, and he was the only family she had. How was Danny to argue with her?

"All right. I'll be right over."

"Thank you. I'm so sorry, Danny, especially since she's been having a rough afternoon."

This was why working during the summer was challenging. It was high season for boating, but it also meant Hannah was out of school. Not only did he need someone to be with her, but she was out of her routine. "Don't be sorry. I'll work it out."

He hung up, and Mrs. Fletcher—Carly—approached him. "Everything okay?"

"I have to go."

"Don't you have another boat to work on?"

"Yes, but it'll have to wait. Mr. Pearson is understanding. I'll order that part for you today, don't worry."

"I'm not worrying about that. I do worry about you, you know. Life would be a lot easier if you had someone to share it with."

Now was not the time to go there. He wasn't going to date someone just to have a woman around for Hannah. It was sexist, and it additionally offended him for people to think he was incapable of taking care of his daughter.

"Don't worry about me. I—we get by. Besides, Tracy is coming home soon."

"Oh, that's good. I haven't seen her in what, a year? Or two?"

"You know Tracy." His sister was a free spirit, to say the least. She moved around so much that putting down roots had to have been her absolute worst nightmare. "I'd better go. I'll let you know when everything is sorted out here."

"Thanks, Danny. Say hello to that wonderful girl of yours."

"I will."

Danny stepped off the boat onto the dock. Pearson's Wharf sat along the southern end of Waverly Lake at the eastern edge of town. It berthed around fifty boats, most of them sailing vessels and dinghies belonging to the locals, while a handful were kept there from Asheville residents who made weekend trips during boating season. It was the largest dock along the one-hundred-plus miles of coastline, of which Danny had seen every inch.

It wasn't despite but rather because of the fact that he'd seen all around the lake that he chose to stay in the town of Waverly Lake. The lake formed a loose backwards L, with the town of the same name near the curved southeast corner. There wasn't much hustle and bustle compared to the metropolitan areas of North Carolina, which were only spreading their traffic and smog and increasing housing costs. But it had the essentials right there and was relatively affordable. Not to mention the views of the mountains north and west, the mountains that held in the freshwater like a curved brim of a bathtub.

He drove his dated but reliable Dodge Ram past the town square to the west side of town. It felt good to have a place of his own, a house where both he and Hannah could relax away from the relatively busier tourist side of town and away from his parents. Moving back in with them after Maggie left had been convenient, yes, but ultimately a disaster. The Bennetts, particularly his mother, Beverly, felt compelled to control every situation, including those outside her own.

He turned toward the lake, then left onto Harrington Place. He pulled into the driveway of a two-story blue cottage set a half-acre back from the lake's edge. He had contemplated fencing the yard, but at the age of seven, Hannah was old enough to know the boundaries. She was never left unsupervised yet anyway. Plus, the view out the back would have been obstructed.

"Hey Danny!" His neighbor, Mr. Carter—Richard, as he wanted to be called—waved on the way from his house to the adjacent shop. Living outside the historical downtown afforded leeway for such things as sheds, workshops and trailers, even the occasional chicken coop.

Danny waved back before heading to the back porch. Rarely did he use the front door. It seemed strange to enter that way, as if he were a visitor to his own home. Besides, Hannah tended to sit out on the back porch most of the time, the ceiling fan churning the humid air, the screens keeping the bugs at bay.

"Hello." He dropped his keys on a table housing a sad wilting fern. Hannah sat on the floor at the coffee table, assembling her puzzle for...well, he lost track it had been so many times. The picture of three sailboats by a lake house was forever ingrained in his mind. Almost as much as the fading yellow shirt she sported, the rainbow across her belly peeling off from more than enough washes.

"I can't wait for your chair to be finished so you don't have to sit on the floor all the time," he said.

"She doesn't seem to mind." Mrs. Warren walked onto the porch from the kitchen, two glasses of lemonade in her hands. The door swung back into place, the loud smack a reminder to replace the tight spring with the newer soft-close kind. The kind that didn't give you a heart attack each time the door closed. Unfazed by it, she handed him one of the glasses and set the other one down on the coffee table for Hannah.

"Thank you." The chilled citrus down his throat dropped the temperature by ten degrees.

"You're welcome. Thank you for coming home early. I know it's not fair—"

"Please." He held up a hand. "Don't worry about it. I got things from here."

She nodded and picked up her bag on the floor by the door. It overflowed with markers and yarn and workbooks and who knew what else. At one point Danny had caught sight of a stapler, some rope, and a spade in there. He didn't want to know.

"I've said it before, but I'll say it again. You can keep those things here instead of lugging them back and forth."

The straps pressed on her soft, plump shoulder. "I know. It's become such a habit that I think I'd feel off if I don't have them with me. I might go into a panic."

Mrs. Warren was very particular about most things. He had never seen her without her silver hair in a bun or mixing up her wardrobe beyond plain calf-length dresses. Her commitment to routine was probably the reason why she was befitting for Hannah.

"I hope everything is okay with Mr. Warren. Tell him hello."

"I will. Have a good evening."

"You too."

She stepped out, manually moving the screen door to a quiet close. Danny sat down on the floor next to Hannah. "That reminds me, Mrs. Fletcher told me to tell you hello."

Hannah paused from her puzzle and looked at him with her sweet blue-gray eyes, swiping her honey bangs out of her face. It seemed like every month her hair turned a shade darker, the blonde slipping away as fast as her youth. "Okay."

"You hungry? Should I make an early dinner?"

"I want spaghetti."

It was her go-to meal. Not technically spaghetti, but his famous out-of-a-jar tomato sauce with penne pasta. He tried introducing actual spaghetti noodles every now and then, but Hannah would gag and say she didn't want to eat strings. And that was only if she successfully captured a bite on her fork. Heck, many adults battled with spaghetti, let alone a seven-year-old with autism spectrum disorder. He preferred penne anyway.

The faint sound of a table saw emanated from outside, drifting into the screened porch with the breeze. Normally, Danny didn't mind any noise Richard made in his woodshop. But the buzzing startled him, kick-starting his pulse into high gear. It was a wake-up call of sorts, one that had to do with something Carly Fletcher had said.

Kara Carter was coming back to town. Which meant she would

probably be staying with her parents. Suddenly, the lemonade and the ceiling fan's efforts at beating the heat were wasted, the realization igniting a fire in his blood.

His ex-girlfriend Kara Carter was coming back to town. The ex he hadn't seen in ten years.

And now they were going to be next-door neighbors.

Chapter Three

TUESDAY, AUGUST 4

IT WAS EITHER THE BUS AND SHUTTLE OR A FLIGHT AND rental car back to Waverly Lake, North Carolina. Seeing as Kara had spent most of her severance paying last month's bills, she opted for the bus, which sincerely pained her. Not only was it crowded with tourists talking about "the big city" and sharing their souvenirs with each other, it made approximately one hundred and seventy-two stops, making it an eternal commute back to her hometown.

Waverly Lake was North Carolina's "Hidden Gem of the West." As in, really hidden. The last thirty to fifty miles, depending on the direction of approach, consisted of winding roads snaking up mountains and dipping down valleys. The roads from Asheville were no exception. Minus the first quarter on the highway, the ride was just short of disorienting. Judging by the road names—like Flanner's Fork and Peekaboo Trail—many of them seemed to have only been made to grant locals access to their remote homes. That, coupled with the fact that it had been almost ten years to the month since Kara had last been in town, fluttered her stomach. She avoided snacking on the bus to Asheville and the van-like shuttle she now rode. The hunger made her lightheaded, which added to her discomfort in returning. She settled on drinking a can of soda, the syrup soothing her stomach and sugar abating her headache.

The shuttle pulled into Bingham Station just as Kara glimpsed the flags adorning Dowager Street leading to the square. It wasn't a transportation hub as much as it was a gas station with a convenience store that her friend Liz's granddad had owned when they were in high school.

It was flanked on one side by Lakeshore Park, the largest park around the lake, with walking paths, pavilions, and a playing field with a clubhouse. Pearson's Wharf edged the other side. The familiar welcome sign still stood between Bingham Station and Pearson's Wharf, an artist's rendering of downtown facades as seen from the water, along with the portrait of Sir Walter Scott. *Welcome to Waverly Lake. Population: 4,382.*

The sign needed updating, judging by the rough edges of rust eating its way toward the center. Not to mention the population number hadn't changed from ten years ago. Then there was the whole issue with its name's origin. In grade school, Kara had been taught that one of the earliest European settlers named the lake after his love for the widely successful novel *Waverly*. However, in high school she'd been told the name meant something about aspen trees and meadows, which made sense looking at the eastern shoreline. That hadn't stopped the shops from selling bobbleheads and magnets of the writer.

The shuttle driver opened the trunk. Kara and two other passengers pointed out their bags, and he unloaded them.

Kara thanked and tipped the driver. A dollar tip in Waverly Lake was a decent bonus. In New York it was the equivalent of finding an old penny on the ground.

Kara stood on the porch of the convenience store, scanning the parking lot leading out to Dowager Street. She could've easily walked the mile and a half to her parents' house, but they insisted on picking her up. Making *that* phone call was excruciating. Nothing like explaining to your parents how you failed.

Mom had sounded near tears. *Of course you can stay with us. Your father and I would love to have some help around here.*

It was only a visit, but Mom would squish in whatever services she could while Kara was home. Coming back hadn't been the easiest decision to make. Marcus had talked her down after being laid off and helped move her things to his apartment. They were going to be married, so why not? It was one less—giant—bill to pay, which was harder to do without a job. He had agreed to give her some time to be away from New York, time to hit the reset button. There was no better way to be motivated than to visit Waverly Lake. Plus, it was time to introduce her parents to Marcus, who was flying down in a couple of days.

"Kara? Is that Miss Kara Carter?"

Kara turned around. An elderly man stood hunched over, wielding a cane in his left hand for support. "Mr. Bingham? Oh my goodness. You haven't changed a bit." He had though, at least in age, his stature lower, wrinkles heavier and white hair starkly contrasting his creamy brown skin. But he still wore a checkered button-down shirt with jeans and suspenders, along with a baseball hat. His uniform for twenty-plus years. Probably longer.

She hugged him loosely, afraid to knock him off his balance. He patted the back of her shoulder. "I can't believe you're still running this place."

"You mean you can't believe I'm still alive!" He shouted the words, laughing at himself. "I'll stop working when I die."

"Or will you die when you stop working?" she said.

He grinned, wheezing a laugh.

"How's Liz doing? Is she living around here?"

"Liz? Oh, no. She went out to California first chance she got."

It made sense. Kara had been friends with his granddaughter for a reason. A twinge of guilt weighed on her. It was something to get out of a stagnant town and away from a broken relationship she didn't want to remember. It was another not to keep in touch with the few close friends she did have.

"I'm glad to know she's doing well." A car horn startled her. Kara's mother waved through the window of the green GMC Yukon. It had been embarrassingly old when she was a teen. Now it was a downright feat of engineering it still had moving parts.

"That's my mother. I'll be seeing you."

"I'll give your regards to Liz."

"Please do."

Kara stepped down from the porch, opened the door of the Yukon, and climbed into the passenger seat.

"I almost didn't recognize you, all skin and bones. Since when did your hair get so long?"

"Hi Mom." Kara hugged her over the gearbox. There were conventions in hugs regarding the acceptable firmness and length of time. Mom violated both, squeezing a bit too tight and staying the course several seconds too long.

Kara patted Mom's shoulder as if she was tapping out of a fight. "I almost didn't recognize *you*."

Sheila Carter had sported a fashionable bob most of her life, dyed a hickory brunette—close to Kara's shade—through Kara's teen years. Her hair now took its natural color, or lack thereof, and brushed her shoulders. She looked like a dignified grandmother.

"I noticed the gray in pictures you sent, but still."

"I got tired of coloring it over and over. And it's about time. I'm creeping up there, you know. I can't expect to be a hip mom into my sixties."

"I don't think any haircut could change your hip status," Kara said.

"I'm not sure whether that's a compliment or an insult. All I know is it's a lot easier, and your father doesn't mind. Now let me see that ring of yours."

Kara displayed the one carat princess-cut diamond on the platinum band as Sheila turned onto Dowager Street, heading west.

"Oh my. I can't imagine your father picking out something like that."

Kara pulled her hand away. Yes, she and Marcus had worked things out for the most part. But a wound had been made that wasn't fully healed yet. The rock on her finger served as a sparkling reminder.

"Anything new with Dad these days?"

"Same old."

"And the shop?"

"Busy enough. I'll let him answer all your pressing shop questions."

Mom's abruptness could've been due to her focus on the road. Or hiding. She never did like to share problems with Kara. Or was it possible she was upset with Kara for being away all that time? Kara hadn't exactly been forthcoming with her life, but she wasn't entirely closed off either. A phone call once a month had been enough. It was more than other people she knew—like Marcus— afforded their parents. Marcus had an occasional texting relationship with his mother, mostly about the finances he managed for her.

They drove through downtown Waverly Lake, a square of shops surrounding a green space with benches in the center.

"You know, plenty of your friends are still in town."

"Not Liz, apparently. She's in California." The other "friends" were more acquaintances, or people she had been forced to know and get along with in high school. It's not that Waverly Lake had a high proportion of unfriendly people. But most hadn't had aspirations for bigger and better, like Kara had. It was hard to relate to them in high school, and most likely harder to relate to them now. Sure, she was back living at home, back into its vortex. But only temporarily.

"Wouldn't hurt to catch up with them. Why, just the other day I saw Maureen. I'm sure she'd love to get a cup of coffee with you."

Kara knew that talk from Mom. It meant Mom had already told Maureen about her return and probably set up a get-together. At least she hadn't mentioned Danny yet. "Yeah, maybe. I'm sure I'll be busy though with the job searching. It'd be nice to find something before I head back to New York."

Kara scanned the façades of the shops in the town square. "It doesn't look like much has changed here."

"Not a whole lot. Jessica Willis opened a bakery. I think she graduated a few years ahead of you. And Richard Bleary took over his father's hardware store."

"Saw that coming."

"What's that supposed to mean?"

"Oh, nothing."

Mom stared her down.

"I don't mean it in a negative way," Kara said. "He worked there during high school. And his father owned it after his father. One of those generational things that I guess I expected to happen."

"So you *do* know how that works, huh?"

Not even five minutes with Mom, and she was hinting at taking over the family furniture business.

"Mom, you know that's not for me."

"I know, honey." She patted Kara's knee. "I'm only saying that the door is always open. Even if you need something for a short while."

"Thanks." She returned the pat on Mom's hand. "But I think I'll manage with something else."

"Your choice."

Dowager Street curved away from the lake as the larger homes overtook the lakefront acreage. They turned right, facing the lakefront before turning onto Harrington Place. The Carters' house was situated on the north side of the street at the end of the road. Compared to the cramped boroughs of New York, the spaces between houses here were forests, filled with alders, oaks, willows, and the supposed namesake of the town and lake—aspens. The spread gave her parents room to make noise with all the woodworking going on. Dad could be up at two o'clock in the morning with the miter saw or busting out the sander before sunrise, because otherwise the sunlight flooding into the workshop windows would bounce off the dust in the air and cloud his focus.

The car slowed, the worn yet sturdy two-story, cream-colored lake house revealing itself at the end of the road.

"How's Mr. Rutherford doing?" Their neighbor, Mr. Rutherford, lived in the blue house next door. He had always been fond of the family, and without a partner or kids of his own, he often came over for dinner and holiday parties as if he was a Carter.

"I hear he's doing well. I mean, I've only visited a few times since he moved to the retirement home."

"He moved? Did you ever tell me that?"

"I'm pretty sure I did."

"Oh." Kara was pretty sure she hadn't. "Who lives there now?"

"Hm? What, honey?"

"I said who lives there now?"

"You know, I've always wondered if you ever talked to that boyfriend of yours from high school since—"

There it was. Took longer than expected to get there. "Danny? No, I haven't. Didn't really care to, considering the way he treated me."

"I would've thought, since you're with Matthew—"

"It's Marcus."

"Right, Marcus. I thought it wouldn't be such a sore subject anymore."

"Just because I've moved on with my life doesn't mean—"

"That you've moved on from Danny?"

"That's not what I was going to say."

"There are some things you should probably know."

Kara stuck her hand up. "Look, if they involve Danny, I'd rather not. Besides, if they're important I'm sure I'll find out about them eventually."

"Have it your way."

They made their way up the gravel driveway, tires kicking up the rocks. Dad sat on the front porch swing, one of the first he had built before everyone in town had to have the Carter Swing for their porches. He rested a glass of iced tea on the brown leather apron over his belly. Completely asleep.

"My welcoming party." Kara smiled. "Was he up late last night?"

"You know your father." Sheila got out of the Yukon, and Kara followed. The slamming of the door jolted Richard Carter awake, causing him to knock his glass off-balance and spill tea on himself.

Kara laughed. "How many spills has that apron seen?"

"You'd better stop it," he said. "Or I'm gonna give you a big bear hug so your clothes can soak up some of this."

He took off the apron and shook it out before setting it on the swing. "Come here."

Kara gave her dad a hug. She took in a breath of his aroma. Dad had two seasons of scent, and he currently wore his summer aroma —tea mixed with wood chips and lacquer. In the winter it was cocoa with a dash of whiskey, also mixed with wood chips and lacquer. The brown dust mottled his short graying hair, which was in fact whitish above his ear and in his eyebrows. "I can't believe you're here."

"That makes two of us." Kara sighed. She was the one who was supposed to "make it in the big city." And now, at the age of twenty-eight, she'd returned jobless with no prospects of advancing her career.

"And going to be a bride!"

Kara nodded. The excitement of the night of the engagement had been overshadowed by the next day's news. It was a shadow hard to be rid of.

Dad's soft hazel eyes, surrounded by more wrinkles than memory served, stared right into her. It was as if the sawdust itself speckled his irises. "We all have our roadblocks in life. I'm just glad yours led you here."

Kara closed her eyes and soaked in the words.

"Your mother and I don't think you're a failure." He slapped her shoulders.

Kara grimaced. "Thanks, Dad." Kara always had a closer connection with Dad. Mom was the one who pressured her to stay and take over the business. Dad got Kara. He understood she needed to leave to thrive, to start her own life. But he never resisted a sarcastic insult. Kara loved him for it.

He broke into laughter. "Come on, Kare Bear. Get yourself settled in." He held the door, and she walked into the house with her bags. As much as the woodshop and Dad had their own aroma, so did the house. That was Mom's doing. But she had all four distinct seasons. Currently, the windows were open, adorned with sheer white curtains. It was fresh and inviting, a mix of cool cucumber and beach with just a hint of pine from a recent mopping.

"You can stay in your old bedroom," Mom said. "And when Max comes—"

"Marcus."

"Right, when Marcus comes, he can have the pullout in the office. You know, the other side of the bathroom upstairs."

"I know where it is." Hopefully, the smile overshadowed her sounding like a whiny teenager. She'd break it later to Mom that Marcus had insisted on getting a hotel. She couldn't blame him. The Carters were a lot to take in, especially for the first time meeting them.

She carried her suitcase up the stairs and turned right. The room had been painted hunter green, with a wallpaper border of trout and sea bass—or whatever those common fishing fish were—near the ceiling and on the baseboards. Completely tacky, but it fit with what Mom had told her a while back about renting out the room on a bed-and-breakfast site. Three cardboard boxes were stacked in the corner, and her closet was filled with Mom's winter clothes.

She set her bag down and looked out the northern window. The lake greeted her below, its silvery surface a familiar yet long-lost sight. It truly was beautiful. She had stared and stared at the waves —rippled with the wind in the fall and spring, calm in the winter with the occasional snow flurries disappearing into its cold depths. And right now, in summer, it beckoned with its inviting coolness from the hot summer sun.

She moved to the east window. Dad had built his workshop separate from the house well before she could remember. She had enjoyed seeing the light on, his shadow in the window, cutting or sanding or whatever he was doing, even if the noise woke her up. Seeing the shop now, same off-white siding and blue shutters as the house, same edge of the bench she had seen so many times from this angle through the shop's window, gave her a twinge of joy.

Dad was back at it. She had interrupted his catnap, but it wouldn't be his last of the day. He held open the door of the shop for a young man, black hair cut short on the sides and a tad longer on top, brushed back a little disheveled. He wore jeans and a navy T-shirt, his body built as if he had labored hard all his adult life. Even from this distance, it was obvious he was handsome. He turned his head up to the window, catching her glance for a second before she backed away.

She had seen his face. It couldn't be. Not here with Dad, just minutes after she'd arrived in town.

She looked out the window again. He stared back, a second longer than an accidental glance. Even at a distance she knew those gray-blue eyes.

It was him. The person she had tried to erase from her memory for ten years. The one who had melted her heart and broke it in the same year. The person she was going to avoid seeing if at all possible —and she had already made eye contact. His stare spun her through those teenage emotions all over again.

It was the handsome face of Danny Bennett.

Chapter Four

SEPTEMBER 2009

"You sure you don't want me to wait with you?" Liz stood next to Kara on the front steps of Waverly Lake High School. Students filed out for the afternoon, rushing to their cars and making a mess of the parking lot.

Kara normally rode with Liz, but today was different. Today was her first day of tutoring pre-calculus. Working at Portside Portrait on the weekends didn't earn quite enough money to buy the Nikon camera she'd been eyeing. Luckily, her parents agreed to let her tutor for an hour after school a few days a week.

"Kara, right?" Kara met the dusky-blue eyes of Danny Bennett. He adjusted the backpack strap on his right shoulder and tilted his head, staring.

"I'll see you later, Kara." Liz raised her eyebrows and smirked.

"Okay." It was all Kara could get out, but she managed a wave.

Danny Bennett. Mr. Sweeney had told her she was tutoring "Danny," but Kara had assumed the *other* Danny in her class. The one who—still, as a senior—flung paper footballs and passed notes in class. It made sense *that* Danny needed pre-calc help. Not handsome Danny Bennett from the football team, the popular one, who probably had no idea who she was.

"So...are you ready to go?"

Kara swallowed the shocking news. *Get it together.* "Mr. Sweeney said we could use his classroom—"

Danny chuckled. "It's rough enough to have to be tutored. And honestly, I don't want to spend another hour in that building we've spent all day in. I'm hungry, you're probably hungry, so why don't we drive to my house? We can have snacks, and you can tutor away."

"I don't—" This wasn't right at all. The wrong Danny. The wrong place.

"Come on. My mom's home, I promise my driving record is spotless—"

"So far." She folded her arms. "You've only had two years of experience, and no major interstate or busy city experience, I assume."

His mouth stayed open, as if shocked at her stance. "Seeing as we're going a few miles from here, I don't think my interstate or city driving experience is relevant."

It wasn't exactly all about safety. She hadn't been in a car with a boy driving. But so what? What was she so afraid of? Liz would laugh if she could hear the inner dialogue. "All right. But can you take me home after?"

"No problem." He ran down the rest of the stairs and strolled across the parking lot. She followed him, her heart pounding with each footstep. He opened the passenger door of the rusted gold Toyota Camry, the door squeaking with strain.

"Thanks." She sat inside, and he moved to the driver's side door.

He sat down, fidgeting with the radio before moving the car to reverse. His hand had almost touched her leg in the process. She swayed her knees to the door and moved her backpack to the left on the floor.

"It's not the kind of car I expected." The radio wasn't loud enough to stop the swirling thoughts, so she had to say something.

"What did you expect?"

"It's practical, that's all. I pictured you more as a Lexus kind of guy or—"

"You pictured me?"

Damn her for saying anything. "I didn't mean like picture, think about you—" This was terrible. "I meant to say that I know who your parents are."

"And they're rich, so they'll buy rich boy Danny a Lexus?"

Kara dropped her head. "I'm sorry. I didn't mean to offend you."

"It's okay. I'm just kidding." The radio definitely wasn't loud enough to fill the void. "They did offer, by the way. They wanted to buy me something more expensive. But I didn't want that." He looked at her, taking his eyes off the road for only a second. "I don't want to be that person, that guy who is handed everything he wants. So I turned them down."

"Oh. That's kind of impressive."

"You think so? I don't know. Either that or stupid."

"It's not stupid." She shook her head. "It takes guts to stand up to parents. My mom's pretty good at putting on the pressure."

"Oh yeah? What does she want you to do?"

"Stay here in Waverly Lake. Work for the furniture business."

"And what do you want?"

This couldn't be happening. She wasn't having an actual conversation with Danny Bennett. Somehow it had gone from nerve-wracking to easy. How were they at his house already? "I want to be a photographer. And get out of here."

"Photography. That's different." He rolled up the driveway and parked the car. "Waverly Lake's not that bad, is it?"

"Oh, I meant out of this car. It stinks a little." She kept a straight face for as long she could before the smile broke her resolve.

"You think you're funny." Danny laughed.

"Sorry. There was an opening, and I took it."

"No, it was funny. Now get out." Another chuckle slipped out, and he shook his head.

They walked the pathway to the front door.

"Just so you know, I am saving up for a BMW."

"A Beemer?"

"Yep. And once I do, I'll make sure to take you on the interstate, or into the big city, just for making fun of me."

She put her hands up in surrender. "Okay, okay."

There it was. Right as she caught his eyes again, before he opened the door. He stared at her, as if studying her face. It stopped her giggle. Stopped her breath.

"Come on in, Danny!" Mrs. Bennett stood in the doorway. "I thought that was you at the door. The ladies will be here for the guild meeting in about fifteen minutes. You two can go out back if you want."

Danny gestured Kara to follow. "First stop, kitchen."

He led her down the hallway to the back of the house. It had to have been twice the size of hers.

Danny stopped abruptly. "What are you doing home already?"

The young girl with poufy, curled hair in a ponytail grinned, her mouth striped with metal. "Orthodontist appointment."

"Please. Like you couldn't schedule it *after* school."

"Don't be jealous I'm a genius." She grabbed an orange off the counter. "Who's your girlfriend?"

Danny shook his head. "This is my tutor, Kara. Kara, this is my deranged sister, Tracy."

Tracy stepped closer. "I guess you want me to leave you two alone?"

"How about for eternity?" Danny joked.

Tracy brushed by him, pinching him in the arm and taking off before he could retaliate. Kara laughed at the sibling rivalry.

"You think she's funny, huh?" Danny grabbed chips from a cabinet. "I'm guessing you don't have siblings then."

"Nope, I don't. Have siblings, that is."

As she stared at him, in disbelief she was in his house, choosing which snack to pick, she kept calm. She only had to make it through the rest of the hour. Just one hour. Then do it over again two other times a week, for who knew how many weeks in the school year. How hard could that be?

He handed her a cold soda, her fingers accidentally touching his and letting go of the can. It hit the floor, bursting into a spray of sugary fizz.

Kara wanted to cry in embarrassment. As Danny reassured her it was okay and helped clean up, Kara was certain of one thing.

This was going to be the longest hour of her life.

Chapter Five

It took Kara more than a minute to compose herself. What was Danny doing here? And why would Dad be all chummy with him when Danny had hurt her? Sure, it was ten years ago, but still.

After a few deep breaths, Kara checked the mirror on the back of her bedroom door. At least Mom hadn't moved that. She pulled her hair back in a quick, low ponytail. It did little to erase the last eighteen hours on a bus. She walked down the stairs and out the front door. She was an adult. She could handle this. Just get it over with. Rip the Band-Aid off. Her compressed anger swelled with each step. Her short-sleeved shirt clung to her, either from the humidity—which she clearly was not used to anymore—or her emotions. By the time she reached the shop door, she felt like shouting.

"Dad, what's going on?" She fully expected Danny to be caught off guard. It would only be right, after all, since she had been.

"Oh hey, Kare Bear," Dad said. "Did you come to check out the shop?"

She folded her arms. Had she been seeing things? It was just Dad and his woodwork, pieces of furniture in all sorts of stages of completion.

"Dad."

"Yes?" He half-sat on a high stool, fidgeting with sandpaper on a block of wood held tight in a vise. Her head commiserated with the wood.

"Was that...Danny Bennett I saw over here a minute ago?"

"Yes." He continued sanding, not looking up.

"What was he doing here?"

"Oh, just checking in on a piece I'm doing for him."

"You're making furniture for Danny Bennett?"

Dad stood up and faced her. "Technically, it's for Hannah. He ordered a piece, and I'm fulfilling that order. That's kind of how this business works." He winked.

"Who is Hannah?" Her voice sounded weak, betraying her. She wasn't supposed to care who Hannah was. *So don't come out that way, voice.*

"Has your mother not told you anything the last ten years?"

"She has. Some things."

"Hm. She tells me that any time she brings up Danny, you change the subject."

"I—not all the time." She shook her head way too much for the words to be believable. In fact, she wanted to switch the subject right now.

She rummaged through the shop, the sawdust slippery under the soles of her shoes. It was exactly as she had remembered. Worktables stretched down the length of the sidewalls. All but the west windows were covered up with shades that glowed amber when the sun hit them. It made the whole room look like the color of lumber, like using a copper-toned filter on a photo.

A long set of objects stretched over a piece the back half of the shop. It had slats arranged parallel to each other every foot or so, each slat curved like the vertebra of a whale. "What is this? Is this something somebody ordered?"

"That? No." He wiped his hands in a towel and set it on a table. "Something I'm hoping to get into." He moved his hands above the object. "Imagine filling across here. Follow the curve all the way down. Can you guess what it is?"

It was amazing she hadn't realized it sooner. That shape was embedded in her memory. She had spent half her childhood knowing its nuances in the waves and how the wind could be harnessed to make it move the way she wanted it to. "Is that...the hull of a boat?"

"Sure is." His smile beamed with pride.

"You're making a sailboat?"

"Well, to be honest, I've already made a sailboat. This is the next in the line."

"You've finished one? Where is it?" The view from the west windows showed no signs of a sailboat, or any vessel, on their short dock.

"Over at Pearson's Wharf."

"Oh. What's it doing there?"

"When I heard you were coming home, I moved it on over."

"Why? You didn't think I'd want to see it?"

Dad's smile turned upward in mischief. He was up to something, and it had to do with that sailboat. And really, the only time he'd sail out of Pearson's was... No. Impossible. He couldn't. Not after last time.

"Better location for regatta practice."

Kara shook her head. "Huh-uh. Nope."

"What are you talking about?"

"I know what you mean, Dad. I know that look. I know how you think. It's not happening."

"Kare Bear..."

"You know what happened last time."

"It's been ten years. I'm sure everyone has long forgotten about your mishap."

"It's Waverly Lake, Dad. Waverly Lake never forgets."

"Then I guess you'll have to go to the committee yourself and tell them we're pulling out."

Of course, he had already signed them up as a sailing team. It took a minimum of two members to qualify as a team, and only the captain had to sign off on the entry. If he had signed a third person, she could back out without him having to forfeit his slot.

"Who else is on the team?"

"Just the two of us."

Kara shook her head. "You're killing me."

"You'll do it then?"

She was staying at his house. He had built the boat *with his bare hands*. But Marcus was coming, they had a wedding to plan—whenever that would be—and she had to find a job.

"We can split the prize money, fifty-fifty."

As if the prize money was enough to buy whatever pride she had left. No, this was all Dad excelling at persuasion. It was a great skill to have when running a business. But a terrible one if you were the recipient.

"Sorry, but I'll be leaving once Marcus visits. The regatta isn't for another week or two after that, right?"

"I know." He hung his head low. "I was hoping I could convince you to stay a little longer. Have one more go at it and redeem ourselves."

Kara shook her head, trying not to smile at his efforts. "Anything else you have set up for me while I'm here? The planning committee for the fall festival, or perhaps Mom's book club I need to hurry and read a book for this week?"

"No, no. Nothing like that." He moved back to the stool by the vise. "But there is one thing. Perhaps to make up for the regatta?"

"Spill it."

"Since you are currently unemployed, and staying in our house, and...to be honest, we had been renting out your room, which made some good extra cash..."

Kara sighed. The regatta was a surprise, but this wasn't. "You want me to help with the business."

"Why, that's a great idea!" He laughed. "I knew if your mom had tried, it wouldn't have gone as smoothly."

"Oh she tried, in her way, in the car. It was much easier turning her down though."

"Great. Now she'll say she warmed you up to the idea before I closed the deal."

Kara laughed. It was funny but it wasn't. A month ago she would've scoffed at the suggestion that she'd be here, agreeing to work for her parents. "I can't guarantee I can make anything—or make it well."

"I had a different idea in mind."

"Don't say it." She may not have kept in touch a whole lot, but she knew Dad's eyesight wasn't great anymore, or his reflexes.

"I figured I'd have you on—"

"Delivery truck."

"Oh, you want to do delivery truck? That's a good idea."

"You know, all you had to do was ask."

"Are you sure that's all I had to do?" He tipped his head down, eyeing her over his glasses.

"No. You're right. But fine. I'll do delivery. Just remember, it's only for a week."

"Great. You can get started tomorrow. I've got one that'll be ready in the morning."

"Where to?"

"Really easy."

"Just lay it on me, Dad."

"Next door."

"That next door?" She pointed in the direction of Mr. Rutherford's old house.

"Yep."

"Can you tell me who moved in there?" She had asked Mom and realized the answer never came.

"I can. But you may not like it."

"Why?"

"Because it's Danny Bennett."

Her stomach dropped to her feet. This wasn't happening. He

was joking. He had finally reached the limit with his sarcasm—or beyond—here.

"That's not funny."

"I didn't say it was."

"You serious?"

"Yep." He chuckled. "And that's where you're going to make your first delivery."

Chapter Six

EVEN THOUGH THE CLOUDLESS SKY GAVE THE SUN FULL reign, the movement of the boat provided a steady cool breeze on Danny's face.

"Faster, Daddy!" Hannah sat in front of him, urging him on. Mr. Pearson himself had given the boat to Danny for his extra hours at the wharf. The simple fishing boat had two bench seats and was not much larger than a canoe. It floated, and the outboard motor was in good running condition. That was all that mattered.

They had boated across the lake, along the northern banks, stopping for lunch on their favorite island. It was quiet, especially during the weekdays, and had a sandier shore on the eastern edge, allowing for easy on and off access. The largest island lay past the wharf, halfway up the upper part of the L. During the summer, boaters frequented the dot of land to picnic or swim, while teenagers jumped off the wooden diving platform on the north end. The larger anchored boats clogged up the waterway and turned Danny off from frequenting the area.

No, he was just fine sticking around home base in the longer stretch of the lake. Other than the occasional water-skier, he didn't have to weave a whole lot to get around.

Hannah liked to go fast, but not too fast. There was a narrow sweet spot for her in terms of speed, and he happily obliged, giving the motor another oomph with the gas. Her bangs flew back in the wind, the rest of her hair held up in two French braids. It only took Danny two attempts this morning to get them roughly straight.

They headed southwest, the outskirts of downtown shrinking behind them. A chain of docks coincided with the end of the commercial—albeit homely looking—buildings, making way for some of the most expensive homes on the lakefront. The homes were relatively modest in size but were surrounded by old growth oaks offering privacy, the planks of the docks peeking into their yards like private driveways.

They splashed along, parallel to the southern bank. Hannah pointed to two birds taking off with their disruption. The thick vegetation cleared as they neared their part of town. Few trees dotted the coast, but Danny liked the openness. It was refreshing and freeing to be exposed, open to the elements. Hannah pointed to their house. She always did when they got close enough to make out the gray roof of the back porch.

He slowed down, focusing on the twelve feet of floating dock behind his house. He had built it himself, with Richard's guidance. It wasn't much to look at, but it served its purpose. He tied up the boat and lifted Hannah onto the dock.

"Wait right there."

"Okay."

He said it every time they returned, as if part of a scripted ritual. Hannah would patiently wait while he'd place the cooler on the dock and hand her the bag of leftover food or trash from the picnic. He'd get out and dump the ice from the cooler on the grass as she'd go inside the back porch.

But the routine was disrupted as Danny looked up at the house. Someone stood in the backyard. A woman. She held her hand up at her brow, shielding her eyes as she squinted at him.

Danny's throat closed up. He had seen that long hickory-brown hair, that perfectly rounded face, briefly through the neighbor's window yesterday. Kara Carter.

"Go ahead in, Hannah."

If Hannah had noticed Kara, she didn't show it. She continued into the house as Danny approached his new neighbor. Oh, how he wanted to straighten his hair, especially after boating, but then she would see how he cared about his appearance.

He swallowed before speaking, the hard kind of swallow that hurt the throat. "Kara."

"Danny."

"I guess *Welcome back* is in order."

She shrugged. It was hard to read her face—she was either scrunching it because of the sun or disgusted to be speaking to him. But it wasn't like *he* was on *her* property.

So many things he wanted to say, to ask. Ten years of questions. How was New York? What was life like for her? How could she go ten years without calling or—

"Your chair is finished." She cut off his thoughts.

"What?"

"Apparently, you ordered a chair from my dad?"

"Oh, right." It was the furthest thing from his mind. "Yeah, I had come by yesterday to pick out the fabric." He had made eye contact with her through the upstairs window during that visit. How he had wanted to stop and knock on the door and say something. Anything. Instead, he'd been dumbstruck and felt like an idiot, staring uncomfortably long.

"My mom finished with the upholstery last night."

"Great. Tell your dad I'll be by to pick it up."

"That's why I'm here, actually." She closed her piercing green eyes and shook her head. She pointed her thumb behind her to the workshop. Were her fair cheeks turning pink?

"Seeing as I'm here, for now, I'm helping out with the business. It didn't make a whole lot of sense to load it in the truck and drive it here."

Danny heard the words but couldn't stop looking at her pretty mouth. Her delicate voice was the same. The same sweetness that could be bitter.

"You? Driving the truck?"

"Not right this second, obviously. But yeah. Why is that hard to believe?"

He raised his shoulders, hands in his pockets. He had walked into a no-win situation.

"What, because I'm a woman I can't drive that furniture truck?'

The chuckle couldn't hide any longer. "Because you're Kara Carter." Back in high school, he had always offered to drive when they went out, not just because he felt the pressure of gentlemanly chivalry from his dad, but because he didn't want to put his life in jeopardy.

"I don't know what you're talking about." She tossed her long locks behind her shoulder, affording a glimpse of her clavicle in the neckline of her purple T-shirt.

"Are you going to help me or not?" Her voice snapped him out of high school. She stared him down, arms folded.

"Of course. Yeah." Danny's cheeks warmed. She was practically a stranger to him. He didn't know anything about her life after high school, despite Sheila Carter's attempts at filling him in. It was better imagining things worked out for the best for both of them than any other truth. Yet somehow, she was picking up right where they had left off as if the last decade hadn't happened.

"No BMW for you yet?" She pointed to his pickup truck in the gravel driveway.

Apparently, her memory was as vivid as his. He had shared how he was saving up for a BMW during that first tutoring session. She called him Beemer for an entire month after that.

"Not exactly. You know how it is. Priorities change. Growing up."

She raised an eyebrow as if surprised and then opened the door to the shop.

"You can check out Steve Albertson's though. Parks it in front of his office downtown. He's a hotshot lawyer now."

"A lot of litigation in Waverly Lake these days?" It was nice to see her face soften with the joke. Or maybe it was the auburn glow of the workshop.

"That's the funny thing about it. Of course not. He drives that thing all over town yet rents an apartment in his mother's complex." He winced, catching the insult too late. "Not that there's anything wrong with living with parents. I mean, before the house, I was with my parents for a while too." What was he saying?

"Help me with this." She pressed her lips together. A habit whenever she was intensely focused on a task. He'd watched her read for English class, always a few chapters beyond what was assigned. She'd press those perfect lips together, and it had taken all his teenage willpower to not interrupt and kiss her.

They each grabbed a side and carried the chair out of the shop. Words ran circles through his mind but did not form any combination of things to say to lessen the awkwardness. The journey to the back porch was a marathon. They placed the chair on the ground.

"Hold on. I'll let Hannah know we're here."

Danny entered the screened porch, the door smacking closed behind him. Hannah looked up from her sailboat puzzle on the coffee table.

"It's just me."

"Okay." She returned to her puzzle. Mrs. Warren was sitting on the bench leaning up against the wall, sipping a glass of iced tea.

"Oh no. Is it time already?" He hadn't even noticed she had pulled up. He checked his watch. The drive to the wharf took on average seven minutes. He had to be there in five. It was tough leaving Hannah at home while he worked. But it wasn't like she could be thrown into summer camp like other kids.

"I'm bringing in your new chair, Hannah. I have a guest with me. Is that okay?"

Hannah nodded, attention on her puzzle.

He slid the lock on the door hinge to prop it open and returned to Kara. "Okay, let's get this in there." There was no time for settling their decade of differences. He lifted the rear legs of the chair. Kara looked back and forth between him and the house, waddling with him as she held the front legs.

"I'll tip it to the side and bring it in reverse through the door. Ready?"

"When you are."

He tilted the chair and quickly moved his grip to the side, muscles straining. Hopefully, Hannah would accept its spot, because he didn't want to have to move the heavy handmade piece of furniture again.

"Coming through! Watch your step, Kara." They carried the chair across the room to the east side and set it down facing the lake.

"What do you think, Hannah?"

She didn't look up from her puzzle.

"I gotta get to work, honey."

He walked to where she was squatted on the floor and picked her up. She put her arms around his neck and let him carry her to the seat.

She lifted her legs when he tried to set her down in it.

"Stand up, please." She stood next to the chair. "Go ahead and feel it."

She rubbed the light pink satin on the seat cushion situated a few inches lower than the standard height.

"What do you think?" He crossed his fingers in his head.

She backed up into the seat and placed her elbows on the cushiony armrests.

"This is my chair."

Danny sighed. "Yep. That's your chair." She had refused to sit in most of the other seats in the house, either because the fabric was all wrong to touch or because it was hard to maneuver in and out of the seat, or both. The Carters understood her needs and had made the perfect chair.

"No more sitting on the floor," he said. "Unless you want to, of course."

"I sit on the floor for my puzzle." She stood and walked over to the coffee table, back to her puzzle.

"I think it's a success." Danny looked at Kara. She had been standing just inside the doorway, watching the interaction.

"I'm sorry. Kara, this is Mrs. Warren." He pointed to the nanny finishing off the ice in her drink. "And this is my daughter, Hannah."

"Hannah is your daughter..." She said the words in a slow drawl.

"Yep. My daughter." Had her parents not told her? Who did she think Hannah was? Judging by the redness of her ears, he had a guess. It made him smile.

"I'm sure your parents filled you in." This was too fun. It was worth being late to the wharf.

"Oh yeah." She waved her hand. "Of course. You had that chair made for her." She stood taller. "Well, I'd better get going."

"Yeah, me too. Guess I'll be seeing you around a whole lot more now."

"I wouldn't count on it."

"Oh?"

"I'm just here for the week. My fiancé, back in New York, he's arriving in a few days, then we're off. And while I'm here I'll be busy."

She was uncomfortable, and whether it was a bit evil or not, that brought him delight.

"You know, I've already taken up too much time, so goodbye." She turned away without waiting for his response.

He couldn't wipe the smile from his face. "Goodbye."

Yep, it was like senior year. Kara Carter was back and just as spunky as ever. And still bearing a grudge.

Chapter Seven

THIS COULDN'T BE HAPPENING. AGAIN. DANNY BENNETT was charming and handsome—even more so with ten years added to his eyes...and arms—but Kara mustn't allow him to fool her. He had done that already. She had trusted him, and he broke that trust.

Nope. No more Danny Bennett.

Kara sat in the idle Carter Furniture truck, staring at Danny's house. He had whipped that smile at her—oh, he knew she had assumed Hannah was someone else to him—which bothered her even more than if he had insulted her. The nerve of him. She had fumbled with the news. Why did she blurt out about Marcus in New York? It was like an unspoken competition that only she was having. *Stop it.*

Her emotions couldn't block out her logic forever. Sure, he had been a jerk back then. But that had been ten years ago. He had a daughter, whom he obviously loved very much, buying a handcrafted chair just for her. High school Danny definitely had been non-accommodating. To Kara, anyway.

The pounding on the truck leapt her out of her seat—and thoughts.

She rolled the window down. "Hi Dad. The chair is successfully delivered." He was probably fishing for details on the interaction with Danny, but Kara wasn't about to feed his curiosity. And how convenient that he was back from his errands right after the delivery.

"Good," he said. "You heading out to deliver the pieces in the truck?" A dresser lay on the no-slip flooring next to a coffee table and smaller pieces toward the back.

"Nope. You know how I like to sit in here for fun."

"Oh how I've missed you, Kare Bear."

She crinkled her nose.

"Clipboard by your seat has all the info. If there's something you can't move yourself, you get help."

There were countless things wrong with that. Did he have insurance to cover employee injury? Probably not. And if someone helped her and got injured? Or damaged the furniture? He really needed to be more careful. Although the last few decades had resulted in zero lawsuits—that she knew of. Perhaps Steve Albertson's services would be needed. Thinking of Steve led to rehashing her encounter with Danny, and she closed her eyes tight to fight it off.

"Be careful, and I'll see you later."

"Will do."

She rolled up the window and rubbed her hands together, psyching herself up to drive the monstrosity. She had driven his last truck once or twice as a teenager, but Dad had been right next to her guiding her through it. At least this one didn't have a choke and wasn't manual. The ride was smoother but just as loud. Too bad the windows weren't tinted.

Out of the two addresses, she opted for Nichols and Dimes Drugstore. The name had amused her as a kid, playing off the name of the owner, Mr. Nichols. As an adult she realized it also played off the old Five and Ten stores from another time. The building sat on the southern end of the square, on the corner of Dowager Street and the offshoot Amble Way, right next to Steve Albertson's law firm. She hadn't seen the sign, but a sporty black BMW was parked on the street.

She pulled around back and parked the truck in the delivery driveway, taking a good five minutes to master backing it up. Between the backup beeping and onlookers helping to direct her, it was as if she was announcing her entrance as the mediocre Kara Carter, master New York failure.

Mr. Nichols stood high on the platform, garage door open. He wore a white apron over his decade-larger round belly with the Nichols and Dimes Drugstore logo, a mortar and pestle in place of the D. Kara got out of the truck and waved.

"I certainly didn't expect to see you today."

"That makes two of us." Kara looked up and smiled.

The drugstore had been an often-visited place on the walk home from school. Back then Mr. Nichols had a big gray beard, and the kids considered him a distant relative of Santa Claus, letting them take an extra piece of candy without paying. His name had helped with the image as well, and he even donned a red suit during Winterfest, embracing the persona. He stood before her now with a clean-shaven face, his looks softer and pudgier. Kara still recognized the jolliness.

She opened the back and hopped up. "Where is this dresser going?"

"I can't let you do that on your own. The thing must weigh a ton."

"I don't think you're allowed to step foot on that truck, liability and—"

Mr. Nichols jumped into the back.

"Don't worry," he said. "If I get hurt—"

"You won't sue?"

"I was going to say I'd call it quits and retire." He cackled, and Kara's worry lessened but still lingered.

He helped her place the piece on a dolly. Kara laid out an aluminum loading ramp to stretch over the gap between truck and ledge, and Mr. Nichols rolled it in.

"Can you open the door? Swings out this way."

Kara held open the back door into the drugstore. The smell of bubble gum and taffy permeated the air, sending her right back to her days with Liz, deciding on whether to spend her change on fruit candies or chocolate and rummaging through the teen magazines that seemed mature and comically naughty back then.

"My office door, right there." Mr. Nichols was red in the face as Kara opened the wooden door. He walked in backwards, rolling the dresser past his desk into an empty corner. "There." He shimmied the dolly free and gave Kara a look of victory.

"Don't think I've ever been in here before," Kara said.

"Probably not. It's where all the accounting and such happens. But sometimes when I get rowdy kids, I have to phone a parent and they sit on the bench of shame, waiting to be picked up." He pointed to the bench in the front of the office by the door.

Kara held her hands to her mouth. She had forgotten about the bench of shame. It was legendary. Sara Ipsom and Dane Pentgrass claimed they had their first kiss on that bench after getting caught stealing cigarettes, and Charlie Garrison infamously sat on the bench for a record thirteen times before Mr. Nichols forbade him from ever stepping into the store again. Or so the legend said.

"Can I offer you a drink or snack?"

"Oh, no thanks. Actually, I may look around and buy one."

"I don't mind if you take a bottle of water or can of soda."

"Mr. Nichols, I think I racked up a hefty tab in suckers that was never repaid. The least I can do is buy myself a soda."

He raised his eyebrows. "Suit yourself. Have a look around and tell me what you think."

Kara stepped into the main area of the store. The same three shelves stood parallel in the middle, with magazines, greeting cards, and books around the periphery. Unchanged from her childhood.

A Coca-Cola fridge sat near the front door, displaying its red and white logo through the front window. She opened the cooler and grabbed one in all its nostalgic glass glory, popping off the metal top on the side of the fridge. She perused the magazines and turned down one aisle, past coloring books and crayons. The puzzles caught her attention. One in particular looked like a generic scene by an Americana artist, with a lakeside house and kids jumping in the water. In the corner, children were racing mini-sailboats. Hadn't Danny's daughter Hannah been doing a puzzle with sailboats?

She added a bag of chips and dropped her loot on the counter, and the young woman at the register rang up her items. Kara stared at the puzzle on the shelf across the way before returning her gaze back to the counter. Was everything reminding her of the interaction with Danny, or was he infiltrating her brain with such veracity that she found reminders around her? Either way, he needed to get out of her head.

"Something wrong?" The woman held the chips out in front of Kara.

"Oh no. Thank you." Kara took the bag and a swig of her drink.

"Find everything you need?" Mr. Nichols said.

"Yes. Got my drink and a snack."

"And what's the verdict?"

Kara looked down at her bag.

"On the store." He chuckled.

"Oh! Yes. It's as I remembered."

He clapped his hands with a smack. "See, Linda? I told you no one notices the new paint color."

"That's because it's only about a quarter shade different than the old paint."

"I think it looks great," Kara said. But she hadn't noticed it, even after he pointed it out.

"You don't think we should get a drink machine?"

"You mean, like fountain drinks, with ice?"

Mr. Nichols nodded. "Had some people complaining I didn't have one. And not enough brand name items. I always try to support locals when I can."

"Just stop before you get all worked up again," Linda said.

"If it means anything to you, I love that it hasn't changed. There's a comfort in that." Her words surprised her. Everything and everyone in this town seemed stagnant, which was why she'd had to get out while she could, and why it was arduous to return. Yet the drugstore had a warmth to it. She knew where everything was. Knew what to expect. And the smells and layout and colors brought her back to fun, happy memories. Maybe it would be different if she had unpleasant memories of the place.

Like with Danny. He definitely didn't invoke comfort. More like frustration, anger, and...what else was she feeling? Why was he in her head so much?

"That does mean a lot." Mr. Nichols smiled. "Especially coming from a big city girl."

"Come on now. What's the saying? You can take the girl out of the small town—"

"But you can't take anyone else out?" Linda cracked.

Mr. Nichols waved her off. "Don't you have some shelves to stock?"

"Well, it's been good seeing you, Mr. Nichols."

"Please...Roger." He held the back door open as she walked through.

"I meant what I said about the store. I think you should keep it the way it is."

He nodded. "I thank you for that."

"In keeping with that comfort, I don't think I can call you anything else other than Mr. Nichols." She chuckled.

"Get on out of here." He jokingly shooed her away, and Kara hopped into the truck. "Tell your dad thank you. It looks great!"

"Will do." She waved and checked the clipboard on the seat, as if she had forgotten the other place where she had to make a delivery.

There were many things she wasn't ready for that she knew she'd have to stomach upon returning to Waverly Lake. And only one place she had told herself to never, under any circumstances, go in: Dye Happy Salon. So what place was next on her list?

Her phone buzzed. Anything to delay the salon visit was welcomed.

"Hello?"

"It's your mother."

"I know. I have your number in my phone."

"Now's not a time for joking."

"I wasn't—"

"Your father had an accident in the shop. He's already on his way to the hospital, and I'm headed there now."

"Is he going to be okay? Is it serious?"

"From what I gather, he fell off the ladder. I was at Bingham's, so I haven't seen him for myself."

Her heart pumped in her throat. If there was anything Mom had passed down to her, it was her knack for assuming the worst possible outcome.

"I'm coming too. I'll see you there."

Chapter Eight

"YOU CAN SEE HIM NOW." THE NURSE PULLED DANNY OUT of the mindless lull of the waiting room television at Lorain County Hospital. He followed her through two corridors to an examining room.

"Here he is, Mr. Carter."

"Thank you." Richard Carter sat up on the inclined exam chair in a hospital gown, name band around his thick wrist.

"What's the verdict?" Danny had seen a fair amount of blood on the shop floor, but he knew cuts to the head could appear worse than they actually were. He was more concerned about the limp leg. He was fortunate to have been outside when the fall happened. Kara's "visit" had made him late for work in the first place. He had called Mr. Pearson, who moved his shift by an hour. On his way out, he heard Richard yelling for help. It took all his might to get Richard in his truck after he had refused an ambulance, his left leg unable to support any weight. Luckily, Mrs. Warren was already scheduled to watch Hannah.

"A few staples to the head. No biggie." He hovered his hand over the back of his head, where blood had soaked a mess through his hair. "Waiting on the X-ray results."

"Are you in any pain?"

Richard raised his left arm, showing off his IV. "They've got me good for the moment. Do you need to head to work?"

"Don't worry about me. I told Mr. Pearson, and we reworked my schedule for the next few days."

A woman in a white lab coat entered the room, followed by a tall man in blue scrubs. "Hi Mr. Carter." She shook his hand. "I'm Dr. Harris. How are you doing today?"

"I've been better."

"This is Dr. Hameed from surgery. We've looked at your X-rays, and it looks like you have a tibial plateau fracture. Now, sometimes these can heal without surgery if the bone is in alignment. However, the X-rays indicate it is not, and we recommend surgery."

"You're saying there's a chance it could heal on its own?"

"I'm saying based on what we've seen, the chances are slim. Given your age with this type of injury, you would be setting yourself up for a high risk of an arthritic knee with possible chronic pain if you forego surgery."

Richard sighed. "You can't just staple it back together like my head?" He smiled, although Dr. Harris didn't reciprocate.

Dr. Hameed chuckled and chimed in. "Slightly more complicated than that, but it could've been worse. I can give you an overview of the procedure, and we'll go from there. Right now, we are going to work on bringing the swelling down."

Richard nodded, and the doctors stepped out.

Danny heard two female voices out in the hallway before the door completely closed. "I think your family is here." The discussion continued another half a minute, the voices escalating then dying down before the door opened again.

"Richard?" Sheila Carter walked in, a large, beige purse over her shoulder. "Oh, honey." She hugged him carefully, and Richard patted her back. "You really did a number on yourself."

"I'll be okay. Just some bumps and bruises."

"A fracture is more than a bruise, Dad." Kara held his right hand and smiled at her father, but her lowered eyebrows gave away her worry. Danny hadn't had the chance to prepare to see her—

not that there was much he could do to ready himself for her wrath. It was more than likely she was going to visit, but her appearance still felt sudden. Maybe the circumstances would soften her attitude.

"What are you doing here?" Her direct stare erased all hope of her softening.

Danny opened his mouth to respond, but Richard beat him to it. "He brought me in, Kare Bear. If it wasn't for Danny, I'd probably still be bleeding on the shop floor."

"Well, we are very grateful for it, Danny," Sheila said. "And for calling me as soon as you did."

"No sweat." Was that the best he could manage? Richard had been like a second dad to him the past couple of years. Surely, he would've done the same if Danny had been injured. But none of that wanted to come out of his mouth. Not with Kara staring at him.

Kara simply nodded. It was thank you enough for now, coming from her.

"We spoke to the doctor," Sheila said. "What on earth were you doing in the shop?"

"I was on the ladder, getting supplies off the top shelf on the wall."

"I told you that ladder wasn't safe." She turned to Kara and Danny. "Darn thing doesn't lock right."

"Well, I fell and hit my head on the table, and next thing I know I'm on the ground shouting and looking up at Danny."

Sheila looked tormented, as if choosing between hitting Richard and hugging him.

"This isn't going to be good for business," Richard said.

"Don't worry about that for now. It's not like we have any new orders to fill at the moment. Just relax."

"Yeah, Dad. You know I'll try and do what I can while you're out."

"Thanks, Kara. But there's something more important you'll have to handle. I'm afraid I won't be able to sail in the regatta."

Kara's shoulders dropped, but not out of disappointment. She looked relieved. "I told you yesterday I couldn't do it."

"But that was yesterday. I was hoping you'd come around."

"Dad."

Richard had worked on that sailboat for the longest time, but this was the first Danny was hearing of the two of them possibly racing in the regatta. Who knew if Kara would ever set foot in a boat, after the last time?

"Withdraw?" Richard sat up straighter. "No, you can't do that. You need to be in that race, with that boat. You'll have to find another partner."

"Dad, that's crazy. It can wait until next year."

"No, it can't." His voice turned firm. Danny imagined if Richard had a heart monitor hooked up, it would've been beeping like crazy.

"The race is weeks away. Everyone who wanted to race would've signed up by now. Even if I managed to stay for it, how am I supposed to find a replacement?"

"I'll do it." The words hit Danny's ears before he even realized they came out of his mouth.

Kara laughed. Not a funny-ha-ha laugh, but a laugh kissed by wickedness. "You sail?"

"I'm a marine mechanic."

"That didn't answer my question."

"Look, you need a partner and I'm standing right here, telling you I'll help. Believe it or not, your dad has helped me in the past." He looked at Richard, who nodded with a grin. "I'd be grateful to do something in return for him."

"You already have by bringing him here."

At least she'd acknowledged his role in helping Richard with more than the earlier nod.

"No, don't worry about it." She turned to her father. "If it's that important to you that I race..."

He squeezed Kara's hand. "It is."

Kara sighed, closing her eyes. She looked defeated. "Then I'll talk to Marcus when he gets here tomorrow. If it works out, I'll try to find someone."

"Good." Richard sat back.

Kara huffed, agitated. "I'm going to get some coffee. Would you like anything, Dad? Mom?"

The compulsion to add his order was immense, but he held it at bay. She could be so stubborn, even when people were offering help. No—especially when people offered help. She walked out of the room, and he exhaled the tension he didn't know had built up in his body with her presence.

"Don't mind her, Danny." Richard held Sheila's hand. "She'll come around."

"I'm not sure about that." It had been ten years, and she still hadn't come around. Why would another few days matter?

"Oh, she will."

"How are you so sure?"

"Because she's looking for a teammate in Waverly Lake." Richard and Sheila locked eyes before they both laughed. "And Waverly Lake never forgets."

Chapter Nine

"How's your dad doing?" Marcus sipped his coffee in the passenger seat of the Yukon. He had wanted to rent a car, but Kara insisted on picking him up at the Asheville airport. It was a bit of a ways and easy to get lost, even with GPS.

Now that he was seated next to her in the ancient vehicle, she felt slightly embarrassed. The frayed seating against his carbon-gray slacks and wrinkleless button-down shirt wasn't lost on her.

"As well as can be expected." They wound along the highway, Kara making sure to slow at the curves. It was all too easy to get nauseous.

Her nerves were on edge. She had filled Marcus in on the accident last night on the phone but didn't tell him about her promise to race in the regatta. That would tack on an extra two weeks to her visit. Surely, he wouldn't want to stay so long, but would he mind if she did? Her gut told her he would, which added a layer of uneasiness.

"This is Waverly Lake." She smiled as they approached downtown on Dowager Street.

"Smaller than I pictured." Marcus looked out the window, scrutinizing the storefronts.

"My house is just over here." She pointed ahead as they reached

Harrington Place. She was dying to know what Marcus was thinking. It was a long way from Manhattan.

"Sheila and Richard, right?" Marcus gripped the door handle and breathed heavily. Was he nervous?

"That's right." She placed her hand on his knee. "It's okay. I'm sure they'll love you." She chuckled.

"What's so funny?"

"You're the first fiancé I've introduced to them, so who knows what will happen?"

"That's reassuring."

They got out of the car, and Kara walked back to the trunk. "Need help with your bags?"

"I got it." Marcus opened the trunk and slung his laptop bag on his shoulder. "Who's that, and why is he staring at us?"

"What?" Kara glanced over Marcus's shoulder. Of course, Danny was outside when they arrived. He couldn't be inside, or better yet, at work.

"That's their neighbor, Danny."

Danny nodded in greeting, and Kara gave a brief, shallow smile.

"You know him well? Seems to be curious about you."

"We went to the same high school. He's probably just wondering about Dad. He's the one who found him yesterday, luckily."

She felt his eyes on her as she led Marcus up the porch. They couldn't clear the front door fast enough. Why did she care? She should've been an adult and introduced him to Marcus. Not doing so made it more awkward.

"Oh, there she is." Sheila Carter had dolled herself up for the occasion, wearing a skirt and gold earrings and a full face of makeup. "I'm Sheila, Kara's mom. So nice to finally meet you."

Marcus extended a hand as her mother went in for a hug. He stood stiff as the two-by-fours stacked in the shop.

"He's not big into displays of affection," Kara said. That made him sound cold. She couldn't blame him for feeling uncomfortable.

Dad sat in his recliner in the living room, wrestling his new crutches.

"Don't get up, Dad." Kara led Marcus over, and Dad obliged the greeting with a handshake.

"Nice to meet you, sir," Marcus said.

"Likewise. Wish it was under better circumstances though." Dad glared at his cast, leg propped up in the chair. "I really wanted to show you the shop."

"I can show him for now." Kara patted his shoulder. "You'll be used to those by the end of the weekend and then you can give him the detailed tour."

"About that..." Marcus tugged Kara's arm.

"What is it?"

Marcus whispered in her ear. "There's been a change of plans." Apparently, she wasn't the only one who left out information on the car ride. "Rick wants me to go to the National Conference on Journalism in Seattle."

"What? I thought he set up a group for that months ago."

"He did. But Hendricks can't go, and I'm the fill-in."

"When do you have to go?"

"I fly out tomorrow morning."

"But...my family. You were supposed to be here until Sunday afternoon. You should've told me as soon as you found out."

"Lunch is ready." Mom clapped her hands, grinning with pride.

"Smells delicious." From the way Marcus slid toward the kitchen, he welcomed the conversation escape.

He wasn't going to get away that easily. It hadn't been right keeping that from her.

"A hand here?" Dad held a crutch out for Kara.

"Oh, sorry, Dad. Sure." She held the crutches under one arm and helped him up to his feet with the other. He adjusted to the crutches and hobbled to the kitchen, the slow pace helping Kara abate her anger at Marcus.

She helped her father into the chair at one end of the table, Mom taking the other end. Marcus sat along the longer side with

Kara across from him. Right where she could laser the irritation directly to his face.

Marcus placed the napkin on his lap. "This looks lovely, Sheila."

Mom's face turned pinker than her blush. "Thank you. I wasn't sure what you liked. I know you and Kara probably eat fancier meals than we ever get around here."

"I try not to eat carbs a whole lot, but these mashed potatoes look irresistible." He smirked at Kara. She was onto him, trying to make up for bailing out of here early.

"So, Marcus." Dad scooped a spoonful of potatoes onto his plate. "Any places you want to visit or things you want to do while you're out here? I was thinking Kara could take you out on the lake."

"There won't be time to do that." Kara stabbed the roast beef on her plate with her fork before slicing it with the knife.

"What's this now?" asked Mom.

Marcus wiped his mouth with the napkin. "Um, unfortunately my trip will be cut short. I'm sorry to have you go through all of this trouble. It's a work thing. I'll have to fly out tomorrow. Kara understands how it is."

She felt his shoe tap her foot under the table. Mom and Dad stared at her. "Yeah, sorry. He'll only be staying the night."

"Oh no." Dad's shoulders slumped. "Here I thought we might convince you to stay a bit longer to catch Kara in the regatta."

"The regatta?"

Kara sat up straighter. Sure, she hadn't told him exactly all of her news either. But she could play his game too. "You know, the boat race? That's why I'm staying a few weeks longer, so I can race Dad's sailboat." She raised an eyebrow, staring wide-eyed at Marcus before turning to her father. "Marcus understands you can't race, and how important it is to you for me to race in your place."

"Too bad you can't stay, but thank you for letting us have Kara a bit longer." Dad squeezed Kara's hand over the table.

She studied Marcus's face, enjoying the small victory.

"Excuse me." Marcus stood. "Kara, can I speak with you for a minute?"

"Fine." Kara followed him into the living room.

"What do you mean you're staying for another few weeks?"

"I'm staying longer, just like you're staying for only one night."

"We should talk about this, Kara."

"I was going to talk to you about it. I wanted you to get to know my parents a little more before springing it on you, so you'd understand how important it is to my dad."

He huffed, arms crossed at his chest.

She gently touched his waist. "Come back to Waverly Lake after the conference. You can make up for lost time, get to know my family, even see me at the race. You've never seen me sail before."

He shook his head. "I can't come back. I need to work, and you should be coming back with me. You can waitress or do whatever to make money, just until we find you another job. You know it's easier to find something when you're there than it is from here." He touched her cheek. "You belong in New York. Not here."

"I'll be there when the race is finished. If I had something lined up, then I'd reconsider. But I don't. There's no harm in staying just a little longer to do this one favor."

"You don't think this is harming us?" Marcus returned to the crossed arms.

"I think you not communicating with me is harming us."

"Come on, Kara, be fair. We already hashed this out. You couldn't have expected me to warn you about the layoff. You think I wanted to keep it secret? My job would've been on the line too if I had told you beforehand."

Kara sighed, massaging her temples. "I was talking about not telling me you're leaving tomorrow."

Marcus stepped closer, holding both her shoulders. "Come on, let's not do this here. Your mom made lunch, which is getting cold. And I'm sure they can hear us in there. This is not the impression I want to leave."

Kara swallowed the tears forming. In two years of dating, they had barely argued. It seemed like all they had done the past month was disagree. Maybe he was right. Time away was tearing them apart. But she wasn't going to let Dad down. Marcus had to understand that. If they were to survive a marriage, they'd have to learn how to get through times like these.

"Okay," she said. "Not right now. Let's try to enjoy the little time you have left here."

"Sounds good to me." Marcus kissed her on the forehead.

They walked back into the kitchen. Mom and Dad struck up a conversation as if they had been chatting the whole time.

Kara sat in her chair and painted a smile on her face. Marcus winked. He held out his hand across the table. Part of her wanted to storm off, leave the table, and scream into the wind. Instead, she placed her hand in his. It was a small step in mending whatever wounds they had inflicted on each other.

Marcus cleared his throat. "Now, how about some more of those mashed potatoes?"

Chapter Ten

THE SOUND OF THE FRONT DOOR LOCK UNBOLTING MADE Kara freeze. She looked up from the computer monitor, the cool air-conditioning of Portside Portrait spreading goosebumps along her skin.

"Kara? What are you doing here?" Mr. Lawson held a tripod and camera case, shimmying through the front door. For sixty, he was fit and lean, and no matter where he was, he wore a baseball hat.

"I—I just—" She stood, not knowing where to place her hands.

"Why aren't you at the prom with the rest of the kids?"

"Let me help you with that." She hurried to the front door and held it open while Mr. Lawson transferred the remaining equipment from his truck to inside.

He set the equipment to the side and stood with his arms at his hips. "Well?"

Kara stared at the floor. "I didn't want to be home." She looked toward the back of Portside Portrait. Anywhere but in Mr. Lawson's face. "I had the key on me."

Mr. Lawson softened and touched her elbow.

She hazarded a look into his eyes. "I didn't know where else to go."

He inhaled as if to talk but stopped, nodding instead. She relaxed and bit her bottom lip.

"Come on," he said. "I'll fix you some tea."

Kara sat at the computer while Mr. Lawson warmed up water in the electric kettle. He returned with two mugs and handed her one, the tag on the tea bag hanging over the side.

She blew on it as he took a seat.

"You don't have to talk if you don't want to."

"I'm sorry. I didn't mean to frighten you. I didn't think anyone would come around. But it makes sense, now that I remember you were taking pictures at prom."

"I don't like keeping the equipment in the truck. Plus, I thought I'd start on processing. You kids want your pictures sooner and sooner. No patience these days." He gave a smile, and Kara assembled what she could of one.

They sat in silence. Kara sipped her tea, the aroma strong but the taste mild. The heat had been ramping up since late April, but with the air-conditioning, the hot tea was welcomed and comforting.

"I was going to go." She looked up. "To prom, that is."

"But?"

"But the person I thought I was going to go with—" She looked down at her mug. "He took someone else."

"I see." He set down his mug and tapped his fingers on the counter. "Was there no one else you wanted to go with? Or a group of friends?"

"Now you sound like my mom. *Just ask somebody else. Go by yourself. You'll regret missing out.*" Kara waved her hand in a circle, as if Mom's comments continued through the air, on and on. "When it came down to it, my best friend had a date, and honestly, I didn't want to have to see...*him*...with someone else."

"Right." Mr. Lawson set his tea down. "Hold on." He walked off and returned with the clunky camera case. "Since you're here, you want to help me with some of these photos?"

Kara considered going home, but she didn't want another dose of Dad's pity or Mom's things-will-get-better rhetoric. This was where she felt safest to just...feel.

"Okay," she conceded. "I'm kind of curious what the dresses looked like anyway."

Mr. Lawson cheered up. "All right."

He guided her through the computer software. Even though the pictures were digital, there still were blemishes and stray hairs and scuffed shoes to correct.

She actually enjoyed scouring the photos. Most pictures taken in front of the backdrop—"The Notebook" theme with river, boat and ducks, even real oars off to the side—were of couples, although some attended in larger friend groups. Tuxes inherently didn't have much variety, minus the chosen accent colors. But the dresses spanned the gamut from sleek animal prints to puffy tiered princess dresses.

The screen flipped to the next couple. And there he was. His arms slung around Caitlyn Hall's waist. Kara didn't care what she looked like. All she could see was his face. His flawless mouth her lips had touched that perfect day not so long ago. The mouth that effortlessly smiled at the camera, as if he were having the time of his life.

And that did it. She had held the tears off all day, all evening. Until now.

It took one look at Danny Bennett's smiling face to release the resentment and hurt her heart let out as it broke for good.

Chapter Eleven

SAYING GOODBYE TO MARCUS HAD BEEN BITTERSWEET. The time he did spend in Waverly Lake proved rocky, at least at first. The rest of the afternoon and evening went without argument. His conversations with Mom and Dad were surface talk—about his job, his ideas about the wedding, his mother. The type of discussions to expect on the first meeting of a significant other's parents. Which was great, except for the fact that he had to leave and couldn't *really* get to know them, or they him.

She didn't know how to feel dropping him off at the airport in the morning. She was still upset he was leaving so soon, but felt relief that...he was leaving so soon. It was complicated. And nothing about dating Marcus the last two years had been complicated.

But she had a favor to fulfill, and worrying about Marcus had to be lowered on her list of priorities for now.

It was midday, and Kara had already spoken to what felt like half the town. She had hoped Linda, the cashier at Nichols and Dimes Drugstore, might have had an interest in teaming up with her, but Linda had no sailing experience, and no time between that job and her babysitting in the evenings to be taught. Mr. Nichols assured her he knew of no one else who could do it, but he would let her know if something came up.

She had worked her way east through downtown, skipping Dye Happy Salon—she wasn't *that* desperate, at least not yet—down to Bingham Station. But Mr. Bingham had no willing employees either. She had turned around, walking the sidewalks along the most historic buildings in Waverly Lake. Flags lined the street, alternating between the Stars and Stripes and the red, white, and blue color-blocked flag of North Carolina. The light breeze from the lake seeped between the brick buildings, offering minimal reprieve from the humidity. She had tied her hair up in a loose bun, but even that hadn't stopped the sweat from beading along her neck.

The bell over the door jingled as she entered Portside Portrait, the air-conditioning raising goosebumps on her bare arms. The walls of the front office showcased the clientele. A high school senior stood under twinkling lights downtown. A teenage girl sat on what could only be one of Dad's swings, hanging from a willow tree, the branches falling in a cascading curtain behind her. The opposite wall had family portraits at the lakeside and several on sailboats on the water.

She had seen all of these, or ones like these, over ten years ago when she had worked as an assistant to the owner, Mr. Lawson. It was her first high school job. It had taken up most of her Saturdays, but it was the one day a week she tasted her dream.

"Why, is that Kara Carter? Hello." Mr. Lawson shuffled up to the front desk. He wore a faded gray baseball cap, with about four days' worth of stubble on his narrow, aged face.

Seeing him brightened her mood. She barely had the chance to know two of her grandparents before they'd passed away. Mr. Lawson was the closest thing she had to a grandfather, the kind she could spend all afternoon with on a porch swing listening to stories. "Is a hug too much to ask for?"

"Get over here, little lady."

She hugged his bony frame, more delicate than she remembered, and walked back in front of the counter.

"Are you here to order some pictures? I'm afraid I'd be too nervous to take your picture, you being a downright professional."

"No, Mr. Lawson. And there is no reason you should be nervous to take my picture. You do have some lovely photographs up here." It was true. They were simple and what the customer wanted, but they also had their own charm.

"I do like the ones you've taken out and about in town." She pointed to the walls.

"Oh, thank you. That was Mrs. Lawson's idea, actually. The townsfolk seem to like it. A lot different shooting outside, I'd have to say."

"Yes, it can be." She couldn't remember the last time she had done an indoor shoot. She tried to capture her subjects with natural light. Sure, certain posed photographs of people often required a little help from light reflectors. But she most enjoyed the off-the-cuff pieces that captured the subjects as they were, in the moment. People assumed those were the easiest—just snap away. But a truly great outdoor impromptu photo required the right eye to get the best light and angle. Shooting wildlife was another story, mainly based on patience and luck.

"It sure is nice to see you back."

"It's nice to see you too." It had been a while since she was immersed in photographs in a studio, and like the visit at Nichols and Dimes Drugstore, she felt at ease. At home.

"It's a shame to see it all go." He took off his cap and scratched the bald spot on his head.

"What do you mean?"

"The wife and I are retiring, dear. After forty-two years with the business."

"Really?" It was a shame. Portside Portrait was at every event that was any event in town. "I'm sure the whole town will be sorry to see you go."

"Maybe. Maybe not. I wasn't exactly the coolest guy. But you know, that makes me think... In planning retirement with the missus, I keep saying it would be great if someone local took over the business. This town always needs someone to do the class photos, sports teams, and the like. Had some weddings in there too." He raised his eyebrows.

Kara held her breath. He couldn't possibly be thinking of her. "I can see how that would be true."

"If we shut it down, it's going to become one of those photo factories that are in and out. Don't even get to know the kids in the pictures, you know what I mean?" He walked around the counter to Kara. "It's a little selfish, wanting to see something I started carry on beyond my time. I'd like to have a little bit of a legacy. Leave my mark, as you will."

"I understand."

"But it's more about this town. Waverly Lake needs someone to capture its people." He pointed to the family portraits. "These aren't of tourists during autumn, standing in a random forest. These are Waverly Lake families, taken in parts of Waverly Lake we all know and love."

His sentiment made Kara smile.

"I know it seems silly, taking senior pictures and elementary class photos and sports team photos. But of all the pictures people acquire throughout their lifetime, those are the ones they'll most likely keep, the ones they display or put in a scrapbook or album and caption them. They look back on those years down the road and laugh at how silly their hairstyle was or reminisce how their kids wouldn't stand still that day. You really are capturing memories.

"And who knows? When I go, maybe some Asheville company will come in for school pictures, processing the kids like a herd of cattle. Maybe families will drive out there to get their photo in front of the Biltmore Estate instead of the lake." He shrugged. "Just something to think about. You'd let me know if anyone fit the bill, right?"

He is thinking of me. She had already called her connections in New York and abroad those last few days in the city, but in photography, she could be called within the next five minutes with an opportunity or never hear from them in the next three years.

Not to mention driving the delivery truck was a surefire way to get her to look for any job other than driving the delivery truck. But taking over a photography studio in Waverly Lake? It just wasn't feasible. His face looked eager, and he spoke so passionately, it was hard to not be more helpful. He had comforted her during a hard time, and the place had been such a refuge for her.

"Sure. But I'm sure you'll find someone, especially with that pitch."

He nodded, clearly disappointed.

"Now what was it that brought you here today?"

"Right." Kara perked up, happy to change the subject. "My dad —you know Richard—had signed up for the regatta."

"How nice."

"Yes. Unfortunately, he had an accident yesterday and won't be able to participate."

"Oh no. Is he all right?"

Everyone had stopped her at that part of her speech. Dad knew everyone, and everyone knew Dad. In Waverly Lake, that held true for most anyone. It was touching to hear their reactions of support. Mr. Bingham had even offered to swing by with a pie.

"He'll be fine, thank you for asking. He broke his leg but is on the mend. The thing is, he pleaded with me to sail the race—it's his own handcrafted boat—and I'm in need of a teammate."

"Oh dear." His gaze turned down to his feet. So far, everyone she had spoken to acted as if they were...uncomfortable with the idea.

"I'm sorry. My son and grandson will be participating, but I'm not sure if anyone else I know could help you out."

She suspected as much. "Well, thank you anyway. I'd better get going if I have any hope of this race happening. It was good seeing you, Mr. Lawson."

He patted her hand. "Good to see you too, Miss Kara."

She walked out, defeated. The marquee of Dye Happy Salon stared her down across the square green space of Dowager Street. "Nope. Moving on."

She entered the next shop down the line. Weeping Wares was

a new flower shop—new to her—in a storefront that had been occupied by a tourist shop. Or had it been an antique store? An overflowing vase of long-stemmed gladiolus all colors of the rainbow sat on a display table front and center. Terracotta pots and garden ornaments lined up against the windows and shelving to the right, while fresh greenery filled tiered tables ahead of her. The store was filled with floral aromas, the sheer variety of flowers surprising for a small shop in Waverly Lake. But the high volume of inventory wasn't messy—it balanced out beautifully.

"Hello, welcome to Weeping—oh my goodness." The nasal yet chipper voice was familiar. "Kara Carter, get your butt on over here." The employee, clad in a green apron, ruffled the longer half of hair on his head, the other half sporting a side buzz.

"Sebastian?" She looked at his name tag to confirm, with the word *Owner* below. He waved his black-polished nails, luring her in for a hug, and she obliged. He squeezed her softly and then parted, standing a foot away.

"How have you been! You are gorgeous as ever, although that bun needs some work, to be honest." He patted the knot on her head, and she laughed.

"Fine, just fine." She pointed to the bun. "Getting used to the heat again."

He swatted at her comment. "There is no getting used to it."

"You're the owner of this place?" Sebastian had been one of her best friends during junior year—part of the bleacher crowd making snarky comments about the popular kids to avoid facing their own unpopularity.

"Don't act so surprised. You knew in high school how I had the horticultural eye."

She did miss his sarcasm. They had grown apart over senior year due to the time she spent with Danny, which, looking back, could've been better spent.

"Actually, I'm co-owner. My partner over there—" He looked beyond the bouquets and indoor shrubbery. "I don't see him, but

George, he's more of the businessman. Anyway, what are you doing here? I heard you were back in town."

"Yeah, just for a little while." She hadn't known Sebastian was around, but he just may be the best opportunity yet for a teammate. "I've been going around town all day, not having much luck."

"What is it? Maybe I can help."

"I'm going to sail in the regatta."

Sebastian chuckled, then bit his lip. "Okay..." It looked like he was about to squeal.

"And I need a teammate. I was doing it with my dad, but he can't anymore."

"Oh, honey. That's just not going to happen."

"What? Why not?"

"Can I ask you a question? How have people been receiving you today?"

"I don't know. Everyone is either already signed up or too busy or—"

"Let me stop you right there."

Sebastian had two sides to him. One, sarcasm. The other, gut-wrenching honesty.

"When it comes to the regatta, you are a legend. And not in a good way."

"You mean, back ten years ago—"

"When you choked? Yes. That's what I'm talking about. They even have a name for it. Whenever someone follows a command the wrong way, they say they did a Kerror. Like, Kara and—"

"Error, I get it." Dad had said Waverly Lake would've moved on. That no one cared about her flub in a race ten years ago. He had only said it to get her on his team.

"I'm sorry. Someone needed to tell you."

Kara sighed, shoulders slumping. "What am I supposed to do? My dad practically begged me to sail."

"Hold on. I have an idea." Sebastian walked to the counter and came back with a flyer. "It's movie night tonight."

"You want me to watch a movie?"

"No. Although I love that you haven't changed your silly self one bit." He nudged her. "The whole town will be there. It'll be much easier to talk to a lot of people because they'll all be at the same place. Maybe you'll get lucky and someone younger who doesn't know about your past will volunteer."

The flyer had a picture of the library with cartoon lawn chairs and blankets dotting the page. Sebastian's honesty could be cruel to hear, but he did have a good idea. She smiled back at his plotting face.

"Movie night it is."

Chapter Twelve

Danny loosened the shoulder pad tie on his chest. Football practice had been brutal. It always was when the Waverly Lake Rangers lost the previous weekend.

He stood between wide receiver Colin Hall and running back Jesse Powers, sharing lockers along the side wall of the locker room.

"You okay, man?" Colin asked.

Danny rotated his right arm, holding his shoulder. "Yeah, I think so. Just sore from Friday's game."

"It was brutal, to lose by one point," Jesse said.

"Don't remind me," Colin said. "Speaking of...what's the deal with Kara Carter?"

The locker room had never been so silent. Except after Coach Wendell gave them "the anti-pep talk" when they lost a game.

"What do you mean *what's the deal*? And how is that *speaking of*?" Danny dropped his shoulder pads on the floor and grabbed a shirt out of the locker. "She's my tutor for pre-calc. That's all."

"Oh really?" Colin stepped closer. "Just your tutor?"

"I'm not buying it," Jesse said. "I saw her at last week's game."

"That's how *speaking of*. I saw her at the home game before that too," Colin added.

"Along with a hundred other students." Danny stared them

down. Hopefully, his face didn't betray his thoughts. The sound of her name got his heart pumping. He had never met a girl so easy to talk to. He was able to be himself around her. None of the tough guy or rich boy act.

And the more he got to know her...

She grew more gorgeous by the day. But he didn't want buffoons like these to tarnish her. She deserved to be around better people—genuine people. And it was none of their business what was going on. Did she think something was going on? Because he definitely felt it.

"Danny!" Colin clicked his fingers in front of Danny's face. "My boy is whipped."

"I am not whipped. You don't know what you're talking about."

"You'll go out with my sister then?"

"What are you talking about?" Danny tied his shoe on the bench. "Caitlyn?"

"Yeah, man. I told her I'd put in a good word."

"You mean she had you in a headlock and forced you to." Jesse grabbed Colin and reenacted the accusation.

"Get off me. No." Colin straightened his shirt as if Jesse had poured sand all over him. "I'm just a good brother like that."

Danny had no desire to ask anyone else out, especially not Colin's sister Caitlyn. He hadn't yet built up the courage to ask Kara. He didn't want to mess things up. He saw her almost every day now for tutoring, which half the time turned into talking or watching television together or even her staying over for dinner. If he made the move and she didn't go for it...

The end of their friendship would be devastating.

No. He had to take it slow and let it happen naturally.

And that meant no Caitlyn...or anyone else.

Chapter Thirteen

Daniel Bennett drove his decade-old Ram pickup to his house, window down and wind blowing. He had spent his Friday afternoon at Pearson's Wharf in a whirl of emotions. For a Friday, work was slow. Usually Fridays meant people wanted their boats ready for the weekend—whether that involved oil changes, tune-ups, or even touch-ups with paint.

The slow pace of work left him with more time to think about the week's events. Three days ago, Kara Carter had walked back into his life. Or he'd walked into hers. Whichever way it went. And it hadn't gone well. Coming to her dad's rescue would seem like something to lessen the anger, maybe accept him at least as a neighbor or a family friend. Was that all he wanted though? Just the sight of her sent his mind whirling and blood racing. He had been uncomfortable in that hospital room when she showed up, yet all he'd wanted to do was reach over to her and wake her stubborn self up.

But there were too many things to blow off any sort of hope. If that was even how he felt about it in the first place. For one, there was the whole breakup thing in the past. He had wronged her. She had no desire to give him a chance—it was laughable to think it, since she didn't even want to be in the same room with him. But he had been a jerk all those years ago. He'd like to think he wasn't now.

Then there was the whole issue of her being engaged. She was smart, beautiful, and fiery as ever. Of course, she'd have a fiancé. But *that* guy? That guy who was over yesterday? No, he had no right to judge. He didn't know the first—or second, or third—thing about him. Scratch that. He knew that guy had braved Kara's driving, so there was that.

Anyway, he had Hannah to think about. She took priority in his life.

"Are you going to just sit there all night?"

Danny sat with his truck in park in his driveway. Tracy smirked, leaning down to meet his face through the window, the wind blowing her curls in her face.

"I'm coming."

"Good. I was starting to think my brother had officially lost it."

Danny got out and followed her to the back porch. "Got yourself a ride here, I see."

"I manage." It was true. Tracy had the ability to wander and roam the world, find a way to eat and explore yet still incur no debt. Or savings for that matter.

"Daddy's home!" Tracy left her bag near the door and clapped her hands. She was an enthusiastic, dramatic person to begin with. But around Hannah, even more so. And for some reason it didn't bother Hannah. She seemed to like the overly blown behavior from her aunt.

"Let's get your shoes on, love." She held her finger down on the shoelaces as Hannah looped them. Tracy was one of the few people Hannah accepted help from. Otherwise, Hannah wanted to do everything herself. But sometimes even ordinary tasks were overwhelming.

"What's with the *love*?" Danny slipped off his shoes. "You go to Australia for three months and now you're speaking Aussie? Is that even Aussie?"

"I can't help that I pick up a piece of culture here and there. It's hard not to when you're immersed in it. But you wouldn't know anything about that now, would you? Waverly Lake all your life."

She had meant it as a light-hearted joke. He was sure of it. But it stung, nonetheless. She knew why he had stayed.

Tracy looked up at him, nose scrunched and mouth winced. "I'm sorry, Danny. Sometimes words just fly out of my mouth."

"I know." He stood in the doorway to the kitchen. "When you get older the filter from your brain to your mouth develops. But you wouldn't know anything about that." He smirked.

Tracy chuckled and stuck out her tongue. "Touché."

"I'm going to change clothes. Be right back."

"Okay. Old man."

Danny walked past the kitchen, through the foyer, and up the stairs. Moving to their own house was wonderful—privacy being the number one upside. The downside was that it didn't feel like home yet. No warm aromas from the kitchen lingering in the curtains or knowing the part of the step to avoid to not creak in the middle of the night. In other words, he had no connection to it. It was like living in a hotel. And Danny didn't quite know how to remedy that, but with time.

He slipped out of his oily work clothes and into jeans and a dark-gray T-shirt. He carried his shoes down the stairs and out to the patio. "Everyone ready?"

"We most certainly are." Tracy stood next to Hannah, her arm over Hannah's shoulder.

"Did you get the blankets?"

"I told her my purple blanket," Hannah said.

"And I told you it's too hot for a blanket." Tracy folded her arms. "Must run in the family. Your dad is wearing jeans for goodness' sake."

"The blankets are to sit on," Danny said. "Plus, I tend to be the target of mosquitoes, hence the jeans. You do know the movie is outside, right?"

"What? You said it's at the library."

"It is. As in outside, in the field behind the library."

"Oh. Well then, that changes things."

Hannah shook her head with her hand on her forehead. "There's no talking in the library."

"Don't you give me sass." Tracy smiled, pointing her finger at Hannah.

Danny found Hannah's purple blanket and picked up a beach towel he kept under a bench seat. They rode in his truck—Hannah in the middle on her booster, Tracy with her arm out the window— to the library on the southwest side of town. It sat next to a soccer field bordered by woods on either side. Waverly Lake had started Films on Fridays this summer, and Danny had taken Hannah the last two weekends.

He parked, and they searched for an open blanket spot. For a brief moment he held his breath, thinking he caught a glimpse of Kara Carter. Of course it wasn't. Kara wasn't the type to go to local events like this. She hated the fact that knowing everyone meant having to talk to everyone. No, she couldn't be paid enough to show up here. So why did his heart sink when he realized it wasn't her?

"Hi Danny." Mrs. Fletcher, the hairdresser, sat with two other ladies in folding lawn chairs. She sipped from her travel mug, probably something fruity and rummy. It would be more of a surprise to Danny if she didn't have alcohol in it.

"Hello Carly."

"Nice to see you and Hannah here. I see Tracy is back in town."

"Do you see me?" Tracy said. "Because you'd think you'd address me, as I'm standing right here."

Danny nudged her with his elbow.

"Well, Tracy, if you ever want to tame those wild locks of yours, feel free to come by the salon."

Tracy tussled her hair with her hands, spreading out the curls even more. "I think I'm good."

"Have a nice evening, Carly." Danny held Hannah's hand and guided her to move on as Tracy followed.

"Why do you do that?" he said.

"What?"

"You know I live here. Just because you're in and out all over the place doesn't mean you get to ruin it for me."

"How am I ruining anything?"

"I see these people on a daily basis."

She stopped and placed her hand on his shoulder, shaking her head. "I am so sorry. Will you ever, in time, be able to forgive me?"

"Cut it out." He swatted her hand off. "I'm being serious. These are all my neighbors. I don't need to be making enemies."

"Aunt Tracy didn't get her filter yet." Hannah rubbed her nose.

Danny laughed. Hannah never ceased to surprise him. Just when you thought she wasn't listening or didn't understand. He knew she was stating it as fact. But he wished she knew how funny it was, and how adorable it made her.

"Yeah. You're right, Hannah," Tracy said. "I have yet to grow my filter. I guess you'll just have to deal with it."

"Deal with it," Hannah repeated.

"Hey now, I'm going to leave Aunt Tracy out of things if you two are going to gang up on me all the time."

Tracy ruffled her hand on Hannah's head, and they walked down the field.

"Daniel! Hannah!"

Danny scanned the field and located a raised hand. Sebastian and George waved them over.

"Got you a spot right here, lovely Hannah," George said.

"Out of Carly Fletcher venom range," Sebastian said.

Danny laid out the beach towel, then worked on Hannah's blanket. "Oh, she's not so bad."

Sebastian and George looked at each other, then back at Danny. He shrugged it off.

"Don't worry." Tracy plopped down next to Danny. "I'll protect him."

"I'm so glad you're back." George kissed her on the cheek. "Is it for good this time?"

"What do you think?

Sebastian pouted. "Take us with you? Wherever it is you're going."

"Stop being dramatic," George said. If opposites attracted, George and Sebastian were the prime example. George was calm and collected, detail-oriented and compassionate. His partner, Sebastian, was everything but. "You know you'd never leave Waverly Lake. Even though you threaten to every summer."

"It's insane that people choose to live in such conditions." Sebastian fanned his face with his hand.

George took Sebastian's hand in his. "It's affordable, we both have jobs here, everybody knows us, and above all, it's home."

"Everyone knowing us isn't always a good thing."

"Well at least they accept us."

"Deal with it," Hannah said.

Sebastian's mouth opened in shock and Danny shrugged, pointing to his sister. "Blame Tracy."

Sebastian softened and rubbed George's back. Danny guessed there was a hurtful story there but didn't want to pry. Unlike Sebastian, George hadn't been born and raised in Waverly Lake.

The surrounding conversations and laughter hushed as the white drape over the library lit up with the MGM lion in black and white, roaring at the crowd. Hannah scooted in front of Danny, full attention on the movie.

Movement to the left, up front, caught his attention. A late arriver was traipsing through the crowd, rummaging for a spot and apologizing at each blanket. The movie watchers shushed and heckled as the person worked across the field.

Sebastian leaned over to George, pointing out the distraction. "That's Kara. The girl who came by when you were MIA. I didn't know if she'd actually come."

George swatted him away. "Are you going to watch the movie or not?"

At the sound of her name, what was a disruption to Danny turned into a comedic bumbling mess. Kara dropped her chair and apologized to the unfortunate victim. She headed their way before finding a spot closer to the middle of the field and farther up. She sat down and looked around at the crowd.

It was shocking. Kara Carter, here, out in the open at a social event in Waverly Lake. The dim light bounced off the library and hit Kara at all the right angles as she turned his way. Her cheek shimmered, and her brunette hair flowed freely down her back over the loose, striped sweater she wore with her shorts. She was stunning.

But where was her fiancé?

She continued to watch the movie, then turned to the left and to the right. Danny had to lean back slightly to see over Sebastian's head to get a view of her. Danny was more of a modern movie fan; the old black-and-white films were filled with too much talking and not enough plot. Which meant he paid absolutely no attention to the film—unlike Hannah, who wouldn't break her attention for fireworks.

"Just go over there already." Sebastian tapped Danny on the knee.

"What? What are you talking about?"

"You're staring. And she's obviously uncomfortable. Poor thing looks like a duckling separated from her mother."

"Shh," a woman one blanket over interrupted.

"I'm here with Hannah," Danny said.

"And with us and Tracy. Hannah will be fine."

"Shh!"

Sebastian whipped around and stared the woman down. She leaned away.

Danny looked at Tracy, who he'd thought was watching the movie but was staring at him. She gave a thumbs-up and winked.

"Oh, and here." Sebastian fidgeted with his picnic basket, which was more like a crate in size than a basket. He pulled out a thermos.

"Should I ask what's in it?"

"It's white wine. My goodness, what do you take me for?"

"Would you please quiet down?" The lady had found her courage yet again.

"We're not *in* the library, ma'am. We're outside. Chill out."

Danny shook his head. "Okay, I guess."

"You guess? Get on over there now, before I have it out with Madam Shush over here."

Danny stood in a crouch, and Sebastian handed him the thermos. He left Hannah and Tracy, and the comfort of his towel, onward to Kara Carter.

Chapter Fourteen

KARA'S EARS WERE ON FIRE. EVEN THOUGH THE SUN HAD set long enough ago to darken the sky, she still felt like the white flashing light of the projector shined right on her alone self.

She had wavered about going to movie night, but Mom had her book club at the house, which meant chatting about how bad health care was for the baby boomers and who had the cutest grandchild, of which Sheila was behind. Kara didn't care to hear it. She joined Dad in the den for about thirty seconds until he pressed her about the regatta.

Now she was all by herself, roaming the middle of a field, the crowd's eyes boiling her skin. If only she had arrived earlier, then it would've been easier to chat with folks. Hopping from group to group was not faring well, the reactions ranging from polite dismissal to downright irritation with her. To make matters worse, she'd caught sight of Danny behind her, sitting next to some woman. Not that it mattered. She was engaged, after all. Kind of. It shouldn't matter whatsoever who that woman was, who looked younger than Danny. But as Kara worked her way through the crowd, she felt Danny's eyes on her, whether or not it was true.

"I know it's short notice," she whispered, her legs tiring of crouching, "but I'm really in need of a teammate."

Steve Albertson, the class introvert now turned town attorney, glanced at his date through his black-framed glasses. The lanky woman rolled her eyes before turning her attention back to the movie.

"I'm sorry, Kara. I'm already racing with my mom, and I think a third person would just weigh us down. But to be honest, I'm surprised to hear you're participating, with the whole—"

"Yes, I know. I messed up. People make mistakes, Steve." The judgment of the town had been irritating at first, but it was slowly chiseling away at her confidence. "Thanks anyway. Enjoy the movie."

"Trying to," his date said.

Kara had a few choice words in response but felt her wrist being pulled.

"Kara, what are you doing?"

She turned around. The light of the film reflected off Danny's strong jawline, his concerned gray-blue eyes the brightest parts of his face. He held a thermos in one hand, his other letting go of her arm.

"None of your business."

"You're embarrassing yourself."

"Oh, I'm embarrassing myself." She stood tall, the words coming out louder than she wanted. A couple at her feet shushed her, swatting her away with their hands.

"Come here." He nodded back.

"No."

"Get a room, you two." The words were offensive, but even more surprising when Kara saw they had come from an elderly woman in a lawn chair.

"Just come on. Please?"

"Fine."

Danny turned, his broad shoulders leading the way. His dark shirt made it hard to see him in the fading movie light. She stumbled on someone's shoe, and in bracing herself she clasped Danny's upper arm. It was only for a second, but the contours of the chiseled arm shocked her. He had been popular in high school but wasn't the jockiest of the jocks—in shape, but gangly. He had definitely changed, at least on the outside.

"Watch it." The disgruntled man flung his hands in the air.

"She's sorry." Danny abated him and turned to Kara. "Here." His hand grazed down her arm, from her elbow to her hand. She wondered if he felt her goosebumps tingling down her arm, raising her skin with his touch like a crowd in a stadium doing the wave. She was too shocked to react as he zigzagged through the maze of people with more ease than she had done. She loosened out of his light grip when they hit the tree line at the edge of the field. Her hand immediately wanted the comfort back.

She half-expected a scolding, with the way he had interfered her search for a teammate.

"Drink?" He offered up the thermos.

Did he pull her out of the crowd for this? "Coffee?"

"No. White wine."

"Is that allowed here?"

"Yes. I just prefer to carry it in a thermos." The corners of his lips turned up. "Why? Are you going to tell on me?"

She broke a smirk. "Don't tempt me."

"You don't drink wine?"

Of course she drank wine. Just not out of Danny Bennett's thermos. But the longer she thought it over, the more appealing it sounded. Anything to ease the tension, or irritation, or whatever it was she was feeling.

She grabbed the thermos and took a sip. It wasn't cold but chilled enough to cool her mouth. The air was stagnant in the field, protected from any wind off the lake. She swallowed, the wine warming her throat and drying her words. Why was she nervous? They could barely see each other, she had wine—which usually relaxed her, not the opposite—and it was Danny Bennett. Just another adult crossing her path in her temporary visit. Who happened to live next door to Mom and Dad.

"I wasn't embarrassing myself, you know."

"Oh, you weren't? Asking anyone who would listen, and probably some who didn't want to, about the regatta?"

"So what? I'm doing it for my dad."

"I told you I would help you as your teammate."

"And I graciously declined."

"Not sure it was gracious." He took the thermos back and drank. "That guy you were with yesterday your teammate?"

"Spying on me now?"

"I just so happened to be in the driveway when you pulled up. Are you hiding the guy?"

"No, I'm not hiding him." She stole the wine back. "He has a name, and it's Marcus. He's my fiancé, who will not be participating in the regatta. And he left this morning. Any other questions?"

Danny smirked. "Have a fight?"

She scoffed, mouth agape. "He had a work thing."

"So that leaves you still with no teammate, right?"

What was it to him anyway? She hadn't asked everyone in town yet. Only most everyone... "There are a few possibilities, if things work out with some people..."

"You've got nothing."

She wanted to wipe the smugness off his face. And her hand through his dark hair. "I don't need your help."

"Maybe not as a teammate." He snapped his fingers and stood taller. "I can help you find one though."

"What do you mean?" His eyes gave away slyness under the offer.

"I know just the thing. You see the projector back there?" He pointed to the back of the field, the movie projector sitting high on a platform. "I know the old man who runs it. I'll have him stop the movie for an announcement."

"You wouldn't."

"It's perfect! We can ask if anyone wants to be Kerror's teammate."

She wanted to spit the wine in his face, but he paced down the tree line toward the back.

"Danny." She chased after him. "Danny! Stop it."

"I'm sure someone will shout out that they'd love to participate."

"Don't make me do this."

"I'm just trying to help."

Kara grumbled. "Fine!"

Danny stopped and turned around. "Yes?"

"You can be my teammate." It twisted her stomach to say it. Her heart slowed its racing, and her hands shook.

"You sure?" He stepped closer. He'd better not make her beg for it.

"Are *you* sure?" She stepped closer. He wasn't going to take a win so easily. "You've got Hannah and I'm assuming work, and we'll need hours of practice." The realization of being around Danny for any length of time churned the little wine she had drunk. What was it she felt tingling her nerves? Excitement?

"If we're going to do this, it's not to complete the race. It's to win it." Maybe he'd back off if it wasn't about having fun—it would be hard work. Hard work with someone she didn't want to work with.

He took a sip from the thermos and offered it back to her. "When do we start?"

Chapter Fifteen
SATURDAY, AUGUST 8

It hit Danny the moment he opened his eyes to the Saturday morning light and remembered last night. He and Kara Carter were teammates. Sure, it had taken some convincing. Okay, a little trickery, but sometimes Kara's stubbornness stood in the way of opportunity. No one would've volunteered to help her, and he didn't want to see her hurt by that. It was all for Richard Carter anyway. So Danny kept telling himself.

Maybe it was Sebastian's wine getting to his head, but he thought he had felt something while holding her hand, a twinge of that electricity they had years ago. Even if it had been real, it wouldn't matter. She was here temporarily. If he knew anything about Kara Carter, it was that her ambitions always shot way past the boundaries of Waverly Lake.

"The door." Hannah marched in his bedroom. "Someone's knocking at the door."

"Who is knocking? Obviously not you." He pushed her nose like the cute button it was. His gut wanted to lecture her on privacy and barging in, but personal space was a never-ending subject. Hannah overwhelmingly valued and controlled her own but could not transfer that desire to other people.

The knocking escalated. His heart jumped, and he threw on a T-shirt and pair of jeans that he plucked off the floor. Would Kara come by here? They had agreed to meet at Pearson's Wharf, and not this early.

"Daniel! It's Mom!" Tracy yelled.

His heart dropped back into place. Of course it was Mom. She was worse than Hannah with the barging and the privacy invasion. Moving away from the Bennett compound had been liberating. However, he had moved into a house that obviously did not put enough distance between him and the Bennetts.

"Come on." He stood in the doorway. "Let's go say hi to Grandma." He followed Hannah down the stairs.

Mom stood in the kitchen dressed as if ready for church—a frilly, black-and-white checkered dress topped off with an oversized, floppy, cream-colored hat. Dad stood with his arms crossed, leaning on the counter and gazing out the back patio in his uniform of khakis and a polo shirt.

"Dad's here too?"

"Good morning, Daniel. And to my little sweetie." She planted a kiss on Hannah's cheek, who seemed unfazed.

"Your father and I are headed out to the church yard sale fundraiser. I thought I'd stop by with some leftovers. I know how much Hannah loves my lasagna."

"Thanks, Mom." No, Hannah did not in fact like her lasagna, but it didn't matter how many times Danny told her. At least Tracy was around to eat it.

She finished placing the containers in the fridge and fidgeted with the empty grocery bag. Classic Mom stalling.

"Anything else on your mind?"

Tracy walked into the kitchen, her oversized pajamas swallowing her frame and her hair disheveled. He didn't know how long she would be staying, but he was certainly glad to see her this morning.

"Oh, I didn't realize you were here," Mom said. "Come to think of it, I didn't hear you come home last night."

Tracy poured herself a cup of stale coffee, microwaved it, and sat down at the kitchen table. "Coffee first," she managed.

"She came with us last night to the movie," Danny said. "Figured, why not stay here? Hannah loves her being around." It was true, but it was also only half the truth. Danny had seen enough arguments between Tracy and their parents to know they clashed. To say like oil and vinegar would be an understatement, since that would imply they could at least exist side by side. No, their relationship was more like oil and fabric—two things better left apart. He just wished he didn't have to be the one to break the news to Mom. It's not like he had a stellar history with her either.

"Anyway, your father and I had a proposition for you. James?"

"What? Oh. Yes. Go ahead, dear. I think I see a loose nail." James Bennett wandered off to the back patio, squinting at a curtain rod. Danny took a deep breath. Dad was rarely invited over due to the fact he would scrutinize every little detail that was off on the house. It was bad enough when Danny and Hannah had been living in the apartment above Mom and Dad's garage. But at least then he could blame the landlord.

"What's your proposition?"

"We were at Nichols and Dimes and saw Tammy Gunther. We got to talking, and her nephew has a friend whose father runs the camp over in Rockford. It's a wonderful summer camp with canoeing, fishing, campfires at night, that sort of thing."

"Where are you going with this, Mom?"

"Well, seeing as it's the last month of summer, the camp is entirely booked. But since we go way back with the Gunthers, Tammy worked it out so Hannah could go for a week."

Tracy gulped. "Yeah, I'm sure it had nothing to do with an extra tuition offer," she muttered.

Beverly stood, mouth agape.

Danny closed his eyes, inhaling patience. "You know Hannah can't go to summer camp."

"Why not? She loves boating with you and being outdoors. I think it would be good for her."

"And you," Tracy managed before burying her face in the coffee mug.

"What?" He threw his hands in the air. "What is happening here? You're supposed to be attacking Mom under your breath."

"You can't always be here for her," Beverly said.

"I'm not. She's with the nanny plenty."

"That's not what I mean. She needs to get out, with other people. Other kids. She doesn't even have any friends."

The battle of home schooling versus public schooling never seemed to end. On the one hand, he knew she was safe and comfortable at home, and Mrs. Warren was excellent. On the other, Hannah didn't have the social aspect she needed if she was going to someday be out in the world without him.

"I told him to join a local support group," Tracy said. "There are plenty of families that get together for play dates and chat about what works, what doesn't work."

"How would you know?" She was right, there were forums and associations for parents and families affected by ASD. But joining would make him feel like a charity case, or like something was wrong with Hannah. It wasn't wrong to have ASD. It was different.

"Don't—" He calmed his blood down from a boil to a simmer. "I'm doing the best I know how."

"No one is saying you aren't, honey. But look. Your father and I will pay for it. Try it out. At least say you'll think about it."

"Think of all that time you could have with Kara." Tracy raised her eyebrows and swayed her shoulders.

Danny whipped her a look. "Isn't it time for you to head on back to Mom and Dad's place?"

"What? I'm just sayin'. Seemed like you two got along pretty well from where I was sitting last night. Enough to be partners in—"

"Tracy," he gritted through his teeth.

Beverly's face turned sour. "I think I did hear she was back in town."

Ugh. This was not how his Saturday was supposed to go. Ten years away hadn't abated his mother's feelings toward Kara. "I know *you* know full well that she's back. And living next door.

She's my neighbor. We're friends. That's all." The last words crackled.

"That sounds believable," Tracy snorted.

"I'd hate to see the same mistakes being made, Daniel."

And there it was. Beverly seeing the line and waving as she barreled right over it. The Kara situation wasn't worth arguing over now. No, he had to save his energy for the battles over Hannah.

"You know what, I'm going to be late. I have to be at Pearson's soon." He poured the stale pot of coffee in the sink. Mom's hand fell gently on his shoulder.

"Just think about it, okay?"

He turned around, Tracy and Mom staring with eyes full of hope.

"Fine, I'll think about it. What week did you sign her up for?"

"She'd start Monday."

"What? As in this week?"

"You still have time to think about it, honey. Just need to know by tomorrow evening, I suppose."

"You're something else."

"We love you too, son." She grabbed his face and kissed him on the cheek. "Come on, James."

"Yes, get him out of here before he decides to knock out a wall," Danny said.

Beverly chuckled. "Call me later." She walked out with James in tow, the sound of the patio door springing back a clap of joy.

Danny swung around to Tracy, who walked to the fridge. "What was that all about?"

"I was waiting for her to leave. You know she'd yell at me for eating lasagna at breakfast."

"That's not what I'm talking about." He leaned on the counter, staring her down.

"I think they just want to do something nice for you."

"I mean you. Since when don't you have my back?"

She scoffed. "I am offended. I did have your back. It just so happens I think it's a good idea for Hannah, and for you. You could use some time to yourself. Maybe get a little romance back in your life."

"I don't need romance."

"Okay, then at least make some friends. Find a hobby."

"I have friends, and my hobbies are Hannah's hobbies."

"You're not getting it." She approached him, her coffee in one hand, the other on his shoulder. "You are a great dad. But even the greatest dads need a break. Plus, they're paying for it. Mom probably spent more on that getup she was wearing. Does the woman own a pair of sweats?"

Danny chuckled. Yes, it was good to have Tracy around.

"All I'm saying is, why not give it a try?" She shrugged and moseyed out of the kitchen, fork and lasagna container in hand.

"You're teaching Hannah bad habits."

She shuffled over to Hannah at the back patio. "Deal with it!"

He stood in the kitchen, alone. They were all going mad. Did they really think Hannah would be okay in summer camp? True, he didn't have a break since...basically, since she was born. But that was the deal in becoming a father.

He shook his head. No, they had it all wrong. Hannah was just fine. He was just fine. There was no sense in changing it up. Summer camp was a no go.

Chapter Sixteen

"YOU'RE NOT GOING TO BELIEVE WHAT I FOUND OUT."

Kara paced her childhood bedroom floor, alternating glances out the north and east windows. She had wanted to ignore her phone, but a part of her hoped Marcus had changed his mind about the conference. It was false hope.

"Apparently, Ned Walburn is leaving *PhotoStyle Magazine*. They have an opening for a photographer, and I mentioned your name."

"You what?" It was one thing to learn about an opening. It was another to declare to companies she was out of work and desperate.

"His name was Ben, I think. When he heard your name, he said you were school buddies."

"Ben...Ben Martinez?"

"Yeah, that's him. He's part of the hiring team at *PhotoStyle* and said he'd love to book you an interview."

Her annoyance with Marcus turned to optimism. "Really?" She and Ben had enjoyed a good rapport throughout school and helped each other out once in a while on projects. It'd be harder to find a better "in" to such a job.

"Yeah. He said he can see you first thing when he gets back from the conference."

"But—that's too soon. I'd have to miss the regatta." She reverted to the east window and pulled back the curtain. She couldn't see Dad directly, but knew he was in the shop, even when he shouldn't be. There was nothing to pinpoint how exactly she knew. It was like knowing if something was alive or not. And the shop looked alive when Dad was in it.

"Kara, I'm worried about you." His tone turned, and she could feel his frustration through the phone. "You're losing focus of the big picture here. This is an amazing opportunity."

"It is, Marcus. But I made a promise. Besides, *PhotoStyle* is a bit out of my wheelhouse." That was putting it lightly. The magazine was famous for being edgy and almost futuristic in its contemporary feel. It focused on art and fashion, which gave it a loyal audience and hence a great way to make a name for herself. But it wasn't like *International Ecologic*. It wasn't introducing problems of the world to its readers, urging them for answers. She had pictured something more impactful.

"Look, I'm trying over here. You have the talent for it. Just give it a shot for a while, get your name out there, and you could move on to what you really want."

Kara sighed and slumped onto the bed. "Okay. I'll do the interview, but only after the regatta."

"Kara—"

"I don't back out of a promise." The silence was too heavy to wait for him to end it. "I'll give them a call to schedule it."

"No, it's okay." Marcus sighed. "It was my f—I mean, I was the one who knew about the layoff. Maybe I should've told you."

It was the first time he had acknowledged any wrongdoing. Perhaps they did have a chance to move on from all of this. She'd return to New York, have a new job, and they'd be back in the comfortable swing of things.

"I'll talk to Ben while I'm here."

"Thank you. After the regatta I'll be free."

She gasped.

Regatta practice. With Danny. He had been charming and

exasperating at the same time last night, getting her to agree to join forces. She had thrown a morning practice on him—set the tone off the bat—but had nearly forgotten.

She checked her laptop's clock, giving her only twenty minutes to make it on time to Pearson's Wharf.

"Look, I'm sorry to cut this short, but I have to get going."

"Call me later?"

"Sure."

"I miss you."

She hesitated, her mouth drying for a split second. It wasn't *I love you*. But it moved them back in the right direction. "Miss you too."

She kept the phone in her hand after hanging up. He was trying to mend things, and perhaps she shouldn't have been so tough on him.

She opened her camera case and powered up the camera, flipping through her saved images on the digital screen. Most of her best photos had been published or sent off with her résumé. She'd need to bulk up her portfolio if she was going to do this interview, but that work would have to wait.

She glanced at the clock again. Seventeen minutes.

She put away the camera and slipped on sneakers, making a mental note to buy some proper boating shoes. They'd get the job done today but wouldn't work well with the water and scuffing, and flip-flops were a downright slippery hazard. She slung the cross strap of her smallest purse over her shoulder and ran out the house.

She hopped on the bike, a powder-blue cruiser that had kept its fair condition despite the years of wear followed by a decade in storage. Her bottom was still sore from yesterday's ride around town. The bike ride provided a nice breeze over her legs and arms until she had to stop at the stop signs and traffic lights—not that there were many between home and Pearson's Wharf. Dowager traffic usually slowed at the square downtown, plus tourists crawled along to find parking during peak times.

She left the bike at Bingham's and walked to the wharf. Dad

gave her the approximate location of the sailboat but hadn't told her the name. As she stood in front of the shiny, splendid vessel, stained deep copper with crisp white lines, she understood why he hadn't. In golden lettering along the stern was the name he had granted his beautiful work. *Kare Bear.*

She walked up the wooden dock and stepped over the starboard side. The sloop was the right amount of steadiness under her feet, swaying slightly to the ripples in the wharf but not enough to worry her about extreme leaning in high winds. "You did good, Dad."

"What was that?"

She startled, grasping the mast rising from the middle like a signpost.

"Sorry I'm late." Danny leaped on board. His hair was still wet, the longer pieces swept back, and he wore a T-shirt tucked haphazardly in his board shorts. Kara looked at his feet. Flip-flops. Of course.

"Just don't let it happen again." In truth, Kara had arrived six minutes past their meeting time of nine o'clock.

The boat dramatically decreased in size with Danny aboard. It was starting to look like a bad decision. Best to get it over with. The sooner they had a feel for her, the sooner they didn't have to see each other.

"Admittedly, it's been a while since I've done this. I was thinking we'd take her out, practice maneuvering close by to see how smoothly we can operate together, then if we have time, take her around the main island and back. Sound all right?"

"You got it, boss. Or Captain, I suppose, is the right term."

Yes, it was the right term. "Kara will do."

"Okay, Kara."

"All right then. I'm confident my dad left things as they should be, but let's check the rigging before we head out."

She started with the running rigging. Danny stood toward the stern, not making a move. It was going to be difficult not to look at him. Was he staring at her? She couldn't *not* look at him. How were they going to work as a team if she avoided the sight of him? She looked up, and Danny turned his head down, hand pushing the tiller back and forth. He had been looking at her. No matter. If they each did their jobs, they could get through this.

"How's it look—"

Danny quickly landed his hands on the tiller, squinting up into the sky.

The realization exacerbated the doubt she had to begin with. "You've got to be kidding."

"Hmm?" Danny took his hands off the tiller, fidgeting them in the air until deciding to land them on his hips.

"You don't know how to sail, do you?"

"It's not that I've never sailed—"

"Oh my gosh. This is insane. You're a marine mechanic."

"Keyword 'mechanic.' As in, motors, all things *mechanical*."

"I thought your parents placed in the regatta, like, every year."

"That is true. I've been on their sailboat. But my parents hire a team every year to sail their boat. So..." He shrugged.

"This can't be happening."

"Look, I said I'm here to help, and I mean that. You've tutored me before."

"Yeah, in pre-calc!"

"Which should be much worse than this situation."

"I can't argue with you there." It wasn't just a jab at the present.

"What is that supposed to mean?"

"I think you know what that means."

"You're going there?" He threw his hands up in the air. "No, you know what? Let's go there. Because if we are going to be a team —an actual functioning sailing crew—you need to get over any of that old stuff you've been harboring for years."

"Yeah, make it all about me. I'm not the one who messed up."

"Would you just listen, please?"

Kara folded her arms and sat on the deck.

"I tried to talk to you. That summer. After graduation. You didn't answer any of my calls. I came knocking on your door. I even threw rocks at your bedroom window like some high school cliché."

She had known about the calls and the knocking, but not the rocks. But if he had, it gave her a little bit of satisfaction knowing he had been out there in the open, unanswered.

"I tried, Kara."

"You didn't try when it mattered." Her voice was weak, betraying her desire to seem stalwart. "You expect me to feel bad for you? We spent our whole senior year together. Tutoring turned into hanging out every day. I went to every single home game to watch you play football. You think I did that because I liked the sport? It was to see you. But you didn't want anyone to see me. Or at least see *you* with me."

"Is that what you think happened?"

"No." That he was acting naïve only made it worse. "I *know* that's what happened. You acted like we had nothing when you know full well it was something. Or that it had been something to me. I had never..." Kara shook her head. That kiss. She blurred out the memory of the setting sun and shore of the lake. It had been the most special moment of senior year, yet Danny had casually thrown it all away. It was both exhilarating and heart-wrenching to think about.

"I never acted like we had nothing. Why else would I try to talk to you after—"

"After you ditched me?"

He stopped and closed his eyes. It was easier to look at him without those intense gray-blues penetrating her armor.

"Are you forgetting that part? You ditched me. I thought after all that time, you would take me to prom. You didn't even tell me you were taking someone else. I had to hear it from Liz."

"I can't believe we're back here again."

"Yeah, we're back here again. Because we never addressed it then."

"Because you wouldn't talk to me. Just say it. Say what you need to say."

She stood, legs wobblier than anticipated before catching her balance. "I know I was the nerdy girl, and you were the jock. You had appearances to keep up. But I fell for you that year. I fell so hard." Her eyes teared, and noticing her vision blurring made her even more upset. But he needed to hear it. "You made me feel like I wasn't worthy of your attention. Of anyone's attention."

The feeling of liberation from saying it was overwhelmed by a sense of vulnerability and embarrassment. It was ten years ago, and she had moved on. She had learned she was worthy of respect and didn't want him to think he had tarnished her life for the past decade. But she was emotional about it because it shouldn't have happened to teenage Kara. Or any teenage girl.

"Can I say my piece now?" He stared at her, eyes wide open. Did he not even care what she had spewed out?

"What I did senior year was wrong."

So far, a good start.

"Spending all that time with you...I did fall for you too. And I knew you were at those games because I looked for you. I knew everything you had done for me and how you felt about me. Yet I still let my so-called friends get to me. Peer pressure. Whatever you want to call it."

He touched her elbow briefly, a sizzle on her skin. "I'm not saying it's their fault. It's my fault. For not being mature enough then. I should've been true to myself. And fair to you. And having Hannah...if anyone ever treats Hannah the way I treated you... Hannah would have to visit me in prison."

He had always been good with words. Not in the fancy wordsmith sort of way. No, Danny Bennett knew how to pack an emotional punch with his words. Back then, it was hard to tell what was fluff and what was real. But now, it couldn't all be fluff. The truth was in his eyes and deep yet mild-mannered voice when he said Hannah's name. He had meant those words.

"If you can't accept that...I'll just have to respect that. But please, let me do this. If not for you, then for your dad. He and your mom really have helped me and Hannah through some tough times. If it weren't for them, I don't think Mr. Rutherford would've even considered the arrangement we made to secure the house. Please, Kara. I want to do this for him."

Kara scanned *Kare Bear*, the curves and lines a beautiful work of artistry. Art her dad had made and desperately wanted to be seen. She knew that feeling, that desire to create and bring joy to others.

She met Danny's eyes. "Okay."

"Okay? As in..."

"As in, I accept your apology." Kara raised her brow. "Did you actually apologize in any of that?"

Danny chuffed. "If I didn't, I'm sorry."

"Sorry for not apologizing, or sorry for the way you treated me? I just want to be clear, if we're going to have a fresh start and all."

"Okay then. I'm sorry, Kara. For how I treated you."

"Thank you." It had been all she wanted to hear a decade ago, but admittedly she didn't give him the chance. It seemed foolish to have craved it years later. Their lives had branched off, diverging and moving past high school. She was going to marry Marcus. High school was a ripple in a life of waves.

"Fresh start, huh?" Danny's mouth curled in that adorable smile. Troubling, but adorable.

"Let's take it one lesson at a time."

"Sure thing."

Her eyes grew wide processing his lack of nautical knowledge. "Of which I think there will be many."

Chapter Seventeen

"What do you mean, you didn't make the delivery?" Richard Carter stood by the Carter Furniture truck in the driveway, balancing his good leg and crutches on the gravel. The first sailing lesson, once it started after an uncomfortable albeit productive discussion, was tedious, going over proper names of the vessel repeatedly and showing Danny the ropes in every sense of the phrase.

"I've got Carly Fletcher calling me up wondering where her new waiting area furniture is, and I'm swearing left and right that my trustworthy daughter delivered them Wednesday."

"I had fully meant to go on Wednesday." Okay, that was a partial lie. She had avoided the delivery—or at least, saved it for last. "But then I rushed to the hospital because that was more important, then Marcus arrived..."

He looked down at his cast, anger fading. It wasn't often Dad was upset. He wasn't that upset now, really. He barely raised his voice. After he would attempt to chew Kara out, whether it had been sneaking out of the house or skipping out on Sunday dinner without telling Mom, Kara always felt like hugging him and telling him he was the best dad. His kind soul was too adorable.

"Then yesterday I was so focused on finding a partner, I completely forgot about the delivery."

"I know there's been a lot going on." He shrugged as best he could with his arms over the crutches. "But here we are, Saturday afternoon, and Carly still doesn't have her things."

"I'll go right now. Don't worry." It was the last task she was up for. Literally, waiting at the DMV on a busy Saturday was more appealing. Or scraping gum off the sidewalks. "You go inside and relax. Stay off your feet."

"Don't worry about me. Worry about the business." He turned around in a hobble. "Keys are in the truck."

"Okay." She walked her bike to the front porch before heading to the truck. She paused by the driver's door. "Oh, and Dad?"

"Yeah?"

"She's gorgeous."

He cracked a smile.

"The name ain't bad either."

He chuckled, and she waved before stepping up into the truck.

Kara drove into town, sighing and whining to herself. It was the one place she had told herself upon returning to never step foot in again. But all roads in Waverly Lake led to Dye Happy Salon. Okay, not roads technically, but all stories, be they true or false, led to or spread from there.

She parked the truck on a side street, the parking along Dowager Street taken up by the Saturday store window shoppers walking their dogs down the sidewalks and eating ice cream sandwiches from the freezer of Nichols and Dimes Drugstore. The black BMW was out of its spot. Steve Albertson must not work weekends.

Her stomach spun in knots as she stood outside the door. Across the square's green space, its benches full of Saturday town revelers, stood Portside Portrait. Mr. Lawson had propped the door open and was wiping the glass. It would be sad to see such a staple of the town vanish. Too bad it was the wrong staple.

Kara inhaled deeply before swinging open the door to Dye Happy

Salon. The interior was shocking in its...decency. The walls were no longer blindingly fuchsia but toned down in a neutral pewter. A sleek, black desk sat in the middle of the entryway, where a young woman stood, speaking on the phone. She put her finger up for Kara to wait.

Even with the makeover—hairdryers hanging from the ceiling over each station, newer unframed mirrors on the wall, unlike the gaudy ornate ones long ago—the aroma broke the façade of newness. No matter how hard an effort was put forth, Kara could still pinpoint the smell of chemical permanent, as if '80s teenagers had signed a hair yearbook in the form of chemicals in drywall.

"Can I help you?" The receptionist hung up the phone.

"I'm here to deliver some furniture pieces. I'm assuming for up here." The assumption had been made because the pieces were two chairs, a coffee table, and a magazine stand, rather than as a statement on the front furniture being in obvious need of an update. Hadn't Dad said they were for the front? Kara realized it may have sounded insulting. "I think they were made for the waiting area."

"Who's that, Stacy?" The voice was undeniably that of Carly Fletcher, shrill yet solid, with an accent more akin to the Carolina Lowcountry than Appalachia, carrying above all the sinks and hairdryers working at once.

"Someone with a furniture delivery."

Carly walked up to the front. The photos of models on the wall may have sported the chicest of modern hairstyles, but Carly still donned her blonder-than-ever-naturally-possible hair. As with the salon updates, it was jarring to see the teasing level cut down ten notches. She looked older by more than twenty years, the black apron barely hiding the bold colors of her clothes. Kara had pictured her as an implant from Boca Raton or some other southern beachy local who somehow found herself in the western mountains of North Carolina.

"Well, there she is, standing right in front of me. Come here, Kara!" Carly squeezed Kara, her perfume as permeant in her skin as the '80s perm odor. "It is so good to see you."

"Where would you like me to—"

"You know, I knew that was you at Films on Friday. I told myself I should've come over, but then you were whisked away by that sweet Danny Bennett. You two. Ugh. It's like you never left."

It's actually not like that. Even though Danny had kept their relationship in high school secret to his social circle, there was no putting anything past the hairdresser. Kara still had no idea how Carly had figured it out before prom.

"Anyway, I have your finished pieces. I'll need help with the coffee table."

"I can have Christian—" She waved to the back. "Christian, you finished with the shampoo?"

A thin man in his twenties wearing black skinny jeans and a black T-shirt approached. His height dwarfed Kara and Carly. "This lovely woman is an old friend, Kara Carter. She needs some help with our new furniture, if you don't mind."

Christian nodded, and Kara was more than happy to lead him out of the salon and into the mountain air. "You seem a bit young to be an old friend of Carly," he said.

"Oh, *friend* is a little..." She waved her hand. "Doesn't matter. She was my hairdresser when I was younger. I'd say she knows my mom more than me."

"She knows a lot of people." Christian's eyes widened, and Kara chuckled.

Kara opened the truck's tailgate. "Coffee table is the heaviest." She climbed into the truck and slid the black-painted table to the edge. In a few minutes, and with some repositioning, Christian helped her get the piece to the ground unscathed.

They each carried a side, Christian offering to walk backwards.

"How did you get involved with the salon? I know Carly doesn't hire lightly."

"Yes, you're right. Unless your mom is her sister, who has an even sharper tongue and holds knowledge of family secrets."

"Ah, I see."

"Just a summer job. My contribution to my education."

"College?"

"Western Carolina. Senior year."

"Well, congratulations."

"It's not over yet. But thanks."

The receptionist held the door open as they delivered the coffee table into the waiting area.

"I can get the rest from here," Kara said.

"Kara, I have the most wonderful idea." Carly waved a bright flyer as she rushed Kara. Hopefully not another movie night.

"I'll get the rest," Christian said. "Looks like you have some chatting to do." Kara shook her head, and he smirked on his way out.

"The Annual Waverly Lake Regatta Parade is coming up." Carly handed her the flyer—a string of cars decked out in various business themes.

"They still do that?"

"Of course! You can't have an afternoon regatta without a morning parade before and an evening social afterward. Anyway, I can still use an extra person for the Dye Happy car."

"I don't think that's—"

"It would be wonderful! You'd sit in the back and wave to everyone, and I'd do your hair to show off the salon. I need someone in your age group, and the town would love to see you participate."

"Unfortunately, I'm actually sailing in the regatta." *That decision finally paid off.*

"Honey, we're all racing. In fact, Danny just finished fixing up *Permanent Vacay.*"

"He worked on your sailboat?" Had Danny been feigning ignorance this morning? If he had lied, boy, was she going to chew him out. But on the other hand, she could bypass a lot of the basics in their practice sessions.

"Well, he worked on the motor. Some shaft or piston or something. I don't know." She waved it off.

He had been telling the truth. Fortunate for him. Unfortunate for the team.

"What do you say?"

"I'm sorry, Carly. I'm not really the parade type."

"Oh, don't be modest." Carly stroked Kara's hair. "Besides, I never did get to do the fancy do I had planned for your prom."

An invite to participate in an event that would be extremely uncomfortable for Kara, with a dollop of sugary insult on top. No, Carly hadn't changed.

"Please. I'll be heartbroken if you don't agree."

And there was the side of guilt. Kara sighed, shaking her head at what she was about to say. "Okay."

"Really? Oh dear, you don't have to unless you really want to."

Kara couldn't decide if her blood was boiling because of Carly or because Dad had made her enter a place she had sworn off. For good reason.

"I'll do it."

"Oh, it's going to be perfect! The parade riders have to be seated by eight, so I'm having the models get here by seven." She fluffed Kara's brown tresses. "Still have thick hair. What most customers wouldn't give for it either. Mm, better make it six. I'll do you first."

"Wonderful." Kara feigned a smile.

Christian finished unloading with the magazine rack. "All set."

"Oh, not there, dear. We're going to have to change this all around." Carly picked up a chair and moved it to the other side of the waiting area.

Kara shook Christian's hand. "Good to meet you, and thanks for the help."

"No problem."

"Enjoy the rest of your day." It was Kara's turn to smirk at him.

"Never a dull moment."

Kara walked out of Dye Happy Salon, grateful for escaping. But in usual Carly fashion, Kara had a return appointment already booked.

Chapter Eighteen

"WHAT ABOUT YOUR RAIN JACKET?" DANNY PACED around Hannah's room while she sat on the floor playing cards with Tracy. It was tough enough sending Hannah to summer camp. Double tough when he decided last-minute. Hannah didn't fare well with plans changing, but luckily, the only thing they had planned for this Sunday was to hang out with Tracy at the house. It was both good and bad when Danny thought about it. Perhaps everyone was right. He was shielding her from people and the real world. Heck, movie nights were the only times he had taken her anywhere with crowds, outside of the rare shopping trip, since Beverly kept bringing food.

Sure, Hannah was protected and safe, but that wasn't much of a life either. That was why Danny had finally given in and agreed to summer camp.

"I think you got it covered," Tracy said. "If you forget anything, I'm sure they'll cover for you at the camp."

"I don't want to take any chances. I'm already taking enough of a chance as it is."

"I hope you're referring to Kara and not your daughter here. Have a little faith in her."

Danny stopped and sighed. "Okay, first off, you know what I

meant." He knelt next to Hannah. "It's not you, Hannah. It's me. You go and be you at camp. I just don't know how I'm going to function without my Hannah here." He patted her knee.

"And second?" Tracy's brown eyes glared at him over her hand of cards, curls spilling out of her ponytail.

"And second, Kara is none of your business."

Tracy silently mimicked his last words, most likely satisfied she got him to address Kara on any level. He didn't want to admit it, but the possibility of spending time with Kara on his own outside of practice was a perk of his decision. Perhaps they'd go out for breakfast before practice, or maybe even hit the fair later this week. But who was he kidding? She was engaged, and she was Kara.

He had told himself last night Kara had nothing to do with the decision, that it had everything to do with Hannah. But it didn't mean that he couldn't try to enjoy his time while Hannah was away. The chances it would be with Kara were low anyway.

Tracy stood and looked out the bedroom window. "Mom and Dad are here. Look at that, a hired car. Pulling out all the stops."

"Okay, Hannah." Danny zipped up her bag. "Time to go."

Hannah followed Danny and Tracy down the stairs to the foyer. Beverly had let herself in the front door.

"There's my little sweetie." Beverly loosely hugged Hannah. "Are you ready to go? You're going to have so much fun!" She held Hannah's hand.

Danny crouched to meet Hannah's eye level. "Now, if you don't like it for any reason, you have the camp call me, okay? I'll have my phone on me at all times."

Hannah nodded.

"Give her a chance, Daniel."

"Mom—"

"Couldn't you dress her in anything other than that raggedy shirt? At least have her look decent."

Tracy stepped in between Danny and Beverly. "It was awfully nice for Mom to set this up, wasn't it?" She glared at Danny.

"Yes," he managed through his teeth. Maybe he'd try out one of those boxing classes while he was at it. He patted Hannah's shoulders as he stood up. "Yes, thank you, Mom. It was nice of you."

"Anything for my little sweetie."

Tracy leaned to whisper in Danny's ear. "And Hannah too."

Danny elbowed her. Since they were kids, Tracy'd had the notion Danny was Beverly's golden boy, and she made sure to express it whenever she had the chance. If "golden boy" meant having to deal with Mom's insufferable control, then yes, he was the golden boy.

"Well, we're off." Beverly opened the front door. "Wave goodbye to Daddy."

Hannah waved, and Danny blew her a kiss. "Buckle up nice and tight. Don't let her skip the booster. She'll try to convince you otherwise."

"Don't worry. We did all right with you, didn't we?"

"Don't answer that," Tracy said through her smile as she waved. The front door closed, and Tracy clapped her hands. "Well, I'm off."

It wasn't worth asking where to. "Are you going to be back late?"

"Aren't you the inquisitive one?"

"I don't care what you do. Just make sure you bring the house key I gave you."

"Ooh, you planning on making it a late night?"

He raised his eyebrows. "I don't want to get out of bed when you come knocking at two in the morning."

Danny shuffled off to the kitchen, fidgeting with the few dishes left lying around.

Tracy grabbed her purse at the sound of tires over gravel in the driveway. "See you later then."

"See ya."

She poked her head back in the house as she exited. "Tell Kara I said hello."

Danny shook his head and shooed her away. The door closed, and he was in his house. Quiet and alone.

IN ONE SENSE, IT WAS HARD TO BELIEVE IT WAS Wednesday already. Hannah had been away three nights, the longest she had ever been away from him. It was encouraging she could experience the joys of camp like most other kids, and perhaps was even forging solid friendships.

On the other hand, the past two afternoons of lessons—not fooling anyone calling them practice—had been grueling. Kara was relentless in throwing new terms at him and quizzing him repeatedly on previous ones. They all started to jumble together. How could such a simple vessel have a million bits and pieces with their own names?

It had been two straight hours of rigging work under direct sunlight when Danny had enough.

"You know if we actually set sail, we might could catch a breeze."

"And if you mastered that bowline, we'd be closer to leaving this dock."

He pulled the line tight, waving the looped rope in front of her face before dropping it and moving aft next to her. She stood when his shoulder brushed hers. "We'll get to that in time."

It was what she had been doing all week. At first, he thought he was imagining things. She had a tight schedule and stuck to it, so she moved on whenever it looked like he was taking a break. But then he put it to the test—sometimes skimming her or fumbling over her feet with his. Nothing inappropriate, only what two teammates would have to put up with on a small sailing vessel. If they were actually sailing.

But every time he neared her, she backed off.

"Kara, I've gotta say something."

"Yeah?" She folded her arms. "What is it?"

Why are you still acting mad at me after we started fresh? Why can't we even sit together without you bolting? Knowing her too well paid off at times—like knowing when not to say everything. "The regatta is a week and a half away."

"Which is why we need to get back to work."

"That's my point."

"Look, if this is too hard for you—"

"That's not it. It's not too hard." He held up his hand to stop her before the backlash. "Don't get me wrong, it's hard. I've learned and unlearned and relearned more things than I could fathom I would in a few days. But if you really want to have a shot at placing in this race, you've got to be comfortable going out there with me on the water." It sounded safe enough. Was it that she didn't trust him not to sink the thing? Or was she scared to be alone with him, with no easy route to walk away whenever she felt like it? If that were the case, not only would it make him feel disrespected, it would also negate the purpose of the lessons in the first place.

"If we're going to be a team, we have to work as a team. That means together. In sync. I know I walked into this knowing next to nothing about sailing, but even I know that's how a team works best."

She bit her bottom lip.

That was it. He had done it.

"I know," she said.

Or maybe he hadn't done it.

"I just..." She closed her eyes, shaking her head.

"What is it? You can talk to me." He stood, taking a step closer. "As your teammate."

"I think all the talk about last time..."

"The regatta?"

"They named it a Kerror for goodness' sake. It got to me. I don't want to mess up again. I don't want to fool myself out there, or fool you. Or worse yet, make my dad look like a fool and give this thing the wrong kind of attention."

It was not what he had anticipated. Seeing her spirit cracking tugged at his own heart. She was the most stubborn, determined woman he had known, and the town had gotten to her head. No wonder she was fighting to get out.

"That's why I've been drilling you on the terms. Because that's where I messed up. We came to the turning point and—"

He put his hand up, stopping her. He knew that part. The boat somehow lost the wind in the turn, angling her and Richard in a precarious position, almost colliding with the vessels behind them. The correction took enough time to lose their second place, dropping it to dead last.

"It's like my head got jumbled up on the terms instead of relying on muscle memory, on just doing it the way I knew how."

"I want to help you, I really do. You're not going to make a fool of yourself if I can help it." He smiled. "I know you're not going to want to hear this, but you've got to relax. Have fun with it. You're on a sailboat on one of the prettiest lakes in the country. We've got the mountains, the blue water—we're standing on a boat that your dad made. With his hands."

Finally, a chuckle. Her eyes shone like emeralds in the sun when she was happy.

"Take it all in, Kara." He spread his arms out to the world. "It's so...hot."

She laughed, a deep one that made him smile without thinking. "It is freaking hot," she said.

"Okay, we definitely agree on something. This is good. Teammates, seeing eye to eye."

"Done for today?"

"Sure." It was a relief, not just because they'd be out of the heat, but because she had opened up. Even if it was hard for her.

"I have a proposition. Something to bring back a little fun in your life. Relax the drill sergeant a bit." It was ironic, given Tracy had lectured *him* about not having fun.

"I...have fun."

"Wow. That was absolutely convincing."

She stood, mouth agape. "Just because I'm a tough teacher doesn't mean I don't have fun."

"Okay. Then prove it." This was his best opportunity. "Let's go to the fair."

"The fair?" Her eyebrows raised, doubtful. "You're serious."

"Yep. I'm Ferris wheel, bumper car serious."

She stared off in the distance.

"Just a fun night out between two new friends. Fun or drill sergeant. Your call." Was she actually considering it? A night out with him, not on the boat? He had thought about it but didn't really think she'd ever agree.

"Okay."

"Okay, as in you made a decision?"

"Yeah."

"Which is?"

"I choose fun."

Chapter Nineteen

WEDNESDAY, AUGUST 12

Kara walked with Danny Bennett through the front gates of the Waverly Lake Fair. Although Lorain County held a much larger fair closer to Labor Day, Waverly Lake insisted on having its own the week before the regatta. It helped spread out the heaviest summer tourist time over two weeks instead of one. Fundraisers were held throughout the year to help pay for it, on top of the cost of admission. Kara had once worked a snowball-throwing booth during Winterfest, in which residents could dunk their favorite—or least favorite—teachers in a "polar plunge." The cost had been five dollars for three throws, but their reactions coming out of the water were priceless.

For a town fair, it was impressive. Food trucks lined the entrance walkway on both sides, permeating the air with the smell of sizzling sausage and peppers mixed with funnel cakes and cotton candy. Being offset from the lake a few miles southeast of the wharf made the fair feel like a pocket of humidity, begging guests to buy tickets for rides just to feel a breeze.

"Rides or games first?" Danny rubbed his hands together. His face glowed like a five-year-old on Christmas.

"Well, if you win anything you'll have to carry it around the rest of the time."

"You mean *when* I win." He puffed his chest out.

"Oh, someone is awfully confident."

"I was pretty famous on the football team, you know."

She concurred with a nod side to side. "True. Can't say it was for athleticism though."

Danny stopped walking alongside her, mouth ajar. "You're rotten."

"I'm just kidding. A little." Kara snapped a picture of him half-offended. If she wanted to enter that contest, she'd need actual photos to upload. Seeing as most of her time was spent on *Kare Bear* or inside the Carter Furniture truck, any other outing was an opportunity. "Come on. Let's ride something. Your pick."

"*Avalanche* it is."

"That doesn't sound good."

Danny led her to a ride on a circular platform, the cars lined one after another, with half the track raised and the other flat like a creased paper plate.

"You'll want to leave your camera." Danny pointed to a set of cubbies next to the ride conductor.

She stuck her camera in the back of a shelf and sat on the inner part of the car, with Danny on the outer side. The attendant checked the meager safety bar that didn't even reach their laps and started the ride. Loud music blared as the ride increased in speed, the cars rotating up the side and over the flat. As the speed increased, the music thumped and Kara felt pulled to the outside, squishing Danny.

"Ah! Sorry!" She closed her eyes and squealed. Danny laughed, pressed against the side of the car. She gripped the bar, but they spun too fast, her hips glued to Danny's. The ride slowed, and Kara caught her breath.

"That was crazy. How are kids not flying out of this thing?" The ride jerked, and the car moved in reverse. Kara clutched the bar. "It's not over?"

"Nope!" Danny claimed his handrail territory, muscular arms taut. "Now the fun part!"

They spun in reverse, the force pushing her hips off the seat while sticking to Danny. He reached around her waist and held her back.

The ride slowed, and Kara's giggles subsided. She sat hip to hip with Danny and looked at him, his face filled with delight. He looked gorgeous. He was relaxed, his athletic shoulders loose, and there was glee in his eyes. Like he didn't have a care in the world.

Kara realized his arm was still around her, and she scooted away. She fixed her tussled hair into a ponytail, and he let go. It felt wrong, like taking a comfortable blanket off and feeling the chill in the air. All week she had avoided his electrifying touch, as if in an articulated dance. Yes, the town had gotten into her head, killing her sailing confidence. But that wasn't the whole story, if she was being honest. She and Danny had only recently reconciled their past. To be so close to him on the boat...it was hard enough looking at him. And it wasn't fair to Marcus.

The attendant unlocked the bar, and they exited the ride. Kara grabbed her camera and walked down the stairs after Danny. Her balance was thrown off, the lights of the fair spinning around her.

"Whoa..." Danny held her arms. "You okay?"

"Yeah. I just got a little dizzy there."

He let go, and she fought the pull to draw him near again.

"Let's get you something to drink, okay?"

She nodded. He pointed her to a bench while he waited in line at a food truck. It felt good to be still, and her brain finally caught up with her body and settled down. She watched as a man struggled to knock down bottles with a ball, a woman standing next to him, more interested in her nails, or quite frankly, anything other than what he was doing. He turned, and she recognized his face—the attorney, Steve Albertson.

Danny returned with a large drink and a big tuft of fluffy blue cotton candy.

"You didn't have to," she said.

"What? This?" He pulled off a big wad and shoved it in his

mouth. "This is for me." The words fought through his stuffed mouth.

Kara laughed and sipped her drink. He tipped the cotton candy her way, and she gave in, the crystals turning the tips of her fingers blue. Danny smiled, showing off his blue mouth and teeth.

"You had to get blue, didn't you?"

"Pink isn't as much fun. No point in eating cotton candy if no one can tell you had cotton candy."

"I hate to tell you this, but we might have to move benches."

"Why's that?"

"Steve Albertson's over there." Steve shelled out another bill for a set of balls.

"Uh oh. You two didn't really hit it off the other night, did you?"

"We were just fine. His girlfriend was the one who had the attitude."

"Ah well, Steve may be awkward, but he's a good guy. He actually helped me through my divorce..."

Kara nearly choked on the candy before composing herself. "My parents actually didn't tell me a whole lot about what happened." She didn't even know he had been married and divorced until a few days ago, when she'd finally asked Mom what the deal was with Danny. Even then, their conversation was cut short when Mom got a phone call. "You don't have to talk about it if you don't want to. But if you need someone to listen, I'm here. You know, as your teammate."

"Does it bother you?"

"What? That I didn't know?"

"That I'm divorced."

"Why would that bother me?" She took another sip of her drink, the iced liquid not helping her flushed face. He had committed to someone—other than her. Not that Kara would've married Danny at eighteen. It was absurd to think it. But knowing he met someone who he was *that* crazy about... She shut out the jealousy before it manifested on her face. Hopefully.

"I'm a little surprised, actually, that you've been married."

"Why is that surprising? I'm a handsome man." He bared his blue mouth again. Damn if he wasn't right.

"It's not that. Not to say I think you're handsome—or not handsome." *This was spiraling.* "I mean, after knowing you, and what happened senior year and all...I guess I didn't see you as the marrying type."

"Hmm. I guess that's fair."

"Is it?"

"I can't say I ever thought, growing up, that I'd get married at twenty."

"I don't mean to pry..."

"But..." He raised his eyebrows.

"But why did you get married so young?"

He shuffled on the bench and lowered the cotton candy. "I guess you can say I fell for Maggie. Hard."

It sent pins to Kara's gut. She had fallen for him hard in high school. But he obviously hadn't reciprocated. What did Maggie have that she lacked? How had she won the heart of Danny Bennett?

"She was someone I thought was gorgeous and wild for life, and I wanted to marry her before she realized I wasn't good enough for her. Unfortunately, she ended up realizing it after we got married."

"That can't be what she thought." She shuffled, the evening heat suffocating. Since when did Danny's confidence in himself buckle? "I mean, deep, deep down—"

"Yes..."

"Abysmally deep down—"

"Hey now." The soft lines around his eyes were adorable.

"You're a good person too. I don't know this Maggie, but it sounds like she wasn't worthy of you and Hannah."

"Thanks." His smirk returned after the sincerity. "I could've used that stellar confidence boost back then."

"What are teammates for?"

Her heart pounded, the sweltering air clinging to her pulsing neck. Danny's jet-black hair lay disheveled over his forehead from the ride and the heat. Short stubble accented his strong jawline, begging to be scratched. This was how Kara had fallen for him, at his untidy and comfy best, as if her head on his shoulder would complete the package. The way he looked back, as if he caught sight of something magnificent that would disappear if he turned away...

Danny's phone buzzed, and she startled back to reality.

What the heck was that? It was hypnotizing—the lights, the music, the strands of hair hanging over his forehead that a simple touch could adjust. She was with Marcus. Marcus. Marcus. Marcus. His name had the tendency to disappear in Danny's presence.

"Yeah, I'll be right there." Danny stood and shoved his phone in his back pocket. "I have to go."

"Everything okay?"

"No, it's not. It's Hannah."

"Oh no. Is she hurt?" He had never been so fretful and worried in all the time she had known him as he was the past three days with Hannah away at camp. He wasn't exactly forthcoming about her, but being separated really drew out his love for his daughter. To see him like that was strange. And beautiful.

"We have to get out of here." Danny walked toward the entrance, as Kara speedwalked to keep up with him. He didn't say a word until they reached the car.

He unlocked the doors and got in. "I'll drop you off on the way."

"Danny, whatever it is, let's go. Don't worry about me."

"No, you don't need to be involved in this." He started the car and peeled out of the parking space.

"Watch it. We're in a parking lot."

"You don't think I know that?" He wouldn't look at her.

Kara clutched the dash, bracing herself. "You were there for my dad. Let me do the same." Whatever was discussed during that phone call, it had completely changed Danny's demeanor. It was a chilling reminder of the old Danny she had known. He was able to completely turn 180 degrees and give her the cold shoulder. It was painful to see that part of him resurface. But something was wrong with Hannah. Could she blame him? "If she's in trouble, don't waste time dropping me off."

Danny shook his head. "Fine."

Chapter Twenty

APRIL 2010

THE FIRST BELL RANG THROUGH THE HALLS OF WAVERLY Lake High School. Kara grabbed the notebooks for her morning classes and closed the locker. Homeroom was down the hall, and the second bell was sixty seconds away from ringing.

It was her favorite part of the morning, those sixty seconds. She clasped her belongings in her arms and walked down the hallway, merging with the students going her way as if they were cars staying in lanes.

Halfway down, there he was. Danny walked with his football teammate Colin, coming her way. She shifted the notebooks to her right arm and let her left hand hang loose by her hip. She inhaled and held her breath, Danny's gray-blues catching hers.

Then she felt his skin. His fingers brushed hers, and she laced them through his—a second, a blink—sending her head into a spiral as tight as the notebook binding. She exhaled when he was out of sight, his touch a fleeting memory on her hand. It was the same every weekday morning. Their secret touch.

But this time had been different. Had it been longer, or was that in her head? He had looked at her differently too. As if it pained him to see her. Maybe he had missed her yesterday. She certainly hated when she didn't get to see him whenever she had to study for exams.

She had worried over winter break that they would part ways. Tutoring was only half of what they did together. Sometimes they'd catch a movie or make an after-school run for burgers. She had hoped it was more than just Danny's way to avoid hitting the books. So when they met up at the park that day in January...she knew. This was right. This was special.

Danny said he wanted to keep it private as much as possible. Last year when he dated Sandra Oakley, the whole football team, cheerleading squad, and basically entire school were in their business. Rumors spread and eventually tore them apart.

He didn't want that this time.

So they took it slow and in secret. For the most part. Of course, Kara was going to share everything with Liz. It wasn't *that* secret.

The homeroom bell rang as Kara took her assigned seat behind Liz.

Liz swung around, resting her elbows on Kara's desk. "How's it going with Danny?"

"Good. Why do you ask?"

"There's something I have to tell you. I didn't believe it at first, but—"

"Ladies, I need you facing forward and quiet for attendance." Mrs. Halsey stood in front of her desk.

"Tell me after," Kara said. Liz had looked so serious. Kara's stomach knotted in worry.

No sooner had attendance finished than a representative from the prom committee entered, carrying a stack of papers.

"It's that time of year. The biggest event—other than graduation—of our senior year." She handed each row a stack of papers to pass down the line. "If you will be attending prom, please fill these out with your information and your date's name. Remember, dates from outside the school are permitted as long as they are also enrolled in an area high school."

Kara looked at the empty lines on her paper. She and Danny had talked about going to prom back in January or February, but had they ever finalized it? She had noticed other students talking about dress shopping the past few days. Perhaps Mom would be able to design something appropriate for it.

She got as far as the D in Danny's name before Liz turned around. "Kara, I'm sorry to tell you this, but you need to know. Now."

"What?" She stopped writing. "What's got you so worried?"

"It's Danny." Liz fidgeted with her braids cascading over her shoulder. "I heard this morning that he's asked Caitlyn Hall to prom and she said yes."

Kara's heart dropped. That couldn't be right. "That's crazy."

"I thought it was too. But I saw Caitlyn, and she has the text messages from him." She shook her head. "I'm so sorry, Kara."

The look of pity was too much for Kara.

"Are you okay?"

Kara nodded. No words were needed. Words would do nothing to pull her emotions out of the abyss they were lying in right now.

She eyed the paper, the penciled letters blurring from the tears. She scrunched the paper into a wad.

The first period bell rang, and students jumped to their feet. Kara scooted past Liz. "Kara, wait!"

"Hand me your completed forms on your way out!" The representative stood up front, a face full of disgusting cheer.

Kara tossed the paper wad in her basket and left the room. Danny had Chemistry first period. It was in the opposite direction of her History class, but that didn't matter.

She weaved through the hallway of students and stood by the classroom door. Another football player nudged Danny in the elbow, and he waved. He turned right in front of Kara.

"Caitlyn Hall? You're taking Caitlyn Hall to the prom?"

He huffed, looking down at his feet. "Yes."

It was all she could do to not slap him. "When were you going to tell me? I had to find out from Liz."

"Please, not here." His eyes wandered the halls. "Can we do this after school?"

"Why, so you can make sure no one knows about us?" She

spread her arms out. It was about time the rest of the school knew their secret. "You wouldn't dare want to take *me* to prom, would you? Then everyone would know."

"Kara, it's not like that." He rubbed his forehead, eyes closed.

Was he tormented over this? Something wasn't right. The look on his face turned her forlorn rage to guilt. "What, Danny?" She stepped closer. "Tell me."

He opened his eyes, his stare aimed at the room behind her. "I don't think you should tutor me anymore."

"I—" She stuck her hand up before anything else hurtful could come out of his mouth. Or was it more to stop herself from crying? "Fine, Danny. I won't be your tutor. I also won't call or maybe I won't even bother to look at you. Okay?"

"Kara, please." He grabbed her cheek, his once fiery touch abrasive on her skin. He was night and day, hot and cold. The last thing Kara wanted during her senior year was to play games with a boy.

She pulled his hand away and stared one last time into those cutting eyes before walking away.

There was nothing left to say.

She had no more words for Danny Bennett.

Chapter Twenty-One

DANNY PUSHED HARDER ON THE GAS, RACING PAST THE speed limit on the highway. He had turned the radio on, then off, and back on. It was better to have the background music than the low truck humming with Kara silent next to him.

He had known better than to listen to Tracy. Or his parents. They, especially Mom, had a way of meddling, screwing up his life. No one knew Hannah better than he did. Why had he doubted himself?

"I know you're worried." Kara held on to her door and the dashboard as if he was about to ram the car into a wall. "But can you please slow down a little?"

He let off the gas a touch.

"Thank you." Her gaze was fixed on him—a searing glare. "What has happened? Maybe you should talk about it before you get there. It may help to process it."

He wanted to shout and slam on the steering wheel. He wanted to stop the truck and speed up at the same time. Kara was probably right. He already had a few choice words to say to the camp director he'd spoken with on the phone.

"Hannah is not adjusting well at camp. She's cornered herself in the kitchen and won't come out. Her group counselor attempted to carry her out, but Hannah was kicking—" He closed his eyes in a long blink, blurring out the sight of poor Hannah in an episode with no one familiar, no one who knew how to take care of her.

"I shouldn't have let her go."

"You can't blame yourself."

"I sure as heck can. Yet again, my parents—my mom, specifically —talked me into another dumb decision."

Kara sat still, quiet.

"She acts as if Hannah is like every other kid. Or it's like she wants Hannah to be like every other kid. She makes me feel guilty, like I'm sheltering her and preventing her from living a full life."

"All kids throw fits sometimes."

Throw fits. He wanted to scream. "You don't understand."

"Then help me to understand."

It wasn't something he cared to share with strangers or acquaintances. They would look at him or Hannah with pity or apologize as if life was something to be sorry about. But Kara was something more than an acquaintance, wasn't she? It didn't matter. She was in the thick of it, and comments like "throw fits" were not acceptable.

"Hannah has ASD."

Kara's mouth closed, and she shook her head.

"Autism spectrum disorder."

"Oh." She turned slightly in his direction. "I didn't know."

"She has good days and then..."

The silence begged to be filled.

"That was the deal with the chair. The one you delivered. She's particular about certain things. She prefers sitting lower. I don't know if it's a vantage point thing or something else. She likes smooth fabrics, but not directional fabrics like velvet or textured like corduroy. And it's why the only movies I take her out to see anymore are Films on Friday, because the enclosed space of a movie theater is unbearable."

"And she gets to sit on the ground?"

"I'm sure that's a factor too." One he hadn't thought of until now. "The bottom line is, she needs routine. And someone who knows how to prevent episodes and help soothe her when she has one. She needs me."

He hit his chest. "I take care of her. No one else."

"You're doing a great job—"

"Am I?" He threw his hand in the air, choking on the fear in his words. It was a common courtesy, something people said. Was he really doing a great job? His stomach knotted, his confidence not enough to face the answer.

He turned off the highway and drove the three miles of windy backroads to Camp Walabash. The welcome sign hung between two totem poles. The dirt road into camp wound to a small parking lot. He got out, Kara's door slamming behind him. He should've told her to stay in the pickup, but he wasn't thinking straight.

They walked past the front office, a lit cabin with no one inside. Across the dirt path was the mess hall, a larger cabin beneath a copse of trees, the front two doors wide open, letting the light spew into the darkness of the camp.

"Hannah?"

A young woman in a green polo shirt sat next to an older man at one of the cafeteria picnic tables in the back. They both stood as he approached.

"Mr. Bennett, I presume?" The older man stretched out his hand. "I'm Brett Hanson, camp director. We spoke on the phone."

Danny ignored the outstretched hand. "Where is she? What happened?"

"She was doing great this afternoon," the girl said.

"Who are you?"

"This is Mandy, her group counselor," Brett said.

"I have a group of six girls, sir. The group is to stay together during all scheduled activities. Hannah had been isolating herself during meals, eating anywhere else but the cafeteria. It was becoming a safety hazard, in organizing staff—"

Brett waved her to stop and move on with it.

"I finally convinced Hannah to try to sit with our group this evening. We were in the middle of dinner, and she...well, she kind of flipped out. She grabbed her ears and chanted to herself. I tried to calm her down, and she got up and ran away."

"She found her in the pantry over there." Brett pointed to a door in the hallway leading to the kitchen. "She's been in there since we called you."

Danny walked to the door and knocked. "Hannah? Hannah, it's Daddy." No answer, but he could hear a tiny voice repeating inaudible words. "Hannah, I'm going to open the door."

"I tried to get her out," Mandy pleaded with Kara. "She was violent, and I didn't know what to do."

"Be quiet, all of you." Danny cracked open the door.

"How about you show me where her things are?" Kara asked.

"Sure. They're pretty much packed already. We couldn't get her to change out of her shirt from Sunday evening."

Kara's footsteps faded out of the mess hall as Danny struggled to keep his fury in check. He had packed her green T-shirt, the one she wore when he washed her yellow shirt. Yet another special instruction of wasted breath.

Danny peeked inside the pantry, an incandescent light overhead casting shadows on the bulk supplies sitting on the shelves. He widened the opening. Hannah sat on the floor in the back corner, rocking back and forth, hands on her ears.

He wanted to rush to her, scoop her up in his arms and take her away from this place. Away from everyone. "Sweetie, I'm going to step closer. Here I come." He lumbered his feet, making sure each step was clear and deliberate. "I'm coming down to you." He lowered to his knees and gently placed his hands on her elbows. She flinched and continued rocking but opened her eyes.

"See, it's Daddy."

Her rocking slowed to a stop. He wrapped her in his arms.

"Too many noises."

"I know," he whispered in her ear. "It's done now. Everyone is out. No one is making any noise."

She lowered her hands from her ears.

"See? All quiet." He nodded. She needed all the reassurance he could give her. "Let's go home."

He stood slowly, urging her to do the same by holding her arms and keeping his face at her level. "Walk with me, okay?"

"Okay." She held his waist, and they walked in unison out of the pantry, into the mess hall.

"We're leaving now." He had a lot more he wanted to say to the director, but not in front of Hannah.

Mandy returned, standing at the hall entranceway. "I'm so sorry this happened. I just don't think she's cut out for this."

He whipped around and stared the both of them down. "No. You got it backwards. This place is not cut out for her." He held her closer. "Come on, Hannah."

They walked out the doors. Kara stood by the truck, Hannah's bags at the ready. She broke a smile as they approached. "Hey, Hannah."

Danny shook his head. It wasn't her place to make this better. And it definitely wasn't welcome if she was going to make it worse.

He opened the door for Hannah and moved her booster to the back, behind Kara.

Kara flipped around the seat. "I'm glad you're okay." She eyed Hannah with soft eyes. Pity eyes. It was why he didn't like telling people about Hannah's ASD. People like Hannah didn't need pity. Only understanding. "I don't know if you remember me, but I'm your neighbor, Kara."

Danny shot her a look. Hannah didn't need to hold a conversation right now, especially with someone she had seen once for a brief moment.

"That place was too noisy," Hannah said. Danny's heart skipped. Hannah speaking meant she had calmed down quite a bit —and she felt comfortable with Kara in the truck. For now.

"You know what? I probably would've thought the same thing." Kara smiled before turning back around.

Where did she get off being the comforter? She didn't get to swoop in and be Hannah's hero. She didn't know what it was like

24/7, taking care of her. It took patience and stability and infinite empathy. Not to mention having to brush off idiots like those two camp counselors. Heck, he had gone through more nannies than he could keep track of before finding Mrs. Warren.

He pulled out of the parking lot and swerved along the windy roads back to the interstate. Hannah hummed softly to herself.

Kara had been quiet but kept turning her head to look at him. "Are you okay?"

"I don't want to talk about it."

"Okay." Kara paused and fidgeted with her hair. "If it means anything, I heard what you said back there, about them not being cut out for her."

"I don't want to—" But she was going to talk about it. Once Kara Carter made up her mind...

"The blame is put on her, or me. All the time. Do you think I didn't inform them before her arrival?" He shrugged. "That's what I do. I inform. They promise. Then it all goes out the window and I'm driving her home in the middle of the night."

"I'm glad you meant what you said. I think you were right in saying it."

He nodded. She had probably meant it as a compliment, but he didn't need her reassurance or praise. "Well, at least I got one thing right tonight."

"What's that supposed to mean?"

"I mean I shouldn't have sent her in the first place."

"You didn't know how—"

"Yes, I did. I shouldn't have sent her away. I shouldn't have been out with you. I should be focused on her." He checked Hannah in the rearview mirror. He couldn't bring himself to look at Kara's face.

"The fair was your idea," she said. "Not the other way around."

"Now everything is my fault."

"Fault? Everything? What has gotten into you?"

He waved his hand at her. "Stop. Just stop. Hannah doesn't need to see us like this."

The words held still in the air. *Me. See me like this*, was what he meant.

Kara huffed deeply before falling silent. This was all wrong. Kara was back in his life, even if just a teammate at most, but enough that he had wanted her to get to know Hannah. Perhaps over a picnic or some other quieter event. Not like this.

The past week had been a whirlwind, and Hannah was in the middle of it. There simply were too many changes for her to handle: Tracy visiting, changing his schedule for sailing practice, summer camp. It was not the right time to bring another person into her life —especially one who will walk out sooner or later. Most likely sooner.

He pulled into Kara's driveway and shifted the truck into park. Kara unbuckled and exited. She popped her head back in. "Push me away all you want. Blame me. I don't really care, Danny. But I'm not sorry I was with you tonight."

She turned and addressed Hannah. "I'm so sorry about summer camp."

Hannah continued her humming.

Kara looked at Danny through her fiery eyes. "So much for a fresh start." She slammed the door and walked away.

Chapter Twenty-Two

THE FAIR DID NOT HAVE A ROLLER COASTER, YET KARA felt like she had ridden one last night. They'd had fun, the ride dizzying yet thrilling, and gotten to talking seriously, even through Danny's blue mouth. The thought warmed her cheeks. Then he got the phone call, and it was like a switch had been flicked in his demeanor. Had he been embarrassed about Hannah? If so, she tried to assure him that there was nothing to be embarrassed or ashamed about. He had come down hard on himself, yes, but somehow, he made Kara feel like she had done something wrong. It was senior year all over again. But Kara had learned from that experience. Just like Danny should have. She knew he wasn't the same person. And she wasn't going to let him revert to his old ways.

Kara had spent the better part of the day helping Dad clean up his shop. It pained him to not work on something, more so than the surgery had, so Kara suggested a compromise. Cleaning was at least productive yet not too strenuous. It also gave him more practice with the crutches.

His desire to get back to work was understandable. Kara had started the day running errands for Mom, then researching everything she could about *PhotoStyle Magazine*. The more she looked into it, the more she...didn't know. Was it the right place for her? Should she accept that anywhere that would take her was the right place? Would they even take her? Marcus hadn't secured an interview yet. It could be worrying for nothing.

Helping Dad got her mind off both the job situation and the Danny situation, at least for a little while. Kara swept the debris away from the far corners of the shop, making piles as she worked her way toward the center. "Dad?"

"Yep?" He polished the circular saw with a dry cloth.

"Is it me or is it a lot cleaner in here than usual?" She had helped him in the summers as a teen and thought the sawdust was endless. But maybe Dad had gotten better about tidying up more frequently.

"Yeah...well, we aren't getting the orders in like we used to. It's mostly the old folks like me and your mother who appreciate this kind of thing. The younger kids want something quick to assemble. Cheap stuff from China."

Kara looked around, really studied the shop. Organized stacks of hickory, cherry, and oak lined the south wall. The machinery was nearly impeccable already, and other than the sailboat hull in the back, there was only one piece in her dad's work corner waiting to be finished.

"Are you guys doing all right? I mean, financially?" It was odd to talk to him like...like an adult. As a kid, the business was something more of a nuisance, something that took up Dad's time and caused her and Mom to argue all the time, since Kara wanted nothing to do with it.

"Ah, we're getting by. You know, we had planned on being retired by now."

"I thought you would be too." Kara flinched at her words. "I mean to say—"

"Because we are old farts?"

"You're not *that* old, Dad."

"It's okay. We know we're getting up there. Which is why it

hurts a little that we're not retired yet. When we had projected our retirement, it was based off the sales we had in the '80s and '90s. But things slowed down in recent years, and we had to put off those plans." He put the cloth down and placed his hands on his waist. "It's one of the reasons I built *Kare Bear*. Sure, it took me a long time. But selling her would be a huge sale and a good start to that venture."

Of course, Kara worried about the regatta and the status of her team, but knowing the truth escalated the worry. "I don't think that's true, by the way."

"Don't think what's true?"

"The younger kids not wanting this. I think there's a whole generation of young adults who would appreciate all this—local, handcrafted, one of a kind. I've certainly come around. I think if they see what you do, if you could get your work out there more...I think it'd be a hit."

"That's why the regatta is so important. It gets our name out there. And if you can place...I know it would sell, and maybe this next one too."

He caught her eyes, and she smiled. He nodded with quiet satisfaction. But the truth added pressure to an already tense situation.

Kara heard the rumble of tires. She froze. Danny was back.

"I think I've got this covered now. Not much else to do around here. If you wanted to go...do something else."

Dad knew she had waited for him to return from work. Dad always knew those things she never said out loud. It wasn't that she wanted to talk to Danny. On the contrary. She didn't feel like talking to him at all. But she couldn't afford to back out of the race now, especially after what Dad had said. Knowing Dad, he'd most likely downplayed the severity of his and Mom's financial situation. Plus, in the emotional roller coaster of last night, she had left her camera in Danny's truck.

"No, it's okay."

"Kara. Ever since you came back from Nichols and Dimes, I've seen you flinch at the sound of the mailman, the UPS truck, and the solicitor who came by today. Now go over there."

She whined. "But he's being a jerk."

"He can be a jerk all he wants. It's how you react to him being a jerk that matters. Don't let him get to you like that. Besides, from what you've told me, it seems like Hannah could use a friend other than her dad."

Something about seeing Hannah last night, vulnerable and unable to express her emotions, tugged at Kara's heart. Not only did she have to manage ASD, but her mother had left her. How could a mother do such a thing? There was no doubt Danny was doing the best he could for her, but maybe Hannah could use some girl influence in her life. Other than wild Tracy. It was what had compelled her to buy the gift when Mom sent her to the drugstore.

"I barely know her, but I get the same feeling," Kara said.

"Don't let her sometimes-acting-like-a-jerk dad get in the way of that."

That was what she had thought, but hearing it from Dad confirmed it.

"You're right."

"I know." He smiled. "And for the record, I think he's a good guy. Sometimes even the good ones mess up."

It was true—she had told Danny he was a good guy to his face. But Dad's words hit her in another way. She couldn't help thinking about Marcus. He had messed up. But he was a good guy. She wasn't treating him like one though. He'd call about job updates and ask what she'd been up to, but Kara cut the conversations short. Besides, what was she going to say? That she had gone out with her ex-boyfriend-turned-neighbor to the local fair, just the two of them? *You know, the guy you didn't like.* Yep, that would go over well. But it hadn't been a date. They were old friends starting a new friendship with their past behind them. How was she supposed to convince Marcus of that?

Danny got out of his truck as Kara approached the house.

"I'm not really in the mood, Kara." He wore torn, stained cargo pants and a T-shirt, and carried a scuffed orange toolbox.

"I'm not here to discuss last night." She pointed to the car. "I left my camera in your car."

"Oh." He set the duffel bag down and searched the passenger side. "Here it is." He handed her the camera.

"Thanks. Is Hannah around?"

"She's inside with Mrs. Warren. Probably out back."

Kara realized it was probably tough for him to leave Hannah today after last night's events. She followed him to the back patio door.

"Listen." He turned around. "I don't think it's such a great idea to come around. I'm not blaming you for last night. I take the blame for it."

"I just wanted to check up on Hannah and give her this." She handed over the sailboat puzzle, the one that had made her think of Hannah in the drugstore.

"That was nice of you, but we can't accept that." He walked toward the back door of the house, but Kara wasn't about to give up. She followed in a scramble.

"It's just a puzzle."

"I want to see it." Hannah stood at the back porch on the other side of the screen door.

"Sure."

Danny eased Kara away from the screen. "Don't do that."

"Do what? Talk to Hannah? I brought her a gift."

"No, you know what I mean. Use her as a tool to get what you want."

Kara's jaw dropped. "I can't believe you. You think so little of me? I bought her a puzzle because I remembered seeing her do one the first time we met, and I thought she'd enjoy it. Seeing as her camp week was cut short. I thought maybe we could even do it together."

He remained still. What was there to think about? It was a simple, kind gesture. And now Kara was getting upset.

"Look, if you want to push me back out of your life again, fine. That's on you. I was doing a nice thing, as a neighbor and, I thought, as a friend."

Danny sighed and shook his head. "Fine. Whatever. I'm going inside." He carried the toolbox in the house and walked through the back patio, patting Hannah's shoulder before disappearing into the kitchen.

It didn't exactly feel like an invitation to enter the house. Kara stood outside the door, wondering if she should walk in or not.

"What is that?" Hannah tilted her head, pointing at her.

"Oh, this?" Kara cradled the camera in one hand. "It's my camera. I'm a photographer." Or at least, I *was* a photographer.

"Like Daddy's phone?"

She smiled. "No, it's not like your dad's cell phone. Only a camera. I can't call people with it or send messages. But I can freeze time with it."

"Really?"

"Yep. You want to see it?"

Hannah nodded and opened the door. Kara peeked in. She set the puzzle down on a small table by the door, next to the sorriest-looking fern she had ever seen. Mrs. Warren sat on a stool at the edge of the kitchen, crocheting.

"Is it okay if Hannah comes out here?"

"I'll be leaving here in a few minutes."

"We won't be long."

The nanny waved her off.

"I'll stay where you can see us."

Hannah stepped out, and Kara walked a few steps toward the lake. She took the camera off her shoulders. "Here we go." She crouched to Hannah's level. "This cylinder here holds the lens. If there's anything you want to freeze, you aim that at it. You look through this hole up here to see what you're going to freeze. When you're ready, you press this button."

Kara scanned the landscape. "You see that bird over there?" She pointed to a warbler swooping at breaking wavelets on the shore below.

"Yes."

Kara aimed the camera and snapped it as the bird returned to the sky. "Now look at the screen." She used her hand to block out the sun over the screen.

Hannah looked at the screen, then back at the bird. "The bird is moving."

"Well, yes. It's still moving. But my picture will always be of that bird, the moment it flew overhead. We might be able to remember when it did that for the rest of our lives. Or not. I know I don't have the best memory sometimes." She smiled, Hannah returning no evidence of emotion. It was a characteristic of ASD, according to the articles she had read online late into the night. "But that picture will never change. It will always be there for us to see and remind us of that moment we had."

"What if you don't want to remember it?"

"We can erase it. Just push that right there."

"No!"

Kara moved her hand away and put it up in surrender. "I won't. I'll keep it there. When I go home, I can put it on my computer and make room for more pictures."

Hannah placed her left hand on the side of the camera, patting it like a kid hesitant to pet a dog.

"That's it. You want to hold it?" Kara took Hannah's other hand. Hannah pulled it away. "It's okay, you don't have to."

Hannah raised her right hand herself and clasped the camera. She looked through the hole with both eyes open.

"That's right. It helps to look through it with one eye and close the other."

Hannah closed both eyes and opened them, going back and forth until she nailed one eye open.

"Good job. Now when you see something you like, push the button with your finger." She guided Hannah's finger over the button, this time with no resistance from Hannah.

Hannah slowly scanned the horizon, rotating from the waist as if her entire upper body was frozen. She pushed the button and backed her face away.

"All right! You want to see your picture?"

Hannah focused on the screen. Kara saw nothing but sky and clouds. "That's a lovely picture."

"It's a banana cloud."

Kara focused in on it, and sure enough, one of the wispy streaks of white looked like a banana. She giggled. "You're right! You got a great picture of it. Can I put that one on my computer to save?"

"Yes."

"Awesome. Should we do some more?"

"Down there." Hannah pointed to the lake.

Kara looked back at the house. "I don't know. I don't want your dad worrying about us if we're too close to—Hannah!"

Hannah walked toward the dock and stopped short of the wooden planks.

"You can take more pictures, but you can't run off like that on me again."

Hannah made no promises or sign of acknowledging Kara's request. Kara wrapped the camera strap over Hannah's head. It was the first time she had set foot on the pebbled shore in ten years. The shoreline hadn't changed much at all. Although the lake experienced a tidal effect, it was so miniscule that it was not possible to tell when high or low tides hit. The only real time she had seen the coastline change was when she was eight or nine, during a heavy thunderstorm. The waves had never been rougher, and the shoreline thinned along western edges of banks and built up along the eastern sides.

Hannah lifted the camera and snapped away, rotating like an automatic sprinkler, taking in all directions.

Kara laughed. and Hannah looked up from the camera to her. "Why do you laugh?"

"Keep going," Kara said. "I want to see all the wonderful things you see."

"What's going on?" The lake breeze blew through Danny's hair, his sculpted arms showing off in the tight T-shirt. Kara stumbled for her words. She pictured him wrapping those arms around her in an embrace before she caught his face.

It was angry.

Chapter Twenty-Three

APRIL 2010

"Daniel, can you come here?"

Danny lowered the phone from his ear. "Be right there!"

"You have to go?" Kara's disappointment bled through the phone.

"My mom's calling me. I'll see you tomorrow morning?" He bit his lip. Seeing Kara Carter in the hallway before homeroom was his motivation to go to school.

"Yep. Good night."

"Night."

Danny walked out of his room. "Mom?"

"In the study."

He took the back stairs and entered the double doors. Richard Bennett's study didn't follow the cliché in movies. The walls were painted powder blue, and the double windows with sheer white curtains overlooking the lake allowed the sunlight to brighten the room.

Mom stood leaning on the front of Dad's desk. "Have a seat, Daniel."

He caught his breath and sat in the navy club chair. "What is it? Something happen to Dad?" Her crossed arms meant something was up.

"Your father is fine." She played with the sapphire dangling on the gold chain around her neck. She straightened up from the desk and smiled. "You've been spending an awful lot of time with the Carter girl."

"Kara? Yeah, she's my tutor."

She raised her eyebrows. "Well, your grades in math certainly have improved."

"She's really smart. And great at teaching."

"That's good."

Danny stared at his mother. "Is that it?"

"Are you dating?"

"Kara?" Mom meddled in his life whenever she wanted. He knew better than to be open with her about Kara. "We are...seeing each other, yes." He leaned back. What was she getting at? Hopefully, he wouldn't regret admitting it.

She stared in his eyes, then shook her head. "Oh dear. It's worse than I thought."

"What is?"

"You've fallen for her, haven't you?"

"Mom." This was not the most comfortable conversation to have.

"I don't want you to see her anymore. There, I said it."

"What?" He bolted out of the chair to his feet. "What do you have against Kara? And who said you can tell me who to date?"

Her voice escalated in volume. "I'd rather you not date anyone right now. High school is almost over, and you need to focus on Duke. You're going to be across the state anyway, so it's best to end this now."

"You're not making sense. If you ever hung around Kara, you'd know she's brilliant and kind and determined and probably going more places than I could dream of."

"But she's not! Sure, she may go away for college. But she'll end up right back here, working for her father, the town furniture maker."

"So what if she does?"

"You deserve better. We've raised you better than that."

Danny wanted to throw up or run away. Maybe both. "You're crazy. I'm taking her to prom. And I'll see her over the summer before Duke. You'll see. You'll change your mind about her."

"You will not be taking her to prom. I already spoke with the Halls. You'll be taking their daughter Caitlyn."

Did he just step into a nightmare? Was this actually happening? "No, I'm not."

"Yes, you are. Because they're the ones who got you the scholarship in the first place."

"What?" He sat back down.

"That's right." She assumed her smug position again, leaning on the desk, arms crossed. "That football scholarship you were awarded was Colin's. But they had other plans for him. So they sent in a good word about you. And here we are."

She sighed, stiff body loosening and voice lowering. "Danny, I'm saying these things because I love you. I didn't want it to come to an argument like this." She approached him and placed her hand on his shoulder.

"Your father and I want what's best for you. I know sometimes it's hard to know at your age what's best. But trust us. This is for the best. The sooner she's out of your life, the easier it will be to move on and focus on college."

He hadn't spoken to Kara about what would happen after summer. What would they do? Keep it going long-distance? It was going to have to end at some point, wasn't it? But there was supposed to be more time. At least have the summer. At least have prom. Not like this.

"You try to get some rest tonight." She kissed his forehead and walked out of the study.

Danny sat in the chair as if glued to the upholstery. His body, his mind, had no idea how to process what just happened. Mom had flown in and demolished his life.

He had to call Kara. He had to tell her everything that just happened. But what was he going to say?

How could he call the girl he loved and tell her it was over?

Chapter Twenty-Four

"I—I'm sorry. Mrs. Warren said it was okay for Hannah to go outside with me. I was trying to stay up there, but she—"

"She's taking pictures?" He moved up to her, the anger at Kara's recklessness receding.

"Yeah. She asked about the camera, and I showed her how to work it. She seems to like taking pictures."

"She does." He changed his stare from Kara to Hannah. "She doesn't take up new interests very often." He had tried with board games and horseback riding to name a few, the former a bore to Hannah and the latter downright torture. For them both.

"Well, I remember I was hooked at her age with my first camera."

He watched Hannah experience a spark of excitement, in her own way, as if she was seeing the world for the first time. What was he doing? Kara had changed—had forgiven him, for starters—and even seemed to enjoy his company last night. There had been a heaviness to the air between them, sitting on that bench at the fair. A heaviness that pushed them together.

"I'm sorry." Danny said the words and stared out at the lake. "I put the consequences of my actions on you. That wasn't fair."

"You were concerned for Hannah. I understand that."

"That may be true, but I didn't mean to push you away. I still feel like I don't know what I'm doing sometimes. With the whole dad thing." *And the Kara thing.*

"Isn't that what being an adult means? I thought I could plan out my life, but life is something that happens to you. Do you think last month I anticipated standing here at Waverly Lake, hanging out with Danny Bennett and his daughter?"

Not in the craziest of his dreams. "Probably not."

"It's a *definitely* not."

"But I'm glad you are." It was embarrassing and cheesy. He had been furious about Hannah, but that was at the world, at the people who couldn't understand her and accommodate her. The ones who couldn't see her as a kid. Not Kara.

"Do you really mean that?"

"I do. You know, if we're being honest and open...there's something you don't know about the whole prom thing."

"We've moved past it. It's okay, really."

It was risky, opening up a wound they had just dressed, but he needed to tell the whole truth. Last night made him think about Beverly's influence. Kara deserved to know.

"I honestly had planned on taking you to prom."

"You know, it sounds like you actually believe yourself." She laughed it off, but her tense body showed it stung.

"I mean it. I'm not joking. I know the guys on the team were giving me a hard time, but I could've lived with that. I didn't care. They didn't know you like I knew you. It wasn't until my mom asked about it, and I told her."

"What did she have to do with it?"

"She didn't want me to ask you."

"That's crazy. I thought your mom liked me, especially since I helped you improve your pre-calc grade."

"Yeah, well, I thought so too. Until she forbade me from asking you." He had replayed the argument they'd had in his father's study many times. "She was afraid I was falling for you and I wouldn't be able to focus at Duke. She said I had to take Caitlyn to prom because her parents had helped me get the football scholarship. But the worst part was that she said she didn't want her son to be with the daughter of the town furniture maker."

"Oh my goodness." Kara stood, mouth ajar, visible fury simmering up her spine.

"Look, I'm not trying to make you mad." If anything, he wanted to hold her and never let go. He had missed his chance years ago. "I wanted to explain. It wasn't nice what my mom said or did. I should've stood up to her, just like I should've said no about the summer camp thing. I'm really sorry, Kara."

Kara inhaled deeply. "That's quite a lot to take in."

"I knew it was wrong, and when I finally couldn't take the weight of losing you, I wanted to apologize to you, sincerely, but you had moved on with your life, out of Waverly Lake." He broke into a chuckle. "I'm sorry. I'm not laughing at you. I'm laughing at me. Here I am, in Waverly Lake, raising a seven-year-old by myself. Because life with *you* would've been crazy." He stroked his hand through his hair. "Then she comes over the other day and what do I do? I listen to her. Against my own gut."

"Danny..." She could've walked away in anger. She could've smacked him or cursed his mom. Instead, she stepped closer in acceptance. "So your mom may not be the best person to give you advice."

He laughed, half with amusement and half to cover the clamor in his chest at her closeness. "That's putting it lightly."

"Yeah. But hear me out. She wants what's best for you and Hannah. You have to listen to yourself, but you can't *only* listen to yourself."

"I can't believe this. Are you saying she was right?"

"No. I'm not saying the pressure she puts on you to do what she wants you to do is right. That part is wrong—and if we're being honest, you should stand up to her when your gut is telling you to. Like when you turned down the new car in high school. You have it in you. I know it's hard to let it out sometimes. You know me and my mom enough to know we've had our moments, so I get it. But what your mom gets right—if that's what she's really after—is that both you and Hannah are worthy of having other people in your lives. You can't keep her to yourself. That's not fair to either of you. Look at her."

Hannah moved sticks on the ground into a pattern before snapping away at the camera.

"She's worthy of new experiences. Some of them aren't going to work out. But that's any kid. You have to give her chances to discover things for herself."

"Now you sound like Tracy."

"Not sure if that's an insult."

"Understandable." He grinned. "She's been on me to join a local ASD group. She thinks we'd both meet more people and have support."

"Do you want to? And do all the women in your life pressure you?"

"I should tell her you pointed out she's more like Beverly Bennett than she'd want to be." He sighed. "It's hard."

"Being a parent is hard. At least, I've always imagined it would be. And there's something else. Something I saw in you last night that worries me."

His breath caught in his throat. She was worried about him? So it wasn't just him thinking about her. He covered the twinge of delight it gave him among the somber conversation. "My driving?"

Kara lost her composure and laughed. It was gratifying to make her laugh. "Let's just say I'm glad *you're* not the one driving the Carter Furniture truck. But I was talking about your self-worth. Just because you're a dad doesn't mean you can't invest in your own happiness."

"I do that." He pointed to Hannah. "Her happiness is my happiness."

"I mean doing things for yourself. Like, you work out, right?"

"Is it not obvious?"

She shook her head at his mock arrogance. "Okay, Dwayne 'The Rock' Johnson. Why do you do that? So you'll be healthy, right?"

"Sure." And most recently, because he'd sworn he caught Kara Carter staring at him more than once.

"Well, your emotional well-being is just as important. You deserve to take time for yourself, doing whatever it is that makes you happy."

Danny's stare lowered to the pebbles at his feet. It was what Tracy had been saying. But Kara made it click.

"Daddy!" Hannah held the camera in both hands as she marched through the sand. "I have ice pictures."

"Ice pictures?" He looked at Kara.

"I told her whenever she takes a picture, she freezes time. You know, like preserving a memory."

"Here, take one of us, Hannah." He put his arm over Kara's shoulder, and she gave in for the pose, her arm reaching around his back. He froze, the floral scent from her hair and the soft silkiness of her skin beneath his fingertips knocking the wind out of him.

Hannah snapped a photo and showed their smiling faces on the screen before taking off again.

"That's a good team photo," Kara said.

He commenced breathing. Apparently, the fair had helped her feel more comfortable around him, which would make sailing as a team all the easier. Unfortunately, it was too late. "About that..."

"Yeah?"

Why was it that he continued to deliver disappointment to her? "Since Hannah's back early from camp, I'm pressed for sitters. Mrs. Warren squeezed in today, but she can't the rest of the week. And Tracy may be able to do a few hours here and there, but she's not exactly the most reliable person."

Her shoulders sagged. "You can't back out on me now."

"I'm sorry."

"I wasn't going to say anything, but my dad sort of confessed that he and Mom aren't doing so well financially. They really need the boat to place to have the best chance at selling it."

He ran his hands through his hair. It was going to be hard enough to get someone to watch Hannah during his work hours the next few days.

"But...we can have three on our team, right? I mean, it shouldn't be a problem to add another crew member."

"You mean as a sub?"

"No, I mean as a crew member. Along with you."

What was this? They were finally getting along well, and she wanted someone else to join the team? "Who are you talking about?"

Kara's sweet mouth curled up in a grin and she nodded to the lake. To Hannah.

"What? You want Hannah to join?"

"Bring her along. Think about it. I saw you the other day in your boat with her. She doesn't necessarily have to learn to sail, but she could ride with us. In fact, she could help on the turns if we need to shift weight on the boat."

It sounded dangerous. It sounded ridiculous. Sure, Hannah liked the wind on her face and going out with him. On the other hand...

The whole point of their discussion was letting Hannah try new things. "It couldn't possibly work. She's too young."

"You said she's seven, right? You only have to be six as long as the parent is also on board. I should know—that's when I started."

"I don't know..."

But she knew she had him. Her smile said it. "It'll be fun. Teammate."

Chapter Twenty-Five

"You've been spending most of your time with an ex and his daughter?" Marcus sounded skeptical and slightly upset over the phone. Okay, more than slightly upset at first.

"Not exactly an ex. An ex-friend, I guess you could say. We've agreed to start fresh as friends." She realized it sounded crazy, like something someone cheating would say. But then again, a cheater wouldn't have said anything at all about another person. She was only being honest and up-front. Well, first she'd had to backtrack, but now she was being up-front about the rest of her time here, however long that was going to be.

"Kara, do I have anything to worry about?" He'd always exuded confidence. This was the first time she'd ever witnessed a crack in his self-assurance. The question sent a jolt from her stomach to her throat. She had convinced herself of the words she told him, but hearing the question from Marcus shook her. Danny was handsome and a fiercely loving father...and they had a history together. It was crazy, though, because she and Marcus had a history. A longer one of togetherness.

"No," she said. "It's just that, being away from New York...life is different here."

"I know," he said. "One day in Waverly Lake was enough to see that. We don't belong there, Kara. We belong here, in New York. Which is why I'm so excited to tell you the news. You have an interview with Ben and his colleague at *PhotoStyle Magazine*."

It was supposed to be good news. Where was the exhilaration, the rush of joy?

"Kara?"

She inhaled and smiled as if on camera. "Great. Yeah, thank you for setting that up. When is it?"

"Monday morning. You fly out Sunday. I already bought the ticket for you."

"Monday?" So soon? She was just getting used to life here, being around her parents, and Hannah and Danny...

Marcus paused. "You said after the regatta, which is Saturday, right?"

She swallowed hard. "You're right."

"Okay, good. I was worried I'd have to rearrange everything. I don't know if they'd make the time twice."

She'd have to tell everyone she was leaving. Especially Danny and Hannah. Danny had made her a part of Hannah's world. He had known though, right? He had known she wasn't going to stay here forever.

"Have you worked on your portfolio yet?"

Kara snapped back to the conversation. "Actually, I have." The idea had struck when she saw her friend Sebastian and his partner, George, out behind Weeping Wares while on one of her outings on *Kare Bear*. They had been arguing over the placement of potted plants in the green space between the back of the store and the lake. Their personalities were disparate, yet they worked: Sebastian the free spirit, who said anything and everything; George the cultivated mature half, who appreciated the value of silence as much as words. With their help, she used the most exotic and unique plants and flowers they had to photograph against the backdrop of the lake and mountains. The juxtaposition of a cactus by the lake and tropical perennials by the Appalachian Mountains. Even the items that didn't belong could flourish with the right care.

"I tried to play on my strengths of nature photography yet show the more artsy side."

"Whatever it is, I'm sure it's great."

She went on to explain it further, but Marcus picked up the dead air. "Kara, there's something..." His voice weakened.

"Are you okay, Marcus?"

"Yeah. No, I'm fine." He cleared his throat, and his strong voice returned. "I just want to hear your voice some more, that's all."

It didn't feel like that was all. "Okay. We'll chat tonight or tomorrow?"

"Sure."

If she wasn't mistaken, he had sounded nervous. He was making an effort to stay in her life. Everything was falling back into place, back on track where she was headed last month. Why, now, did the possibility of forever in New York—with Marcus—leave her uneasy?

They said their goodbyes, and Kara checked the time. Three minutes past nine. "Ah!" Already three minutes past their meeting time. She grabbed her camera and purse and rushed down the stairs. She reached for the front door and realized she hadn't checked the mirror. She took out her cell phone and set the camera on herself. She tucked the layered strands that didn't fit in her ponytail behind her ears before exiting the house.

"Don't forget about dinner tonight," Mom yelled from the kitchen. "Remind Danny."

Dinners with the parents had been fine at the start of her stay. But it was obvious Mom was getting antsy about Kara's future plans. Or lack thereof. At least tonight she'd have a buffer in the form of Danny and Hannah. Dad had called it 'feast before the fleet,' seeing as the regatta was tomorrow.

Kara closed her eyes and took a deep breath. "Yes, I know! I won't forget."

Danny and Hannah waited outside the truck next door as Kara ran down the front steps. Danny tapped his wrist on a nonexistent watch.

"I know, I know. Lost track of time." Seeing Danny and Hannah, time was all she could think of. And how they were running out of it. She couldn't tell them right now though. No sense in overshadowing the practice run with the news.

Danny opened the door for Hannah.

"Hi there, Hannah." Kara waved and moved to the passenger side. They all buckled up and headed to Pearson's Wharf.

Kara shuffled her purse from the seat to the floor by her feet. Back in high school, early in senior year when he had started giving her rides from school to the house for tutoring, she had been a tangled ball of nerves in the car. She'd been so tense, shoulders stiff, legs and arms nowhere near the console. He had driven a stick shift then, and there was no way she was going to risk a brush with his hand. She would have simply died.

Of course, it all seemed ridiculously childish now. What she would've given to skip the whole awkward growing pains phase in adolescence. If everyone did, then they probably would've all been friends at school. Less snarkiness and cliques and bullies. Then again, that all still existed to a certain point in adulthood.

"I think I recall you and Liz getting up to things over at Nichols and Dimes." Danny pointed to the storefront as they passed along Dowager Street.

"What? Never. We were too set on getting out of Waverly Lake, and studying was our ticket."

"You never were much of a fan of Waverly Lake, were you?"

"You know, looking back, it's not that it was a bad place." With Hannah in earshot, there was no sense in being all doom and gloom. It was Danny and Hannah's home, and her own views had matured. "It was more about the size, and the feeling of being locked in by the mountains. I wanted to see other places. Waverly Lake does have its redeeming qualities."

He put his right hand up. "Let me stop you there. According to Kara Carter, what are Waverly Lake's redeeming qualities?"

She opened her mouth, but no words came out.

"Do go on." Danny laughed, turning the truck into the parking lot of Pearson's Wharf.

"Maybe back then, yes, I was a downer when it came to being around here. Face it, my parents had a business they wanted me to be a part of—or mostly my mom wanted me to be a part of—and as a high school student, you feel stuck in the routine of things. But as an adult, sometimes the routine things are the redeeming qualities." It was a strong quality of her relationship with Marcus.

Danny went for another interruption, but Kara stopped him with her hand. "Qualities like reliability. Neighborliness. Everyone may know everybody's business, but sometimes that can come in handy." The scene of Dad's shop played in her mind. "To be honest, if it weren't for the local people, those who embrace what it means to be a neighbor and be reliable, I'm not sure my parents would still be in business."

"Well, soon they may be the premier handmade sailboat manufacturers in all the Carolinas."

"That's right." She chuckled, and they got out of the truck and walked the planks of the dock to the ship's berth. *Kare Bear*'s mast stood tall, as if she awaited her crew with pride. They used the last week to learn, practice, and perfect sailing. Yesterday had been their one day off, and not just because the clouds drizzled rain all day. She had insisted on a day of rest before a final run-through, as if training for a marathon. They were even having a big dinner tonight, though Kara doubted it would be carb-loading. More like feasting on as much meat as possible, knowing Dad was in charge.

Danny lifted Hannah into the boat, life jacket snug.

"At your mark," Kara said. Hannah had been frustrated the first day of sailing, since the sloop didn't move as nimbly as Danny's motorboat. But Danny was great at helping her soothe, and once Kara and Danny hoisted the sail and Hannah felt the wind, she was hooked.

Hannah sat aft, near the bow, while Danny took up position starboard, untying the line to the dock, with Kara in front of him. They cleared the dock and headed west past town, toward the smaller islands in Waverly Lake. The corner of the backwards L was the start of the race, but Kara knew her competition—they had spying eyes, watching how her crew maneuvered the route.

There was one spot that was the most crucial—between the third and fourth straightaway. The westerly wind across the lake made for an easy north-south sail. On the east-west axis of the lake, sailing was more difficult. To top it all off, they had to turn 180 degrees from a near direct headwind to a tailwind while minding oncoming zigzagging vessels. They had practiced tacking and jibing over and over at that spot. It was the only maneuver Kara wanted to run through today. If it wasn't ingrained in their muscle memory, and they didn't move smoothly together as a team, they'd never have a chance to place. She knew that for certain. It was where she had messed up ten years ago.

They tacked three times over before reaching the full turn. Kara waited to gain speed before giving the signal. "Ready about."

Both Hannah and Danny shouted, "Ready."

"Tacking."

To any onlooker, they probably looked like a whirlwind of movements—headsail swinging, Hannah ducking, Danny scrambling. But to Kara, they were an orchestra, in tune with the boat and with each other.

"Good, good." The boat edged the turn, leaning to port. They had to jibe fast—a stark contrast with everything taught in beginner's sailing—not just because of the turn and the wind pushing their weight to port. But because it was Kara's little secret. A secret weapon to win.

"Prepare to jibe."

The response was immediate. "Ready."

"Jibe-ho!"

If tacking looked like a whirlwind, jibing was utter chaos. But the movements were deliberate—quick, calculated, and smooth. As they headed east, with the turn behind them, Kara examined her crew, smiling.

"Hannah, check." It was a routine she had picked up, one that

Hannah responded to best. Although Kara and Danny did the majority of the work, Hannah had to pay attention during the maneuvers or she could get hit by the boom, among other accidents.

Hannah gave a thumbs-up.

"How was that, Captain?" Danny smirked, fist on his waist and leg bent, as if he belonged on a rum bottle.

Kara didn't know if it was Hannah's presence or not, but Danny had come miles from not knowing anything about sailing to the knowledgeable sailor he was today. He listened, acted, reacted. And Kara's demeanor had changed. They practiced harder than ever, yet she ended the day with a smile. She was having fun.

Kara nodded. "We're ready."

Chapter Twenty-Six

"Danny!"

"What?" He sat on the dock, paintbrush paused on the hull's trim of *All Mine*. The sleek, antique, wooden, twenty-two-foot Chris-Craft looked to be straight out of *Indiana Jones*. It belonged to Huck Pearson, the man who owned the wharf and currently stared down at Danny, hands on his hips. He let no one touch his baby, except for Danny.

"I think you're done for today," Huck said. "She looks good. But if you put one more coat of paint on that same two-foot patch, I'm going to throw you in the lake."

Danny set the brush down on the paint canister. "Sorry."

"Get out of here. Get some rest before the big day tomorrow. You have a girlfriend to impress."

Danny stood, wiping his forehead with the towel hanging out of his pocket. Pearson knew everyone who was in and out of the wharf, but it was surprising to hear he was paying attention to Danny's lessons.

"She's not my girlfriend."

"So...you wouldn't mind if I asked her out?"

Okay, the question did rile him up. Not because it was from Huck though. Huck was blunt in personality and looks, and twenty years older than Kara, so no, Danny wouldn't mind. In fact, Danny would take pleasure in seeing the encounter.

But Kara had been on his mind all afternoon—that smile she threw at him after they had made the turn. It was an arrow to the chest, rewarding yet painful. He had stopped seeing her as a teammate days ago. Perhaps he had never truly seen her only as a teammate.

"I'm going to take the silence as a yes, you would mind."

"I'm sorry, Huck. I've had a busy day." Sailing this morning, work in the afternoon, and he still had an errand to run before dinner at the Carters'.

"Which is why I said to get on with it. I'll take care of the paint."

"Thanks."

"No problem."

Danny checked his watch. Nine minutes to five. Weeping Wares would officially be closed at five o' clock, but that didn't mean George wouldn't stick around.

"And Danny?"

Danny stopped his near jog along the dock. "Yeah?"

"Don't worry. I won't ask her out."

"Good. I'm sure her fiancé would appreciate that."

Danny kept his truck in the parking lot and rushed along the sidewalk of Dowager Street into the town square. The storefront had "Weeping Wares" in yellow letters arranged in an arch. During the day, two tables sat on the sidewalk with pots of annuals, but George had already brought them inside. The front door was locked, with a "Sorry, We're Closed" sign visible through the glass.

Danny peeked past the long stems and greenery. He caught the back of George's balding head and knocked on the door.

George waved and opened the door. "Daniel. This is a surprise."

He was the only other person outside of his family to call him by his full name. "Hi George. I know you're closed, but I couldn't get off on break any sooner."

"For you, no problem." George wore a maroon button-down

sweater, the store's iconic green apron off for the day. Carolina August may have been hell's furnace outside, but the shop felt cool and damp.

"What can I do for you?"

"I want to place an order for tomorrow, if that's doable."

"As long as it's not something out of season, should be okay." George cocked his head to the side. "Does this have anything to do with a certain neighbor of yours?"

"Actually…"

"Mmmhmm. I see."

"Hey now. You and Sebastian are always on me about me…" *Putting myself out there. Dating.* "Being more social."

"Not always."

Danny rolled his eyes. "Come on. It's me you're talking to."

"We just want to see you happy, that's all."

"Not everyone can easily find their perfect match like the two of you."

"Now, don't even get me started. I was thirty-nine when I met Sebastian. And he was a young twenty-five. I wouldn't say the odds were for us. Nothing came easy for us. But that's a topic for another day. We were talking about you and Miss Kara Carter."

"Were we?" Danny laughed.

"What is going on between you two? Sebastian has spotted you more than once out on the water."

"You know we're racing in the regatta together."

"Are you telling me you're strictly race partners?" He gave Danny the doubt eyes.

Danny shrugged. "Trio actually. Hannah is with us too."

"Daniel…"

"Look, would it work out with Kara? I don't know. Does she get along with Hannah? Better than I could've imagined. Does she have a fiancé back in New York? Yes. But does she make me feel queasy and excited and scared all at the same time?"

"Oh Daniel."

"I know."

"Are you sure you're here for the right reasons then?"

"I don't know what I'm doing." Danny scratched his head and leaned up against the register table. "I haven't dated in forever. All I know is that Kara and I have something. She pulls me in whenever she's around me. I can't help it. I'm falling for her."

"She's engaged."

"Does that mean I can't spend time with her at all?" Danny rubbed the back of his neck. It was like George voiced his conscience. "I keep telling myself to walk away. For me, for Hannah. But then I think, she's not married yet. What if there's a chance?"

George picked up the mini-sprayer for the hanging plants. "Look, I can't tell you what to do or not do. But I can tell you I don't—and Sebastian too—we don't want to see you hurt. From what I understand, there was a falling out in high school, and she left town without even saying goodbye."

"Word spreads around here, doesn't it?"

"Word spreads around Sebastian. Which is how I know enough to worry about you. How long is she staying? How do you know she won't pack up and leave tomorrow morning? She sounds about as adventurous and as high a flight risk as your sister."

"I don't know," Danny said. "She does have a sense of adventure, which is one of the things I like about her the most."

"I don't know if she told you."

"Told me what?"

"She was in here a few days ago, asking for our help. She said she was working on her portfolio. Sebastian spent more time with her, but in the time I did spend, I got the feeling she was hoping it would help her get back to New York."

It did hurt to think she had her eye yet again on leaving. But what were the chances that's what it was for? "She's changed. It's just a feeling, and I know how crazy I sound. But I think she values family and friendship more than she lets on."

"I don't really know her all that well. But I know you. Just make sure whatever decision you make, it's the best one for you."

Danny nodded. "You've been talking to Sebastian about me and Kara?"

George sprayed down the line of hanging plants. "Don't get me started. Or him. He's crazy about you two. If you talk to him, he'd convince you to have her move in with you, get a dog, and invite us over for Tuesday potlucks."

Picturing it all warmed Danny's face. He didn't want George to see it, which of course made it worse.

"Just take care of yourself, and that wonderful girl of yours, okay?"

"I will."

"Speaking of Kara." George set down the sprayer on the counter and slapped down a small pouch of fertilizer.

"What is this?"

"She told me about the code red on your fern."

"What? My fern is...it's a little wilted but it's fine."

"Daniel. Don't let it suffer any longer."

He shook his head and laughed. "Okay, okay."

"Good. Took care of the fertilizer. Now what was it you came for in the first place?"

Chapter Twenty-Seven

DANNY STOOD AT THE FRONT DOOR OF RICHARD AND Sheila Carter's house, Hannah standing at his side. Kara opened the screen door, taking the fresh lilies in the other hand. The flowers had to have come from Weeping Wares, judging by the meticulous packaging and bow around the stems. Plus, she had seen the blazing mottled peach petals during her photography session the other day and complimented George on their beauty.

Which meant Danny had told George or Sebastian where he would be tonight. Which meant Danny had been talking about her.

"Thank you for those!" Sheila plucked the bouquet out of Kara's hand and rushed to find a vase.

"Come on back." Kara led them to the kitchen, the five-foot table in the eat-in area crowded with place settings and condiments.

Through the French doors, Richard was tending to the smoker, the round, black metal a giant overturned can of meat.

"Whoa. I hope he didn't do all that for us." Danny pointed to Richard through the window.

"I'm sorry," Kara said. "Usually my mom is the cook, but Dad got a little excited about the feast before the fleet."

"That's what he's calling this?"

Kara nodded. "Bet you didn't know anyone pre-gamed eighteen hours before a regatta."

He turned, eyes striking as his gaze met hers. "No, I didn't."

He still held Hannah's hand and brought her to a chair at the table. Her hair was in two pigtails, and she wore a flowery dress. It must've taken some convincing to get her out of her T-shirt and shorts. "Why don't you have a seat? Looks like dinner will be ready very soon."

She investigated the solid oak chair before sitting.

Kara nudged Danny and whispered in his ear. "I took off the seat cushions, just in case."

He nodded in appreciation.

"Yes, it's nearly there," Sheila said. "Just fixing the drinks. Would you like sweet tea or lemonade?"

The only two options in the thick of Appalachian summer. It was hard to turn down Mom's iced tea though. New York's silly excuse for sweet tea wasn't worth the outrageous price.

"Hannah will take lemonade," Danny said. "I'll have the tea."

Mom was at her best when she was busy—cheerful, positive, humming to herself. But the humming came from two sides of the room.

"Hannah, honey?" Danny sat down next to her. "You okay?"

She rocked in the chair, humming louder.

"Hey Mom, is it okay if I open these doors?" Kara pushed open the French doors. Hannah wasn't feeling okay, and the best way to soothe her was to open up the space and quiet down the noise. Luckily, the smoke from the meat factory Dad was managing blew away from the house, toward Danny's.

Hannah made circles in the air with her dangling feet, the humming mixed with the beginnings of a helpless whine.

"I'm going to take her outside." Danny guided her out of the chair and through the doorway.

"Is she okay?" Sheila whispered at Kara's shoulder.

"Yeah. It's her way of expressing discomfort."

"Oh no. She's been here before, well, in our living room. I didn't think having it at our house would be an issue."

"No, don't worry about it." Kara popped her head out the doorway, the evening heat overtaking the kitchen. The sun had already made its way over the western mountains, yet the air refused to let it go. Hannah sat at the patio table outside, Danny beside her. She wasn't rolling her foot or rocking.

"You know, Mom? I think we should take advantage of this weather and move this outside."

"Really? I already set the table."

"I'll take care of it." Kara lifted a plate and its corresponding silverware. She was going to explain the situation when Mom met her gaze. It was a simple nod, but it was one of understanding. Nods like that from Mom didn't happen very often. But Kara was happy this one did.

The wooden picnic table looked neglected—not in the sense of faded paint and rough lumber but rather in the way it sat on the side of the bricked patio, unused and lonely. It had been one of Dad's first pieces to keep at the house. But apparently neither Richard nor Sheila found much use for it when Kara was away.

"How's it going?" Kara set the place setting on the bench.

"We're good." Danny smiled. Hannah was going to be okay.

"I thought we'd have a little picnic out here. Take in the colors of the sky, the sounds of the birds hunting at dusk. What do you think, Hannah?"

"I'm hungry," she said, head down.

"Well, let's remedy that." Kara returned to the kitchen and picked out a blue tablecloth, the white border speckled with yellow sunflowers. Danny helped her arrange the tablecloth and laid out the place settings she brought out.

"All set." Richard clicked his tongs and closed the smoker. He balanced a heaping plate of ribs and turkey breast in his free hand, making Kara nervous as he limped with the crutch in the other.

"Let me get that, Dad."

"Don't you dare. I got it." He set it down as the glorious centerpiece for their feast.

Mom brought out the buttered corn on the cob and potato salad.

Kara sat on the other side of Hannah, while Richard and Sheila took to the opposite bench.

Richard raised his iced tea. "I just wanted to say thank you to you, Kara, for never giving up on the regatta. And to you, Danny and Hannah, for helping my dream come true."

"To the regatta," Sheila said, glass in the air.

"To Team Kerror." Dad stared, a grin growing on his face.

Danny's gaze burned at Kara's cheek. Richard burst into laughter, and Kara couldn't help but laugh. "To Team Kerror."

They clinked glasses.

"Because of the terror they'll all feel when we sail past them," Danny said.

"Oh!" Richard and Sheila bubbled at the joke.

Kara dug into the turkey, Danny opting for the ribs. She tried not to stare as the sauce made its way from the corners of his mouth to halfway across his cheeks. It was almost as adorable as the blue cotton candy had been.

"What are you going to do once the race is over, Danny?" Dad took a bite of potato salad. "Think you'll continue to sail?"

"I'm not sure." He wiped his face and hands with a napkin, much to Kara's dismay. "Kara has certainly taught me a lot."

"Well, I can see why you wouldn't continue."

"Dad!"

"I know how you can be, Kara." He winked.

"I have to say, at first I wasn't sure if I was going to...let's say, live up to her expectations." Danny shot her a glance, albeit a benevolent one.

"Fine. I was a little harsh. Regimented."

"That's a bit of an understatement."

She stared, mouth agape. "Is this pick on Kara time?"

"I want more corn, please." Hannah reached for the plate, and Kara helped her.

"I bet Hannah wouldn't say such things about me."

"That's because you were nicer with her on board."

She considered flicking a chunk of potato salad at him, but instead snickered in jest.

"Well, who knows how long your teacher will be around?" Mom hadn't said much all dinner, but this was how she interjected. With a sprig of venom.

Kara shifted on the bench. The race was tomorrow, and that was her focus. She didn't want to think about beyond that because when she did, sorrow sailed in. She had gotten used to their company. They had worked on puzzles a few times and had a picnic or two. But sailing lessons would be missed the most.

She didn't want to face the truth, that the prospect of less time with Danny felt worse than not finding a job.

"Oh, I meant to ask you, Kara," Danny said.

Kara welcomed the redirect.

"George said something today about some portfolio work for New York?" He said it nonchalantly, but the look in his eyes, the expression on his face, painted it with something else. Was it hurt?

She sat up straighter. "I was going to tell you and Hannah, but there never seemed to be a right time."

"I guess now would be good," he said.

They were outside, yet the air felt suffocating. "I have an interview at a photography magazine."

"That's good news, right?"

"It's back in New York."

He played with the condensation on his glass of tea. "When is it?"

She took in a breath of courage. She was going to have to tell him sooner or later, but it wasn't supposed to feel this disheartening. "Monday. I fly out Sunday."

He looked up from his glass. "In two days?"

She nodded. *Say something, Danny.*

He cleared his throat and leaned away from the table. "If your photographs are anything like what I've seen in *International Ecologic*, I think you have a real shot."

She nearly choked on her tea. Harsher words were expected. Not those. "You've seen my work?"

He smiled, but his eyes held sorrow. "Of course."

"I'll take it you'll accept the job?"

"There's no way of knowing if I'll be offered. But yes, that's the idea, isn't it?" It was asked to no one, yet she hoped he would give some sort of answer. What did she expect him to say? What did she *want* him to say?

"Well, Kara knows she's welcome to stick around." Mom couldn't help herself, could she? "It'd be nice to continue to have help around here, especially with your father. I'm sure this broken leg won't be the only accident."

"Are you trying to say you're going to get rid of me?"

Kara laughed. He knew how to brighten the mood and set Mom in her place. She loved him tremendously.

Dad leaned back as much as he could, seated at the end of the bench with his healing leg swung out, and patted his belly. "What's for dessert, Sheila?"

Mom stood, grabbing her plate. "Not until the dishes are done."

"I'll get the dishes." Kara and Danny both stood up and offered at the same time.

"That's very kind of you two." Sheila sat back down. "You go ahead. We'll watch Hannah."

Danny hung his head in a slight bow, his lip curling in a grin and eyes devilish as he stretched out his arm. "After you."

Chapter Twenty-Eight

"Looks like we'd make a good dishwashing duo too." Danny washed and rinsed the dishes as Kara dried and put them away. The window over the sink afforded a check-up on Hannah, who sat on the pebbles of the lakeshore. The sun must've completely set, the sky hard to delineate from the ridge of the mountains across the lake. Richard switched on the patio light, which flicked with the colliding of moths.

"You should come every night." Kara grabbed the wet tongs. "Then it wouldn't take me so long."

He could picture doing the dishes with her every night, but he didn't want the warmth rushing his face to tell her that. "You do the dishes every night?"

"Whenever I'm here for dinner. Which, let's face it, is most of the time." She stacked up the dried kitchen gadgets in a corner. "I don't mind helping out. Honestly, it helps me pull away from whatever conversation I need to get out of."

"You and your mom seem to be getting along well." He raised a brow, and she rolled her eyes.

"It's hit and miss. Dinner tonight...was miss."

Sheila had thrown an underhanded comment about Kara leaving. It wasn't the most tactful way of addressing the topic. "I don't know. Maybe she's just sad at the possibility of you being away again."

"The way she talks sometimes pushes me away."

"Perhaps it's easier for her to cope that way."

"What is this?" She waved the towel along with her hand gestures. "You couldn't possibly be defending controlling moms."

"Giving you a dose of your own medicine."

She whipped his shoulder with the towel and laughed.

"If I come over for the dishes, will you come over to water the fern?"

Kara tipped her head back in laughter. "So you did see George."

"Yep." Danny grinned. "Only added ten dollars to the order."

"I'm sure the fern will be happy about it."

"We'll see." He joked about it, but it was thoughtful of her, and it meant she was thinking about him and Hannah even when they weren't around.

"Thanks for accommodating Hannah tonight." The change of subject lowered her cheerfulness, and he wished he had held onto it longer. "My ex-wife, Maggie, didn't have the capacity to do that. Speaking of irritating mothers."

"I guess relatively speaking, Mom isn't so bad." Kara sounded solemn, her face serious.

It was why he didn't bring Maggie up much with anyone. After the phone calls had stopped, and she hadn't visited in a year, he had given up hope she was coming back. Only then was he able to mourn and begin to sort out his new life as a single dad raising Hannah. But it was the look Kara gave now, the one of pity and sorrow, that he didn't want from people.

"Danny, what happened?" Kara leaned against the counter. Her green eyes were enough to light up the kitchen. "You said you divorced?"

"Yeah. You know, we married young. And shortly after, we had Hannah. It wasn't until Hannah was about two years old that things deteriorated, around the time Hannah started showing symptoms of ASD. She wasn't smiling or laughing or looking us in the eye. And she was very clumsy in walking." He chuckled, her chunky legs marching down the hallway a clear picture in his head. "We shrugged it off. But it was taking her longer to reach each milestone, and eventually we knew something was wrong." He swallowed hard. "Not as expected. I don't like to say *wrong*."

Kara replied with a soft nod. "And Maggie?"

"I had always seen her as a free spirit. Wild and full of life. But when the responsibilities became greater, and harder, I eventually saw her for who she was—an immature girl, not willing to step up when she was needed the most."

"Did she not want any visitation or joint custody?"

"That was the most hurtful part. Not that she was leaving me. But that she was leaving Hannah. That she could walk away from this beautiful girl we created. She wanted nothing. With either of us."

"I'm so sorry."

"I know that's the right thing to say, and that's why people tell me it whenever they hear about it. But really, don't feel sorry for me. At first, I wanted people to feel sorry for Hannah. But now I don't really feel that way. In the long run, I think we're better off. Hannah doesn't seem to remember Maggie, and it's probably best. It would've been harder if she had stayed and her attitude deteriorated more with Hannah old enough to remember."

"If that's the way you feel, you're probably right." She grabbed a wet plate. "Do you still think about her?"

"Only when I'm asked about her." He regretted it as soon as it came out. That wasn't fair to Kara. "No, I don't, much. At first I did. But I've had plenty of time to cope with it and move on." It wasn't just something he told people. It truly was how he felt. Maggie was not a good person for him or Hannah. The sooner he had realized that, the easier it was to move on.

"Have you...dated at all since the divorce?"

The answer was embarrassing. In five years, he'd had two relationships that didn't even deserve to be called that. One of the two had been over the course of five days on a cruise ship. More of a tryst than a relationship. The other was with a bank teller who, after two months, moved up to management and onward to Charlotte. "A few times, here and there. Apparently, I fall for women who don't want to stay."

His heart thudded in his chest. The words lingered, and he pulled the drain, the noise masking the uncomfortable silence. He picked up another towel to help with the drying. "Okay, I've had my moment. Now you."

"Me?" She tilted her head, as if she was shocked and had nothing to tell. "What about me?"

"Yes, what about you? You were quick to tell me you had a fiancé when you arrived but then…" He stared at the ceiling before meeting her eyes. "No, I don't think you've said anything else about him."

Her cheeks flushed, and she looked at her feet. So he wasn't the only one who felt awkward in all of this. "Well…his name is Marcus, and we dated for two years before he proposed last month."

"That's a pretty substantial amount of time." It hurt to hear it. Engagement usually meant serious, but two years confirmed it.

"Yeah. It is. Which is why it's complicated right now."

For some reason, Danny imagined she meant he complicated things, but that wasn't true. She didn't know how he felt. She looked so fragile right now, standing in front of him.

"Complicated?"

She shook her head, biting her lip. "Our anniversary was when I was laid off. And Marcus had known about it but didn't warn me."

"Ouch." Danny wasn't a violent person, but the guttural urge to punch the well-dressed man he had seen get out of the car that day was real. "That's what brought you back here."

"Mostly the not being able to afford New York brought me here." She chuckled. "Honestly, I needed a break."

"From New York or Marcus?" If it was the latter, maybe he had a chance. But Marcus wasn't the only hurdle. She was leaving Sunday. How was he to convince her to stay? He didn't have the right to ask her to stay. That wasn't fair to put Kara in such a position.

Why was it that he hadn't known for sure how much he wanted to be with her until she made it clear she couldn't be with him? If there was anything he learned from the experience with Maggie, it was that a partner needs to figure out herself before any serious relationship with him could work.

"People do make mistakes," he said. "Take me, for example. I messed up the day of the fair. I know we talked about it before, but I still feel like you need to know I'm sorry how I treated you that night."

"Water under the bridge."

"I know, I know. I'm just saying, mistakes happen. And I do know what it feels like to be Marcus."

"What's that supposed to mean?"

"On the other side of Kara Carter's wrath."

She opened her mouth, scoffing. "Well, apparently, I fall for men who don't know a good thing when it's right in front of them."

It came across as a joke, but her smile faded, and the kitchen, the air, the noise all stood still. Her body pulled at him to break the distance between them. His pulse rang in his ears. Somehow the words managed to come out. "You're right. It just takes some longer than others to realize it."

She closed her eyes and shook her head before stepping back. "You think I should go easy on Marcus?"

No. That's not what he meant. He countered her step away. "I think that you already know how you feel."

What was she thinking? It was hard to read her face, her eyes distant yet on him.

"Oh, look how clean!" Sheila Carter clapped her hands, smiling at the kitchen. "Who's ready for dessert?"

Kara slipped away from the conversation. It had been a moment, but it was over.

Chapter Twenty-Nine

"Come on." Danny waved her over to the playground. Lakeshore Park was nearly empty, even though the six inches of snow the New Year's snowstorm dumped had melted.

Kara was ecstatic he had called her over break. She had wanted to call him, but still wasn't sure where they stood—more precisely, how *he* felt about *her*. After the first time he called—it was better than her actual Christmas gifts—they had chatted on the phone almost every day. Today was the first day they finally had a chance to meet up after all the holiday family visits.

Kara sat in the swing, her jeans doing little to keep her legs warm. "I can feel how cold the chains are through my gloves."

"Don't be a party pooper." Danny kicked his legs, pumping the swing back and forth.

Kara kicked off, the wind in her face tearing her eyes. Her scarf did its job, but her exposed nose and cheeks were feeling the nearly freezing temperature.

Danny huffed and puffed next to her. "Is it me or is this harder to do than when we were kids?"

Kara jumped off as the swing hit its farthest point forward, sticking the landing.

"Showing off now." Danny waited for the right time and leaped off the swing. He landed, knees slightly bent and arms in the air. He straightened. "Perfect ten!" He ran in a circle in victory.

Kara giggled and ran off to the slide.

"Hold on, wait for me." Danny climbed up the tall ladder after her.

She clunked her lace-up boots in front of her as she sat down.

"Scoot up a little." Danny sat behind her, his legs beside her hips and under her arms.

"I think we're too big," Kara said.

"Count of three," Danny said. "One—two—three—"

They pushed off, creeping down the slide, the soles of their boots squeaking across the metal. Kara laughed in between fake screaming, raising her arms as if they were on a roller coaster.

At the bottom, Danny grabbed her gloved hand.

"Where are we going?"

"To the beach." Danny pulled her along, and Kara ran after him. The sand wasn't as forgiving as in the summer heat. It stayed mostly in place, hard under Kara's boots.

They stood side by side, staring out over Waverly Lake. Danny kept her hand in his, and she had no desire to let go.

"I think I like it best in the winter." Danny's warm breath matched the clouds streaking the sky. The sun had already crested the mountains, the sky pink and violet. "On days like today it almost looks like ice crystals are floating on top."

He turned to Kara. "Are you crying?"

Kara used her free hand to absorb the tears in her glove. "They're just watering from the wind and cold. Are my lips actually moving as I'm talking?"

Danny laughed. "Here." He loosened her red scarf, the layers hanging lower on her chest.

Kara raised her eyebrow. "How does that help?"

Danny took her head in his soft gloves, his palms warming her cheeks. He stepped closer, drawing her to him and pressed his lips against hers.

Every inch of Kara stood still. All nerves in her body were

focused on this. His lips were cold at first but warmed within a second. He backed away and met her lips again, a new flurry of delight melted down her neck, her back, her arms. Her hands came alive as she held onto his jacket.

And just like that, he stopped. He stepped back and smiled, looking into her eyes. "Did that do the trick?"

She tried not to smile at his confidence, but she had just kissed Danny Bennett. This smile wasn't going anywhere for a long time. "Hmm. I'm not sure. I think I feel a little frostbite coming on." She stared at the tips of her gloved fingers.

Danny chuckled and hugged his arms around her puffy-jacketed waist. "I guess we'll have to remedy that."

Chapter Thirty

SATURDAY, AUGUST 22

KARA SAT IN THE PARKING LOT BEHIND DYE HAPPY Salon, the sun barely peeking over the horizon enough to send a soft glow on the brick building. Her early arrival had secured a spot, something that wouldn't come so easily once it got closer to parade time. Dowager Street would be blocked off several blocks west and east of the square, along with the south artery that fed it.

She questioned why she had agreed to do such a thing. But she knew why. There was no telling Carly Fletcher no. Carly knew everyone in town. Plus, she was a customer of Dad's. There was nothing to gain by saying no, except a free morning and keeping her dignity.

She walked to the front of the store and knocked on the locked door. Waverly Lake had been its usual August self, but the forecast threatened an uptick in temperature over the next few days. The early heat and humidity signaled it was going to be a scorcher by the time of the regatta. A bad omen for sailing.

The cool air-conditioning welcomed her as Carly opened the door. "Good morning, Kara."

"Morning."

"Just have a seat in that first chair. You can put your purse on the ledge."

Kara sat in the newer seat, a sleek, black ergonomic chair with a mesh-like back rather than the hard timeworn seats with flower cushions from her childhood. Sometimes, as in Nichols and Dimes Drugstore, it was charming for things to stay the same. In Dye Happy Salon, it was encouraging that changes had occurred. Kara had worried throughout the night she would walk out with a perm, or big '80s hair, or the crazy up-dos she had seen during prom season that looked like antebellum southern belles had transplanted to the present.

"I wasn't sure if I should wash it this morning or last night..."

"Let me see." Carly grabbed a brush and ran it through Kara's hair. "Did you have a style in mind? Or do I have free rein?" She smiled, as if the second option was the natural choice.

"I—I'm not sure..."

She must have sensed Kara's worry. "Do you trust me?"

Don't answer that.

Carly moved in front of the chair, blocking the updated mirror on the wall. She ran her hands through Kara's hair, pulling pieces up and putting some back down. Kara could only imagine what bouffant she was going to end up with.

"I think it looks good as is for what I'm going to do." She twirled Kara's seat around so her back was to the mirror and put her hands on Kara's shoulders. "Just relax. I promise it'll be tasteful and elegant. You'll love it."

Kara sighed. She had agreed to this. At least Carly wasn't reaching for the scissors.

"I'll grab you something to read."

Carly came back with a stack of magazines and a bin of hair supplies with brushes and pins and clips in a jumble.

Kara flipped through the first pages of an entertainment magazine. It was hard to turn off her photography brain when looking at published photos, even if they were fluff pieces on celebrities. But it was easier to flip through that type of magazine than fashion or home décor ones, and nature magazines were off-limits at the moment.

Even though it was early, it felt good to sit in the chair and have time to herself.

"So I saw you yesterday." Carly ran the brush through hair toward the front of her face and twisted it up, pinning it to the top of her head.

The magazine time was too good to be true. "Oh, you did? I didn't see you."

"Well, you seemed busy with Danny and Hannah. Looked like you were docking as Donald and I were heading out."

Maybe if Kara didn't respond, she'd drop it.

"How's that been going? Ready for the race?"

Of course she wouldn't drop it.

"As ready as we can be." Yesterday had been such a success, they now actually had a chance to place.

"I know you have the experience, so I'm not taking your casualness seriously. Even with the whole...well, you know."

She wanted to shrink in the chair, but Carly pulled on her strands.

"I think you'd make a great sailing coach. If you could teach Danny..."

Danny hadn't been a difficult student. Sure, he had known next to nothing at the start, but he listened and worked hard. None of which needed to be said, because Carly switched subjects like a NASCAR driver switched gears.

"You know, Christian asked about you the other day, and I couldn't for the life of me remember what it was you were pursuing out in New York before you came back."

Insult hadn't been the intention. It was just the way Carly was. It didn't make it hurt any less.

"Photography."

"That's right! I knew that." She worked quickly but gently, Kara losing count of how many pins were going in her hair.

"You know, it's good to see Danny out and about, learning something new. He doesn't really get out, at least not since Maggie."

"Did you know her?" Admittedly, she had piqued Kara's interest.

"I did. As much as a hairdresser could know a client."

With Carly, that meant she was probably the officiant at the wedding.

"What was she like?"

"She had a rebel streak in her. A bit like you in that she had the bug in her to be out in the world, away from Waverly Lake."

I fall for women who don't want to stay. Danny had said it bluntly in the kitchen. It had somersaulted her stomach and ached her soul.

"But to do that to Danny..."

Did Danny view her that way? Her situation was so different from Maggie's. She would never abandon someone, especially her child, suddenly and completely.

"So terrible," Carly said. "He took it hard. It really was sad to see. I wish I could say I didn't see it coming."

"What do you mean?"

"I only did her hair a few times. The first time, she was all excited to be in Waverly Lake, newly engaged to Danny. We got along just fine. But—and don't tell Danny I said this—I didn't see the connection between the two of them. It was more infatuation on Danny's side. He was smitten and she...well, she was a little abrasive, in my opinion. She and the bridal party had their hair done in *Westerville*."

"I'm sure you were okay with that." Kara gave her big eyes.

Carly laughed. "It wasn't that. Okay, it wasn't only that. But it showed she didn't value anyone or anything here. Anyway, she seemed positively ebullient for the wedding."

"What happened?"

"That's the thing. A wedding is only one day. A marriage on the other hand..."

It was as Danny had described last night. It was heartbreaking— even if Danny didn't want her to think so. He deserved better. Hannah deserved better.

"It wasn't like the two of you." Carly warmed up the curling iron and tested it with a quick touch of her fingers.

"Oh, there's no two of us," Kara said.

"Honey, you can tell yourself whatever you want. And you can think I'm just the dumb town gossip. But what you and Danny have...I've seen you together. I've known the two of you since you were kids, even if you've been gone for forever." She nudged Kara's shoulder with her elbow. "I don't know if you believe in God or some higher power or what, but there is a force between the two of you. Something that keeps pushing you together. We're all just waiting for you to get to the point where you stop fighting it."

"*We're?*"

"Oh, don't act so surprised. This is Waverly Lake, you know."

Carly's nephew Christian, the student who helped Kara with the furniture, walked in along with two other women whom Kara assumed were fellow parade models. The street was brightening from the rising sun, and people began to line the sidewalks.

"Get to prepping them first." Carly pointed the women to two seats opposite Kara. "I'll do you last."

Christian nodded.

"Wait, you're doing the parade too?"

"Of course," he said. "We needed a male model so naturally..." He pointed his thumbs at himself. "You're looking brighter or something this morning, by the way."

"Thank you." She probably hadn't looked her best their last meeting, delivering furniture. She took the opportunity to stay on Carly's good side. "I guess praise should be given to Carly for that."

"Don't sell yourself short," Carly said. "This is just the cherry on top. Not the whole sundae. But I must say, one look at you and Danny will come to his senses. If he hasn't already."

Christian perked up. "Um, who is this Danny you speak of?"

"I'll fill you in later."

"Danny is a friend," Kara said. "Besides, I have a fiancé back in New York." Whom she would have to return to tomorrow, but that was all Carly would have to hear to go on a rant.

"Oh really?" Carly put down the curling iron and fluffed Kara's hair. "I'm no fool, you know. I noticed that ring the day you walked in here. But tell me, why did it take this long for you to mention him?" She raised an eyebrow.

Maybe because I couldn't get a word in. But that wasn't entirely true.

"Here we are." Carly turned Kara's seat around, adding drama to the big reveal in the mirror. Kara's sides were swept back loosely, with the rest of her long hair in soft, barely-there curls. Carly gave her a hand mirror and spun the chair back around. Kara checked out the back, her hair pinned in swirls and draped down in beachy imperfect waves. It was elegant and modern. Not at all what she had expected.

"It's...it's gorgeous."

Carly slapped her shoulder. "Well, don't act so surprised."

Kara lowered the mirror. "I love it."

"I'm happy with it," Carly said. "Too bad it's going to be a hot mess by the time the social rolls around this evening."

"Oh, I hadn't planned—"

A knock on the door startled her. It was Danny, holding Hannah's hand.

"Speaking of Danny..." Carly caught Christian's attention and pointed to the door.

"Ooh, this is Danny?" He approached the door and unlocked it.

"We're here to see Kara?" Danny looked embarrassed, with all eyes on him.

"Right here." Kara stood and straightened her shirt and shorts.

"Wow," he said, mouth agape. "You look...really nice."

"She looks better than really nice," Carly said. "Hello there, Miss Hannah. Gosh, you get prettier by the day. I have a guess how you got that gorgeous golden hair, but darn it if you don't have your father's eyes. Are you going to let me do your hair like this one of these days?"

"Yes." Hannah looked away from Carly. "But no haircut."

Carly sighed. "Okay. I know, you hate the scissors. You're

beautiful just the way you are anyway. I especially love those pigtails." She winked at Hannah, even though Hannah's attention wasn't directly given back.

Danny smiled, then stared at Kara in awkward silence. "So...why did you want us to come by?"

"Oh, right." Kara reached in her bag and pulled out her camera. "This is for Hannah." She handed Danny the camera. "If it's okay with your dad, Hannah, I'd like you to take care of my camera this morning. Do you think you could take some pictures of the parade for me?"

"Yes!" Hannah clapped.

Kara bent to Hannah's level. "Great. Take real good care of it."

"I know," Hannah said. "Put the strap over the head."

"That's right. Always have that strap on in case you drop it. Take all the pictures you want. Anything you find interesting, go for it."

She stood and caught Danny's eyes. "Meet up with you afterwards?"

"Sure."

"Now, now." Carly waved her hands. "Everyone needs to be on the float within the hour. We still have a lot to do."

"I guess that's my cue to leave." Danny opened the door, and Hannah walked through. Kara grabbed the door handle and held it for them. Danny stopped, his face close to hers.

"You do look really beautiful."

The words covered her arms in goose bumps, yet she felt the heat forming sweat on her forehead.

"See you after."

She nodded, and Danny walked out of the salon.

Carly and Christian stared, Carly's plucked eyebrows raised high. Christian folded his arms, a smirk on his face.

Kara's face scorched. "Oh, shut up."

Chapter Thirty-One

"How about here?" Danny stood on the sidewalk two buildings east of Dye Happy Salon, holding one of the noise-protector muffs off Hannah's ear. Hannah was being particular about where to stand for the parade. The first place had too tall a person next to her. The second place a building over had a tree with branches hanging over their heads that she didn't trust.

Hannah waved, and Danny searched for her recipient, hoping out of the handful of people Hannah waved to, it was Tracy. Beverly and James Bennett stood across the street, waving back. His shoulders sank. They waved him over.

"Come on." He picked up Hannah, her seven-year-old body getting no lighter as time went on. He wasn't going to be able to carry her like this much longer, and it was joy and pain at the same time. Parade volunteers kept their eyes out for wanderers. The parade was about to start, and they wanted the street clear. He rushed to the other side and put Hannah down.

"Well, hello there!" Mom shouted, cupping her hands on Hannah's cheeks. It may not have bothered her, but it bothered Danny.

"I haven't seen you since you've been back from summer camp. How did it go?" It was more a question for Danny, since the ear protectors were quite effective at drowning out the noise, but Beverly's strained voice showed her lack of understanding.

"Yeah, about that," Danny said.

The parade started with a cadence of drums, then trumpets blaring. The Waverly Lake High School Marching Band in their navy uniforms took the lead with a patriotic medley, slowly marching eastward on Dowager Street, cutting on the southern stretch of the square.

Hannah clapped her hands in response to the crowd's cheers and let go of the camera. It fell to her waist, the strap luckily around her neck. It was nice of Kara to let Hannah use it to her amusement, but it was nerve-wracking to make sure Hannah didn't damage it.

"It wasn't right for her."

"How so? I told them about her condition. It's not like they didn't know—"

"Just because you tell them about her..." He hated that word, *condition*, among many others to describe his daughter. "...Doesn't mean they're equipped to respond with sufficient care."

"What do you mean?"

"She had an episode, Mom. A bad one. I got called halfway through the week."

"What? And you didn't tell me until now?"

It was none of her business. It wasn't like she had followed up with her camp connections to check on Hannah. Maybe if she had, she'd understand.

"I got called last Wednesday night, and I had to drive up with Kara—" The name slipped out, and he winced. It was the last thing Mom needed to know.

"Kara. Kara Carter? You went out with her?"

"Mom, don't start."

"Don't tell me not to start." She nudged Dad, who didn't seem to want to join in on the conversation. Either that or he was genuinely mesmerized by the parade. "Did she convince you to pull Hannah out of there? She always knew how to meddle in our business."

"What are you talking about? She had nothing to do with it." If anything, Kara had stood up for Beverly to some extent. But she had also asked why he didn't follow his gut and stick up for himself and Hannah. *Good question.*

"How is Hannah supposed to know how to act normal if she's never around normal children?"

His jaw dropped. *She did NOT just say that.* His ribs weren't strong enough to keep his raging heart in his chest. This was beyond unwanted lasagna. Beyond summer camp and prom dates and football scholarships. These were the most ignorant words out of Beverly Bennett's mouth.

"You know what? I don't need to explain myself, or Hannah, to you. You need to trust my decisions. I'm an adult for goodness' sake."

"Did you buy Hannah a camera? Does that seem like a good choice?" It was as if she hadn't heard a word.

"Cut it out!" Danny waved his arms. Hannah continued to take pictures, and Dad turned his head their way, the din of the parade escalating. "The camera is borrowed, from Kara. Hannah loves it actually. She found something other than puzzles that keeps her attention, so let her be. And no, Kara doesn't meddle in our business. If anything, *you* meddle in our business."

He was shouting over the parade and over the aggravation coiling up his spine. "You were the one to convince me to stay away from her in the first place ten years ago. Remember that? And why? What damage could she have done? Look at me. I'm a single dad. Stuck here in Waverly Lake. And my daughter's mom ran out on us. Is that what you envisioned for me? Because that's how I ended up. No matter how much meddling you've done. Or perhaps because of it."

The song had stopped, allowing his last words free rein in the air. A soft cadence ensued, guiding the band in their continued march, and a gap followed before the first parade car approached. Danny caught Sheila and Richard Carter waving to him from the other side of the street, where he should've stayed to begin with.

He waved back, painting on a smile.

"I guess nothing has changed with you and that girl," Mom said.

"You know who hasn't changed? You, and your uppity attitude. You don't care about what's right for Hannah. You just want her to do all the things your friends' grandkids do, the stuff they harp about at your luncheons and gatherings."

"That's—that's not—"

"How could you be so cruel to the Carters? They're literally some of the nicest people you'll ever meet. They're hardworking and friendly and loyal. They've helped both me and Hannah out as my neighbors and as my friends. I'd rather have Hannah know that kind of love than the conditional love you have for me and her. If you could even call it love."

He scooped up Hannah in his arms. "Come on. Let's go see Miss Kara's parents."

"Daniel!"

He pushed through the two volunteers trying to stop him and crossed the street in between Mr. Bingham's vintage rusted pickup truck and Steve Albertson's BMW, the only parade car not decked out with streamers and banners. The sight gave Danny a chuckle, and he wondered if Kara found it amusing too.

Whether from seeing the car or the exhilaration of finally giving Beverly what she deserved, Danny beamed, his smile unwavering.

The Carters made way for him and Hannah on the sidewalk.

"Hi Danny," Sheila said.

"Hey there, Miss Hannah," Richard said, waving his hand in her line of vision.

"Everything okay over there?" As hard as it was for Danny to believe, Sheila Carter had been friends with Beverly Bennett long ago. Now they barely talked, but evidently, Sheila knew enough to recognize Beverly's attitude.

"Yeah. Sometimes it's not the best living near your parents."

Richard pursed his lips together and shrugged.

"No offense, Richard. I'm sure Kara and you are different when she's in town. At least, I'd hope so."

"Speaking of Kara." Richard pointed to the Dye Happy Salon convertible, all sleek and black like the new interior of the building, a black cloth sign on the side of the car with white lettering. Two women sat on the divide between the front and back rows, their feet on the front seat by the driver. In the back sat Kara and the young man he had seen this morning.

"Daddy, I can't reach." Hannah tugged at his shirt. She held the camera up to his face. "You take the pictures."

"Oh." He grabbed the camera. "Okay." He looked through the viewfinder and focused on Kara. Her dark, wavy ringlets blew in the light breeze. With her hair held back, her face shone. She caught them in the crowd, her smile growing from a canned parade smile to a genuine beam. He waved with one hand while snapping with the other. She was gorgeous, and his chest hurt just looking at her.

"Give it back. Daddy! Give it back." Hannah reached for the camera. He wrapped the strap over her head.

"How about I lift you up?" He picked her up, Hannah facing the parade. She took a picture before waving back to Kara. His heart melted. She had never waved to Kara before.

"Can we go now?"

He lowered Hannah and leaned to Richard. "I think we're going to head out now."

"Okay. Thanks for coming over to join us."

"Of course." He shook Richard's hand.

"You know, we loved having you over for dinner last night. You and Hannah are always welcome to come visit us. I know we're neighbors, and you might get sick of us…"

"Not at all. At least, not yet." He smiled.

"Well, in any case, don't be a stranger."

He patted Richard's back. "Thank you. I appreciate it."

"We just love that little girl," Sheila said. "You're not bad yourself either."

"Thanks."

"I think Kara wouldn't mind you coming over either," she said. "You know, when she visits."

"Now, Sheila. Don't embarrass Kara."

"She's way over there," she said. "I'm not lying. There's nothing wrong with telling the truth."

"Actually, there is something I wanted to discuss with you. It's about tonight. I think it would help if you two were in on it."

"Oh?" If Sheila Carter's ears could perk up like a deer's, they would've, judging by her excitement.

"We're always happy to help," Richard said. "Right, Sheila?"

"Oh yes. But tell us. What exactly are your plans?"

Chapter Thirty-Two

"Well, how'd I do?" It took Kara a few minutes to find her parents after the parade.

"You were great." Mom kissed her on the cheek.

Dad gave her a pat on the back. "I have to admit, I never really pictured my daughter would ever be in a pageant car."

"It wasn't a pageant, Dad. Just a parade."

"Well, you are all dolled up like a pageant. I bet you'd win."

People pushed past them along the sidewalks of the square. "Where are Danny and Hannah? They were with you, weren't they?"

"Yes." Mom batted her eyes with her big grin. It was awkward-Mom fashion. Kara had seen her like this before, when she got tickets to see Eric Clapton for Dad and couldn't contain her excitement.

"Dad? What's going on with Mom?"

"Nothing," Mom said.

"I think the crowd got to Hannah," Dad said.

"Oh, okay. We said we'd meet at Pearson's anyway. You're going to watch the regatta, aren't you?"

"Wouldn't miss it," Dad said.

"You'd better not. I think the juniors have already started, so I'd better go."

Kara walked east along Dowager. A good portion of the parade crowd remained along the square, but many had spread out to the periphery. As the morning stretched into the later hours, families made their way to Pearson's parking lot for face painting, relay races, and water balloon fights amid the food trucks, many of which Kara recognized from the fair.

The Waverly Lake Regatta stretched from mid-morning to late afternoon. The local racing competition encouraged children to race individually by hosting a juniors competition at the start of the festivities. Kids eight years and older sailed solo, with either their own vessels or the training dinghies used by Pearson's sailing classes, as long as vessels did not exceed eight feet. Dad had encouraged Kara to race in the juniors once she was old enough, but she had already raced with him in the Open Sail two years before. Juniors stayed within the corner of the lake, and having already tasted the biggest of the races, there was no way she would downgrade.

Already the more serious regatta viewers were setting up their blankets and lawn chairs at Lakeshore Park, close to the starting line. By the time her heat would be up, it'd be hard to spot a patch of grass in the playing field.

Kara scanned the crowd but had a hunch Danny would be by *Kare Bear*'s slip. She bought three sausage subs from a food vendor and carried the foiled sandwiches behind Pearson's. Sure enough, Danny was lying on his back, feet flat and legs bent, with Hannah seated next to him, camera around her neck and muffs at her side.

"Well, if this doesn't look like the most excited bunch of sailors I've ever seen." She stood beside Danny, and he covered the glare from the sun to see her.

"Brought some lunch." She handed him a sandwich and placed Hannah's beside her.

Danny sat up. "I think I'm good."

"You'll need to eat beforehand, and let it settle a bit before we get on. I know it can be hard sometimes when you're nervous." She unwrapped her sandwich and took a bite, the sausage hot but not spicy.

"Are you nervous?" Danny asked.

"I'd be fooling myself if I said no. I think it's good to feel nervous a little. Gets the adrenaline going. Are you telling me you're not?"

"Oh I am. That's why I already ate two slices of pizza, a corndog, and a funnel cake. So please, no more food."

Kara laughed. "Okay." She moved the sandwich away from him.

"I appreciate the thought though."

"No problem."

They watched what they could see of the juniors competition, won by Mr. Lawson's grandson apparently, since Mr. Lawson greeted him with a hug after the awards ceremony. At one o'clock, Danny had retrieved a final copy of the schedule and heats for the fleet racing. A total of thirty-two teams had signed up, split into two heats of eleven and a third of ten. *Kare Bear* was listed in the second heat.

"It's good placement," Kara reassured Danny as they untied *Kare Bear* and headed out of the slip. "We get to see how the first heat's start goes." But the size of the heat was worrisome. Eleven vessels at once? Ten years ago it had been six, and they had fought for starting position. Eleven seemed borderline dangerous. There simply wasn't enough space to fit all eleven in a line, at least not safely between the buoy and committee boat—which meant some had to be forced farther back.

The first blast went off as they motored away from the wharf west.

"Hannah okay with the blast?" She eyed Danny, and he gave her a thumbs-up. She had hoped as much, since wearing the muffs would be dangerous. If the blasts were too much for Hannah, then it would be over before it began. Hannah's safety was more important than winning. It was that simple.

Sailing vessels clustered in position in the holding zone for the heat. Kara had never seen so many boats occupying the same space. "We're going to really have to keep our eyes out for other boats."

Danny nodded and turned to Hannah. "You think you can help us with that?"

"I don't want to crash."

Danny smiled. "No. None of us want to."

"But I want to go fast."

He patted her shoulder. "That's my girl."

They cleared the thick of the racers and turned around, motoring idly toward the back of the fleet through the long blast. "First heat is up in one minute." She had opted for a tank top, the black parade shirt's fabric roasting in the sweltering mid-day sun. The choice meant bathing in sunscreen, but it was worth the extra exposure, now that they bobbed on the lake like a rubber duck.

Kara stood on the bow, stretching to see the racers. The minute up to the starting flag and blast was almost as crucial as the final turn.

"What's happening?" Danny stood behind her.

"I can't see exactly. But looking at the race committee's boat and where I thought I had seen the buoy..."

"That boat in the middle there is too far."

"Looks like it." She watched as the blue-and-white race committee's flag swung down and the starting blast sounded. The leading boat looked ready to tack. "They were too far. They were penalized." The boat had to make a full 360-degree turn before continuing on, which was annoying at the least and nearly disqualifying, since most of the other racers in the heat had to clear out first.

The start of the first heat meant they had five minutes to prep for position. The fleet of second-heat dinghies and cutters drifted closer to the starting line. The Open Sail allowed any single-mast sailing vessel to enter, which meant crews and boat owners argued over which length performed better, while others swore width or depth was more important. *Kare Bear* sat somewhere in the middle of lengths. The largest vessel in the heat was nearly two times her length. They finished hoisting the jib and mainsail and cut out the engine, joining the zigzagging ships. The one-minute blast sounded, and she hit her watch button.

This was it. The moment she and Danny and Hannah had prepped for. The moment Dad had waited for over the long months of building *Kare Bear*. Kara glanced to her right at Lakeshore Park. It was impossible to find anyone in the crowd.

"They're getting an edge on us." Danny pointed to a cutter at their portside that veered straight on to the starting line. *Permanent Vacay*.

Carly Fletcher's blonde hair immediately identified her. The burly tall man with her must have been her husband, Donald.

"Carly, you're coming in too fast!" Danny waved his hands to get her attention.

"Don't listen to him," Donald shouted to Carly. "He's upset we've got prime position."

Danny watched portside as Kara kept starboard clear. The race sailboats lingered in all directions waiting for the start. It took skill to position the boat forward, catching the wind, yet not move across the starting line. Kara looked at the race committee's boat to the right and starting buoy to the left. The invisible line between the two points formed the starting line, and *Permanent Vacay*'s bow was about to cross it.

"We should go," Danny pressed.

Kara checked her watch. Twenty seconds left. "No. Stay the course. They're going to hit it too early."

Her watched ticked down. *Ten seconds. Nine. Eight.*

"Kara." Danny was ready to swing the boom, to catch the full force of the tailwind. *Six. Five.*

"Now!"

Danny made the play, signaling Hannah, who moved out of his way while watching the other boats. *Two.* The race committee flag flew in her periphery, the invisible line so close. *One.*

Flag down.

Blast.

They crossed the line, ahead of most of the fleet but half the boat's length behind *Permanent Vacay*.

"Penalty." Danny pointed to Carly's vessel, Donald swearing left and right at having to go around full circle.

"You were right." Danny smiled.

Kara nodded. They were off to a good start. They led the heat past the main island and through the turnaround, and even past a lackey from the first heat, whether they had been penalized or just lacked the experience. The wind was not as strong as it had been during the practice run, which meant the last turn would be more difficult. They were at risk of being in irons, at a stalemate with dead wind.

"Starboard!" Hannah shouted. A white fiberglass sloop angled toward *Kare Bear*.

"Good eye! Danny, they're going to try to slow us to cut in front. Do not waiver."

"Aye." He winked.

She had forgotten how thrilling the race could be. It was fast and hectic, with competitors nearing the line of cheating as close as they could to gain an advantage. It was incredibly fun.

"That's my parents' boat." Danny's voice lost some of its strength. "That's Joshua and the captain, Garrett. They're coming in hot."

"Let them." It took years on the water to accurately judge distance and speed with confidence. Luckily, Kara had just that. *Kare Bear* was straight and steady. If the other boat stayed its course, their bows would meet—a clear impeding of an opponent on their part. But it also meant *Kare Bear* would suffer damage, ending the race for them. It was a game of chicken.

"Come on," Kara gritted through her teeth. The other vessel kept its aim.

"We're steady!" she shouted, the hired crew of the Bennetts close enough to hear. "Don't do it, don't do it."

Kare Bear angled off its course to the right. Kara looked back. "What are you doing?"

Danny controlled the rudder, shooting fire from his eyes to the other crew. Joshua and Garrett looked at Danny in horror as the third crew member wised up, veering the rudder and killing the wind in the sails.

Kara stood in shock as Danny repositioned *Kare Bear*, leaving the Bennett vessel behind.

"What—I—"

"Sorry," he said. "I thought they could use a little lesson."

Hannah laughed with a screech. It was the first time Kara had ever seen her giddy with joy.

"That was dangerous."

Danny nodded back in seriousness, and Hannah calmed down.

"And awesome." She laughed and Danny lightened back up, Hannah clapping.

They raced onward to the horizontal part of the L, facing the headwind in their move west. The leaders of the first heat soon sailed past them on the way to the finish. "They're moving fast."

"They have the tailwind."

She nodded, but she sensed the wind had died down from heat one to heat two. Perhaps not measurably. She just knew. It didn't only matter how they placed in their heat. They needed to place with their time overall. If the first heat or even the third heat behind them had an advantage, placing first in the second may not be enough to place overall.

"Here we go." Danny gestured up ahead. The final turn.

"Keep up the speed." She didn't need to say it. Danny was already doing it.

"Ready about!"

"Ready!" her two teammates replied.

"Tacking!" The reaction time, the swing of the boom, the glide of *Kare Bear* over the water had been perfect, but there was no time to praise just yet.

"Prepare to jibe!"

"Ready!"

"Jibe-ho!" The movements, the wind, the water—she couldn't have asked for a better maneuver. "Hannah check." Thumbs-up.

The Bennett vessel finished its tacking behind them. "Time to leave them. What do you say?"

Their practice had paid off, quickly harnessing the tailwind and increasing their lead.

They were going to win.

Chapter Thirty-Three

THEY HAD WON THEIR HEAT.

It felt good to achieve such an accomplishment, having never sailed. Good to beat out Beverly and James Bennett's hired crew. Good to help Kara be elated.

They had shouted with joy, Kara and Hannah jumping up and down on *Kare Bear* before lowering the sails and churning the engine. They pulled into the slip at Pearson's Wharf, Richard and Sheila Carter awaiting their arrival, beaming from ear to ear.

"You did it!" Richard looked like he wanted to jump up and down too, but he resorted to pumping his crutch in the air.

Kara hopped off and gave him a giant hug, and Sheila patted her back. "Are the results in yet? Has it been five minutes?"

"Let's go." Richard led the way off the dock to where Bingham Station's parking lot met Lakeshore Park. The awards podium stood with its three levels, and a digital leaderboard timer posted the finish times of racers.

Kare Bear stood at second overall.

"Oh my goodness." Kara turned around. "I can't watch." She covered her eyes and peeked through them. "Did the third heat's winner cross yet?"

"I don't know." Danny scoured the leaderboard and looked out on the racers. A gap existed between the current one crossing and the next two, sailing neck and neck. "They may be up next."

"I can't take this."

Danny laughed. "It's okay." He grabbed her hand, squeezing it in his as she turned back around.

"Looks like we have a close one for first place in the third heat," the announcer added to the tension.

The sloop cut away in the final seconds from the competing cutter, the leaderboard going blank before the update.

"That's it, folks. We have your top three overall times. Congratulations to the winners, and let's keep greeting our sailors for a wonderful regatta."

The leaderboard lit up. *Kare Bear* kept its position in second.

"Ah!" Sheila screamed, and Richard looked like he was about to cry. Danny lost his grip on Kara's hand, her arms flinging around him in a hug.

"I can't believe it!"

He took in her scent of light flowery salon product—*damn you, Carly*—and nerves and hard work. He held on for as long as he could. Longer than he thought she'd hold him. She backed up, arms still around him and face gleaming.

"I can believe it," he said.

Her smile waned to a sweet curve of her lips, and her eyes grew serious. Everything faded—the crowd, her parents shouting, the beating of his heart that had been thrashing his chest.

Hannah tugged at his shirt, her muffs over her ears.

"Oh Hannah, we did it!" Kara crouched and held up two fingers. "We got second place."

"We get a trophy," Hannah shouted.

"We certainly do," Danny said, holding out her muffs. The moment with Kara had fled as quickly as it had appeared.

"You can keep the trophy, Hannah," Kara said. "You were such a great sport through all of this. We don't really need the trophy anyway."

"Hey now," Richard interrupted. "Speak for yourself."

Kara laughed along with Danny. "Okay. Maybe you all can work out a sharing schedule."

"All right." A middle-aged man with a Waverly Lake Regatta staff shirt approached. "We need our heat winners and our overall winners for pictures."

"I guess that's our cue." Kara hugged her dad and led the way to a group gathered by the podium.

They waited for the first heat winners to finish with the pictures before stepping onto the tallest podium. Danny lifted Hannah, who didn't seem to mind both the height and the attention.

Mr. Lawson of Portside Portrait directed their mini photo shoot before getting back down, only to get back up on the second-place platform for the overall winners picture.

Danny considered telling Kara about tonight when Mr. Lawson got her attention.

"Hello there, Kara. Congratulations!"

"Oh thank you, Mr. Lawson. Congratulations to your grandson for the juniors competition."

"Oh yes. We are very proud of him."

"Congrats to you as well, Danny. And Hannah." He smiled at Hannah, who was holding Danny's hand. The excitement of winning seemed to be overshadowed again by the noise and busyness of the crowd.

"Thank you."

"Kara, any thought on what we discussed a while back?"

Danny raised his eyebrows. "What would that be, if I may ask?"

"I was telling her how I'm retiring but would really love someone local to take over."

Would she really take over Portside Portrait? As in, stay in Waverly Lake? There went that thrashing in his chest again.

Kara bit her lip before responding. "I—we—were so focused on the race, I haven't really had time to think about it."

"Well, the time is approaching sooner rather than later."

"I understand. I'll let you know if I think of anyone."

Mr. Lawson nodded and moved on to shots of the remaining stragglers in the regatta.

"Are you actually considering running the photography studio?" It sounded too good to be true. "Or were you just saying that to get rid of him?"

"I get the feeling he'd like me to." She tucked a loose strand behind her ear, face solemn. "Maybe I know someone who would be good for the job."

I know someone good for the job. If he had to say it out loud, then that meant she wasn't serious about considering it. Why was he pursuing—or whatever it was he was doing—someone who wasn't serious about being here for good? He certainly couldn't follow her to New York, or wherever else she wanted to go to pursue a high-profile career. Beverly and James were deeply frustrating, and perhaps standing up for himself would eventually change that dynamic, but that didn't mean he could take Hannah that far from her grandparents. He had a house, a job with flexibility, a wonderful caregiver for Hannah. He and Hannah belonged here.

Maybe he was making a mistake. Maybe his plans for tonight were all wrong.

Perhaps it was the adrenaline of the race. Perhaps it was the fact they had finally built up a foundation of a relationship, one that had been faulty and cracked. Or maybe, plainly, it was the notion that losing her again was terrifying. But his mind threw out the doubts. Tonight would be his last chance—his opportunity to assert the unspoken.

"Kara—"

"I was wondering who could give me a description of—" A thirty-something woman read off a notebook in her hand. "The vessel *Kare Bear*? I'll be using it in the paper and on the site to highlight the winners."

Kara's attention turned to the reporter.

Danny stepped aside, goading Hannah to pursue whatever it was she had her eye on.

"Danny?"

He waved his hand. "Go ahead. I'll catch you later." It was what Kara had worked for. What they had worked for.

Kara nodded in goodbye and turned to the reporter. "I would love to."

Chapter Thirty-Four

MAY 2010

"You sure you don't want any?" Colin waved the engraved flask in Danny's face.

"No, I'm good." Danny wiped his clammy hands on his rented tuxedo pants. They were almost at the banquet hall, the limo ride a ten-minute journey that took nine minutes too long.

"Are you sure, because you've been nothing but quiet since we picked you up."

"And grumpy," Caitlyn Hall added. Danny had nothing in particular against his date, other than the fact she wasn't Kara.

"I just want to get out of this limo."

"Well, we're here, so you'd better cheer up." Colin slapped Danny's knee and escaped out the door, the limo's wheels still coming to a stop. His date Eileen laughed, as she had done the entire ride.

Danny let Caitlyn go before him and followed the group into the hall. The building sat in the far west reaches of Waverly Lake, halfway up a hill. The height, coupled with the arched windows, gave a glorious view of the water. Even though the dance floor was set up on the far side of the hall, past the round dinner tables, the music managed to shake the floor below his feet.

"Danny!" Caitlyn tugged at his arm. "We're up next for pictures."

"Oh, okay."

She pulled him to the backdrop, the lights bright. Danny knocked over an oar propped up against the wall and shuffled to set it back in place.

"If you could stand behind her," guided Mr. Lawson. "That's it. Put your hands on her hips."

Caitlyn covered his hands with hers and struck a pose.

Behind the camera, Colin bent forward and waved his butt in the air, his date and other kids waiting in line laughing. Danny shook his head. How was he friends with that guy?

Suddenly Colin froze, and Danny saw why—a large tear zigzagged up his pants, splitting the seam.

Danny broke out in laughter. Caitlyn pressed on his arms tighter. "Come on, Danny. He's taking the picture."

Danny sucked it in for the second it took Mr. Lawson to snap the camera. It had made him feel better—happy even—for a moment.

They ate dinner, or at least Caitlyn and everyone else at their table did. Danny's stomach was empty, but he couldn't take down a bite. It didn't feel right being here. Everywhere he looked he was reminded of Kara. He couldn't look left where Mr. Lawson finished packing up— Kara worked at his photography studio. He couldn't look right where couples danced, the ones who cared for another dancing too closely for the chaperones' comfort—as close as he and Kara would have been. He certainly couldn't look out the windows to the lake.

That's where he had kissed her for the first time. She had been freezing, and he held her, kept her warm. If only they could go back to that. Back to him holding her.

That was when it hit him. At prom, sitting by himself at the table, all the other students dancing, sneaking booze, hiding away for kisses. And it wouldn't matter if his friends got in his business about it, or what Mom would say or have arranged.

If he ever had the chance to hold Kara again, he would never let go.

Chapter Thirty-Five

KARA SAT AT HER DESK, RUMMAGING THROUGH THE photo files on her laptop. The regatta had been exhilarating, but between the hysteria of the race and the early parade prep, she was exhausted. To top it off, she hadn't finalized her portfolio, and she was leaving tomorrow.

An interview with PhotoStyle Magazine... *It's what you've been waiting and working for. An opportunity like this may never come again.*

Everything she kept telling herself was true. *PhotoStyle* was at least one level, if not five, above *International Ecologic*. It wasn't capturing nature and culture and peoples from around the world. It was an opportunity to create art. To be noticed.

It was what she had to do, yet she couldn't shake the one returning thought. Her relationship with Danny and Hannah. It had been a whirlwind of emotions, but they were finally at a good place. There was a connection there, to both of them, but she knew how it would go if she left. She would go back to her life, and the Bennetts to theirs. The connection would weaken and eventually vanish.

She collapsed on her bed in the hope a little sleep would cure everything. It was a restless slumber, her mind filled with unease.

How was she going to say goodbye to Danny? To Hannah? The silence and isolation only made it worse. Surrendering to the restlessness, she showered, but otherwise hadn't budged from her room.

Mom tapped on the open door and poked her head in. "I've got something for you."

Kara remained at the desk but opened the door wider. "Well, let's have it."

Mom carried a blue something on a hanger in a dry-cleaning bag.

"What's going on?"

"I know I'm springing this on you. I was going to tell you when we arrived home, but you seemed so tired I didn't want to bother you. Danny got your father and me involved."

"Involved in what?"

"A redo."

"Mom, please tell me what you're talking about."

"The Waverly Lake Regatta Social is tonight. Danny asked if I would help convince you to go. I thought maybe you would want to wear this. It's Grandma Alcott's dress, and I mended it some time back for when you—" She sighed. "I planned it for your prom."

"Mom." Kara sat next to her on the bed. "You never told me that. Is that why you were so intent on me finding another date?"

Sheila stroked Kara's cheek. "You've grown to be such a beautiful woman. Not that you weren't a beautiful kid. But I mean it. You are a wonderful person. I want to see you do wonderful things with wonderful people. If that means it's here, I'd be so happy."

"Mom—"

"Let me finish. It also means that if you're happiest in New York...I'll be happy too. As long as you are appreciated and loved. I mean that now, and I felt the same way back then. I thought you were happy with Danny, but when it didn't happen, I didn't want you to regret missing prom."

She hugged Kara. Sheila Carter was a protective and loving

mother. She was a mastermind at laying on the guilt, but even that was out of a good place. They had had their share of fights, but Kara hadn't been mature enough back then to see her mother for who she truly was.

"Just go and have a good time tonight. Make up for that other time."

It would be her last night in Waverly Lake for who knew how long. Of course, this time she wasn't going to wait ten years to return. But still, they deserved a celebration. And she still needed to talk to Danny.

Kara shook her head. "I don't know. I didn't even style my hair." She ran her hands through her air-dried hair. Between the products from Carly and the windblown stress of the regatta, it deserved some basic TLC.

"I can help you with that." Mom worked on unwrapping the dress.

"You sure that's going to fit me? I'm not exactly the size I was in high school."

"Oh, don't worry. I let it out some this afternoon."

"Mom!"

"I may be reminiscent, but I'm also practical, honey."

Kara scoffed, and Sheila laughed. It took her mom under half an hour to pull Kara's hair into a loose, windswept French braid down her back, the shorter raven strands relaxed around her face. Kara had worried about what to say and how she was going to say it to Danny. A simple goodbye wasn't enough. But sitting in quiet, with Sheila's fingers gently swiping her scalp, lulled her into a trance.

The doorbell rang, jolting her to attention, the worry returned.

"Better hurry." Sheila pinned the last strands of hair around the bottom of the braid, concealing the skinny hairband.

"That's Danny?"

"Should be. Your hair looks great." Mom moved to the door and poked her head out one last time. "A little color on the lips wouldn't hurt."

Kara shook her head and changed into the dress. The

cornflower satin chiffon flowed seamlessly to the floor, the bodice gently hugging her waist. The cap sleeves flittered over her shoulders. She felt like a Hollywood movie star, awaiting her man to return from war.

She stared at her painted toes. "Shoes. Uh oh." Maybe Mom would happen to have a pair, even though Mom's feet were two sizes larger. She opened the door. "Mo—!"

Two silver shoes lay on the carpet in front of her. She picked them up and examined the strappy heels. Her size.

She slipped on the shoes, glanced quickly in the mirror, and grabbed her purse. She rummaged through the bag and pulled out the only lipstick she could find—a shade somewhere between lilac and lavender—following Mom's advice.

"Kara?" Mom shouted from below.

"Coming!"

She took the stairs slowly. Heels were rarely worn while walking in Manhattan, and certainly not adorned during shoots, so the carpeted stairs took some getting used to. She cleared the last step and looked up. Danny stood in a deep-navy blue suit with a matching steel-blue buttoned shirt and tartan tie.

"You look beautiful."

"Thank you." *You look dashing.* "No tux?"

"I couldn't decide—vest versus cummerbund."

"It's the age-old question." She laughed, and he smiled. "You clean up nicely."

"Thank you." He brought his arm from behind his back and revealed a corsage with white freesia and orchids that bled powder blue to violet from to center to tip.

"I'm starting to see the theme here. School colors?"

"Closest thing I could get to them."

"You didn't have to do that."

"I kinda did." He opened the plastic. Dad held the container as Danny placed the corsage around her wrist. Danny scooted her in front of him, his hand on her waist. It was all she could think about.

"Say cheese." Dad stood across the living room and snapped a picture.

"This is embarrassing."

"Good!" Mom clapped. "Just like a real prom night."

Kara and Danny laughed.

"Ready to go?" he said.

"Please."

They exited onto the porch, and he helped her down the stairs. She checked out their surroundings.

"What are you doing?"

"Just making sure you didn't get a limo. I draw the line there."

He slipped his phone out of his jacket pocket and held it to his ear. "Call it off, guys. No go on the limo."

Kara laughed.

"No. I mean, what girl doesn't dream of being swept off her feet in a Dodge Ram?" He held the door open for her, and she stepped up into the truck. If she hadn't been sick with nerves, this would have been exciting. Back then she would've been nervous Danny Bennett was taking her out. Excited to be in the truck with him. Giddy to think about dancing close and if the night would end with another kiss like the one lakeside. But this was a different set of emotions altogether.

He sat in the driver's seat as she buckled her seat belt. "Where's Hannah?" The words cracked out of her dry mouth. She'd have to tell Hannah goodbye too. The last thing Hannah needed was another woman in her life leaving without explanation.

"Hannah is home with Tracy." He pulled off Harrington Place, toward Dowager Street.

"You're okay leaving her there?" It was more about wanting Hannah around at the same time she said farewell to Danny, but the more she thought about it, Tracy wasn't exactly the most mature and reliable person to watch Hannah.

"I'm trying not to overthink it." He winced. "In all seriousness, she's one of the few people Hannah seems to take to. And you, of course."

Kara bit her lip. She had felt they connected the moment Hannah asked about the camera. They didn't talk about how they felt, or if they enjoyed each other's company. They simply did, without needing to verbalize it. That Danny noticed was enough reassurance.

"So just us?"

"Yeah. Well, half the town will be there. So there's that."

"You really didn't have to go through all this trouble."

"Look, I know I screwed up back then."

"And we talked about it and moved on."

"Yes, but...sometimes talk isn't enough. From now on, when you think of prom for whatever reason, I want you to think back to this night instead of the one ten years ago. Okay?"

It was hard to argue with that. "Okay. Where is this dance?"

"We're here." He pulled into the parking lot at Bingham Station, and they got out of the truck. The humid air lay thick over the ground, and the cicadas buzzed their evening tune under the sound of the music. A couple walked to the party, a din sprouting from the back deck of Lakeshore Park's clubhouse. One guest was dressed in shorts and a tank, the other in a skirt and short-sleeved shirt.

"Aren't we a little overdressed?"

"Incredibly." Danny whipped that charming smile. He slipped off his suit jacket and threw it in the back seat. He undid the buttons at his wrists and rolled up the sleeves. He was maddeningly handsome. "Come on." He grabbed her hand, and she let him, as they walked through the cleared-out playing field, past the playground, to the clubhouse.

Maybe it was the sight of the swings or being back here where she realized she had fallen for Danny Bennett. But it was as if nothing else was happening in the world outside this moment.

She put all her focus on the touch of his hand—his rough mechanic hands, holding her fingers in a firm yet gentle grasp. It was hard not to think how this could have worked if the circumstances were different. That they could be together, were it not for her career and ambition and Marcus. Tallying the reasons didn't help with the feeling that no matter how she said what needed to be said, it would hurt Danny. And herself.

"Over here." Danny led her up the stairs, around to the back deck. Lights strung across all four corners of the deck and converged in the middle, where a larger light hung shining on the dance floor.

"Care to dance?"

"I don't know—"

"Come on." He spun her out to the middle of the dance floor, where some seven or eight couples moved around to a live band playing oldies music.

"Guess they got over the penalty," Danny said. Carly Fletcher and her husband, Donald, danced a form of the shag, Carly's blonde hair bobbing with the beat.

"Looks like it."

A group of teen girls huddled by the drinks table, busy on their phones, while their counterparts stood along the side of the boathouse, leaning up against the wall.

"It really does feel like prom," she said.

"What?"

She nodded to the teens. "I guess technology hasn't helped them in the dance confidence department."

"We'll just have to show them how fun it is when you don't care who's watching." He twirled her and pulled her close, then let her loose before pulling her back in. The quickness of it all, mixed with the music and lights and summer air, made her want to scream, as if she were spinning around on *Avalanche* at the fair again.

They weren't perfect dancers, nearly knocking into the Fletchers at one point and a younger couple when they corrected for the first error. Kara stepped on Danny's shoes a handful of times, but he didn't seem to mind. It was fun to be dancing—not just dancing, but dancing with Danny—that she nearly forgot the gravity of this last night.

The song ended and Kara puffed, catching her breath.

"We're going to take a five-minute break. We'll return with all your favorite classics."

The crowd clapped the band off the stage. Kara watched them exit as if her security blanket had slipped off her lap.

"Want a drink?" Danny asked.

"Sure." She needed one. Or two.

Danny wandered off to the drinks table. Kara smiled, for the teen girls giggled as Danny approached. He was a dream, as if age had only bettered him like wine. It hurt to look at him, his firm arms in his rolled sleeves. He loosened his tie and unbuttoned the top shirt button. His raven-black hair, disheveled from dancing, asked to be tussled.

"Why if it isn't Ava Gardner." Kara turned, and Sebastian stood by George, arm over his shoulder. "You look gorgeous."

"Oh thanks. It was my grandmother's apparently."

"It suits you," George said. "So does the corsage, but I knew it would."

Kara stared at the flowers on her wrist, then back at George. "Of course. You arranged this, didn't you?"

"Oh yes. Danny came by yesterday. I was closing shop but when he told me what he was up to, how was I to say no?"

"You couldn't," Sebastian said.

"I know what you mean," Kara said. He had gotten her out here *and* she danced. Knowing what George meant was an understatement.

"Are you saying he had this all planned out?"

"I—"

Sebastian placed his finger on George's mouth. "He's not saying any more. You two have a great time. I just love seeing Danny have fun for a change."

They walked off, and Danny came back. "Here you go."

Oh, how she hoped it had alcohol. She sipped. "Hmm."

"What? Not good?"

"It's good, if you want a kid's juice box. Kinda doesn't feel like prom unless...you know."

"Kara Carter, are you trying to get us kicked out of prom?"

"I mean..." She shrugged.

"Hey, Sebastian!" Danny waved.

Sebastian came back over. "Hello Danny."

"Can you share that flask of yours?"

"What flask? How did you—oh, all right."

Kara laughed and poured a little in her cup, then in Danny's.

"You two still owe me for the wine, you know."

"Thank you, Sebastian." Kara raised her glass in a toast to him and drank a sip. Or a gulp disguised as a slow sip.

Across the dance floor, Carly Fletcher made a beeline toward Kara and Danny. *Oh boy, here we go.* Kara turned around. Maybe if they didn't make eye contact...

The band returned. "We're back. We're going to start off slow and work our way up this set."

Danny set his drink down and took her free hand. "Shall we?"

"Yes, please." Kara placed her cup next to his, and they moved toward the center of the dance floor, Carly backing off.

Kara laughed. "Thank you for that."

"For what?" Danny asked.

"You saved me, well, probably us, from Carly Fletcher." *Us.* It tingled her face and ached her heart.

"You're welcome." He held her hand, other arm across her lower back. Her feet laced between his.

"You had this all planned out, huh?"

"What do you mean?" He spoke in her right ear, his face nearing hers.

"I mean the corsage, getting my mom to prepare this dress..."

"A few things here and there." He was so close that she sensed his smile without looking. "Sheila told me what color the dress was, but I had no idea."

"No idea, what?"

He pulled away and looked at her mouth, then met her eyes. "No idea it was this stunning."

They swayed to the music. A slight breeze kicked in, grazing her neck and flittering the cap sleeves on her shoulders. It mixed with his scent of faint rosewood and a hint of citrus. They danced closer, not knowing if he had pulled her closer or if she pressed closer to him. His clean-shaven face brushed against her cheek as he pulled slightly away. She didn't want him to pull away. Didn't want him to let go.

He looked into her eyes. The arm on her back lifted. His fingertips caressed up her spine, over her shoulders, and up her neck. She sighed at his touch. With both rugged, worn hands, he cradled her head as if holding the most precious fragile object in the world. The anguish made her nearly cry as he leaned in and pressed his lips against hers.

She kissed him back, a trace of spiked punch on his warm lips. They had stopped dancing. The world had stopped dancing. Both hands held her cheeks and she held him, pressing him tighter, as if her strength couldn't move him close enough. She had let him in. She had surrendered her soul for the split-second, the minute, the slow-burn day, month, year of this kiss until that voice inside, that pesky, irritating, rational voice, spoke loud enough.

"I can't." She shook her head. "I'm sorry." She rested her forehead on his chest, his arms around her.

"Kara."

"Please." She touched his chest and gently forced space between them. This was not how she had wanted her time here to end. It wasn't supposed to happen this way. That kiss. That kiss wasn't supposed to happen. But here he was, standing in front of her, heart on his sleeve.

A heart she was going to break.

Chapter Thirty-Six

To Danny, the evening had been perfect. The corsage, the weather. Her dress. He was finally going to have a chance to tell her how he felt, but instead of telling her, he showed her. It had felt right with the music, the darkening night sky and the lights. She had responded by showing him she felt the same—the pull of their magnetism, the thirst for each other's souls. But only for a few fleeting seconds.

He followed her through the other dancers, close yet miles apart without her touch. Sebastian and George no doubt noticed their abrupt departure, standing on their tiptoes to catch a glimpse of the aftermath. When Danny looked back, a teen couple brave enough to dance the slow dance filled their vacant space.

They reached the car, and Danny moved to the passenger side.

"I got it," Kara waved him off. He got in and started the car.

"Talk to me, Kara. Are you telling me you feel nothing for me?"

"I'm not saying that. It's just—"

"You do feel something for me? It certainly felt like it back there. It's felt that way since you returned to Waverly Lake. I can't explain it, but when you showed up, something awakened in me. I haven't felt such a connection with anyone since—"

"Danny, please. I can't. I'm with Marcus, for one."

"Do you love him? On the rare occasion you do mention him, your face doesn't light up. You don't gush or turn pink when you talk about him. You don't seem to feel anything for him. I kind of feel bad for him because if you acted like that with me, it would crush me. At least when you were angry with me, it meant you felt *something*. I don't think I'd be able to stand the indifference you give to Marcus."

"Please stop!" Kara wiped the tear away before it could fall. "I'm flying back to New York tomorrow."

There it was. The reason he had convinced himself for an eternity to hold back and not feel anything. He felt like a fool.

He maneuvered out of the parking lot.

"I'm sorry, Danny. I have to go back."

He drove through Waverly Lake's town square. He couldn't look at her. Tonight, she was the most beautiful person he had ever seen. He had felt magic with that kiss, a confirmation that they could be...together. Looking at her now would be the cruelest form of torture.

Danny couldn't reach the Carter house fast enough. He parked the car and sat still. "To say you have to go is ridiculous. You have a choice, Kara. I don't know how he feels about you, but you know how I feel about you. You've got to by now."

He turned to her. "I don't want there to be any doubt what would be here if you chose Waverly Lake." The blue dress kissed her shoulders, and her dark hair brought out the green in her eyes. It tormented his core.

"Kara, I love you."

She opened her mouth, but Danny stopped her. "I haven't felt this way in a long time. Maybe ever. You are brilliant and adventurous and creative and talented. All the things I'm not, and you make me a better person, a better man. A better dad. You were right. I deserve to have a life outside of being a dad. I deserve to be a man with his own identity. But I also deserve someone who will return my love."

Kara's resolve broke, her face falling into her hands, the tears rolling.

"If you stay..." The strength in his voice cracked. "If you stay, you will have me—my heart, my love, the good with the bad. I can't give you the big job interview in New York. I can't give you a fancy studio apartment. I can't give you a BMW or whatever other riches and opportunities you would have in New York. What I can give you is all of me. I'm a flawed, truck-driving, marine mechanic dad. But with me, you'd have love. Forever."

"I never wanted to hurt you," she said between sobs. "Or Hannah." She said the words as if no decision existed.

"I'm telling you there is a decision to make, and letting you know what it means to choose here. But don't base it on Hannah." He swallowed hard. "I know how you feel about her. I see it in how you treat her like any other person, any other child. You don't see her as someone with a disability. You see her as Hannah. I know she doesn't say it or show it in the usual ways people are used to, but I know—I know—she loves you too."

She shook her head, wiping her tears. She pulled at the truck door handle and stepped out. "If I stayed," she said turning back to him, "I would always wonder."

"That's the difference between you and me." He looked at her, took her in, this crying young woman who was about to walk out on him for a second time. "Being with you would be enough."

Chapter Thirty-Seven

KARA HASTILY CLICKED THROUGH THE SUMMER'S collection of photographs. The portfolio was the last thing on her mind, hence the haste, but if she bombed at the interview for not finishing it, she wouldn't be able to forgive herself.

She stopped on one of Hannah's earliest photos of a bird flying over the shore of the lake. It was simple—a shot of the bird with its wings spread out. Nothing fancy. But it was clear. And it was as if it was taken from Hannah's eyes. Kara couldn't pinpoint the reason why—perhaps the angle or the slightly off-center orientation. She could've tried to imitate it, crouching low or sitting on her knees. But it wasn't replicable. It was uniquely a child's viewpoint.

She saved the photo in the desktop folder and moved on. She rummaged through the photographs, many from the days out on the lake over lessons with Danny and Hannah. She stopped at one of Mr. Bingham. He stood tall, his weathered face stalwart, his cane a pillar of strength. Another one of Hannah's.

She rifled to another, of Nichols and Dimes Drugstore, the candy display filling up half the shot with Mr. Nichols bent over the display refilling the goodies. She moved it to the folder with another shot of flags held high in the parade's crowd, the parade an afterthought in the background, the faces in the crowd smiling and cheering. These were the pictures of a small town. Her small town. From the eyes of an innocent child. It wasn't the storefronts or the views of the lake. Hannah had captured the essence of Waverly Lake. The people. Perhaps she'd print and mail them to Hannah. Honestly, she wouldn't mind framing a few for her own use.

She hit another photo, and her breathing ceased. It was the one of her and Danny the day Hannah had touched the camera for the first time. She scrolled past it, the memory too painful.

Finally, she reached the collection of photographs from Weeping Wares. Five stood out as the best. She would randomly choose five more. It didn't matter at this point—she had to use what she had.

Kara quickly loaded the slideshow software, selecting photo titles from the desktop folder to upload. She didn't have time to make prints, but most companies wanted to hire tech-savvy photographers anyway. She moved the cursor over "Preview" to double-check the upload when his voice stopped her.

"Please, I just want to talk to her. I didn't exactly get to say goodbye." Danny's words echoed through the front door to her bedroom.

The green checkmark confirmed her entry, and Kara closed her laptop and zipped up her suitcase. Danny pleaded with Mom at the front door. Kara wanted to hug him, comfort him, tell him everything would be okay eventually. That he'd find his person to be with, for him and Hannah. That he'd forget again about Kara. Perhaps for good. But hearing his voice broke her resolve, and she couldn't leave for the most important interview of her life with lingering doubt.

"I'm really sorry, Danny. She's fixing to leave any minute now."

"Maybe I can take her to the airport."

"I appreciate the offer, but I don't think that's best right now."

Kara didn't hear anything else out of Danny. She had never been more thankful for Mom intervening, even though she heard the regret in Mom's voice warding him off. There was no way she would've been able to endure telling Danny herself, no matter how weak that made her.

The front screen door swung closed, and Mom bolted it. Even through the security of her bedroom door, it was the hard sound of finality. He was gone.

Kara closed the east window, refusing to look out at Danny retreating. She moved to the north window, taking in the faint morning breeze off the lake. Soon the leaves would dry up into hues of rust and honey, the wind louder, rattling the crunchy nothings. But the summer wind had its own sound, the weighed branches swaying slowly, singing a heavier, fuller song. She closed the window and moved away from the sound, the past, the memories.

She lugged her purse and bags down the stairs.

"Ready, honey?" Mom stood with her purse on her shoulder, car keys in hand.

"As much as I can be."

Mom held the door for her, and they walked silently to the car. Kara loaded the trunk with her belongings.

The artificial light in the shop barely broke through the morning sun's rays on the windows. "Let me say bye to Dad."

Mom nodded. "I'll wait in the car."

Kara entered the shop, hands in her front jean pockets. Dad stroked the curved back of the unfinished sloop, moving his hand back and forth over the same spot, feeling the bows and arches of the wood as if his palm had a sixth sense.

"I always liked watching you during this part." Kara leaned on a stool next to Dad.

"I didn't even hear you come in."

"I know. You get in this zone of yours. That's why I liked watching you, completely absorbed in it. I could always tell you liked your job."

"The minute you don't see your job as a job is the minute it becomes enjoyable."

She smiled. He had never complained, as far as she knew, about his job. He had chosen it, not the other way around. No matter how tough times may have been or how great, he had never worn the work to the dinner table. Even if Mom sometimes did.

"Is that how you feel about photography?"

"What?"

"Photography?" He stopped sanding. "Taking pictures." He traded the sandpaper for a towel and wiped his dusty hands in it. "When you're out there with the elephants or birds or whatever it is."

Kara rolled her eyes. Dad knew every published project of hers. "Why do you like playing dumb like that?"

He shooed the comment away. "Does it feel like a job?"

"Sometimes no. Sometimes yes. I guess it depends on the day. On the assignment."

"With this new job—"

"I don't have it yet."

"Okay, well, if you do get it, would it be the kind of assignments that make it feel like it's not a job? Sometimes you have to ask yourself if the work excites you or if the idea of the work excites you."

She folded her arms and stared at the dust-covered floor. Her shuffling foot made a path through the shavings.

"It's a great opportunity."

"Are you sure I'm the one playing dumb?" His cell phone buzzed, and he checked the screen. "I gotta take this. You be safe, you hear?"

Kara obliged with a big hug. "Bye Dad."

"Don't wait another ten years to come back."

"I won't."

She inhaled the aroma of his hard work one last time before heading to the car.

"Better get going," Sheila said.

"I'm coming." Kara sat in the ancient SUV and buckled up. Mom headed east, through downtown Waverly Lake. Sunday mornings were quiet, but today eerily so. The flags fluttered along

Dowager, no tourists or locals milling about. Perhaps it was the best way to leave town, slipping out in the stillness.

"You know, there's something I never told you," Mom said.

"Oh?" Kara was thankful for the distraction. "Should I be scared?"

"It depends."

"Depends on what?"

"If you've truly moved on from ten years ago."

Kara sighed. She had moved on from ten years ago. Danny was forgiven, and they had mended their relationship. Maybe a little too tightly. She had braved the seat at Dye Happy Salon and showed her face to the whole town at movie night. It wasn't the town's fault for her feeling the way she had about Waverly Lake the past ten years. She had feared failure and feared confronting the pieces of her she had left behind. "You can tell me, Mom."

"You probably know about Danny's mother Beverly? How she told him not to take you to prom?"

"Yes. I mean, I didn't know then, but Danny told me recently."

She nodded. "Well, he may not know the truth himself."

"What do you mean? What truth?"

"The reason *why* she did that."

Kara shook her head. "Mom, you didn't tell her to do it, did you?"

"What? No. Nothing like that. But I do feel I had something to do with it."

Kara waited for an explanation. Mom took her time composing herself, equal parts staring at the road and staring off into nowhere.

"You see, your father and I, and Mrs. Bennett—Beverly—went to school together."

"Yeah, back when Waverly Lake High School and Middle were in the same building."

"You also know I didn't grow up here. Grandma and Grandpa Alcott moved us when I was sixteen, so I was the new girl at school." She merged onto the highway, northeast to Asheville Regional Airport.

"The thing is, your father and Beverly were dating when I had arrived."

"What? Mrs. Bennett and Dad?"

"I'm not making this up."

"What happened?"

"Apparently, they were not in a good place by the time I showed up. Your father was one of the few friends I had made. We spent more and more time together. Eventually, things fizzled with Beverly, and Richard and I started dating."

"Are you telling me you broke up Mrs. Bennett and Dad?"

"Maybe. Maybe not. What I am saying is that Mrs. Bennett had seen it that way, and she kept a grudge for many years. Then you and Danny came along, and I guess she saw the perfect opportunity."

"You think she did it to get back at you?"

"I'm sorry you were in the middle of it. I had never said anything because I couldn't look you in the eyes and tell you then. You were so heartbroken and hurt. I didn't want to admit I was the cause of it."

"Oh Mom." Kara grabbed Mom's hand, grasping it in hers. "It's okay. It wasn't your fault. It wasn't Danny's fault either. He was young—we both were. There were pressures on all sides, whether this whole thing with you and Mrs. Bennett existed or not. And I could've been a better person about it too." She squeezed Mom's hand.

Mom smiled, eyes watering. "I know you and your father are very close, and I'd never get in the way of that. But good night if I'm not jealous sometimes."

"Mom." Now the tears were welling in Kara's eyes. There had been something holding her back from connecting with Mom. She had never been able to define what it was. Maybe it was this guilt Mom had felt for so many years. Whatever it was, for the moment it had vanished.

"I'm sorry, Mom. For being away so long, and not being a good daughter."

"Oh honey."

"I know my actions—or inactions—hurt you. I'm really sorry. I know words may not mean much at this point, but I'm going to be better about it from now on."

Mom squeezed her hand one last time before taking the wheel again. They sat without talking the rest of the ride, the radio playing the greatest hits of yesterday, each song transporting Kara back to another childhood memory. Her soul was at ease. It was unfortunate that such a moment happened on her way out of Waverly Lake, but she was grateful it happened nonetheless.

At the sight of the airport in Asheville, the unease returned.

Chapter Thirty-Eight

MONDAY, AUGUST 24

"Kara!" A black sedan pulled up to the entrance of Salisbury Hotel. Marcus waved his hand out the rear window. "Hold on." He got out and kissed her cheek. "Good to see you back."

The car horn honked. Marcus turned around. "Hold your horses! Didn't you miss it here?" He winked and held the door as she got inside.

Kissing Marcus felt almost foreign. Did he sense she had kissed someone else? No. Impossible. It wasn't like she had initiated the kiss anyway. Not that she hadn't kissed back at all...

"Kara, where's your mind wondering?"

"What?"

Marcus held her hand in the back seat and stared at her, eyes seeing too deep into her.

"Sorry. I'm a little jet-lagged, that's all, and I didn't sleep a whole lot last night."

Marcus smiled and kissed her hand. "Well, you look great, and you're going to be great. Nothing to be nervous about."

"Good. That's the kind of confidence they'll like to see."

Marcus meant well, but his words felt a little patronizing. She knew one of the interviewers, Ben Martinez, from her grad school days at NYU. And it wasn't like she hadn't completed interviews before.

The car made its way on West 57th Street and turned onto Seventh Avenue. The rough stopping and quick accelerating added to Kara's lingering nausea. She looked out the window to the horizon, or what she could see of it between the buildings. For such a big city, New York felt so closed off, especially during Monday morning traffic.

The journey was more than walkable, but Marcus had insisted on the ride. It was the least she could allow for not staying at his place—their place—last night. With her share of the regatta winnings, she had afforded a hotel nearby. It took some convincing to appease Marcus's worry. She had told him she wanted to spend the night alone, with her thoughts, to prepare for the interview. In reality, she tossed in bed, forcing the thoughts of Danny out of her head. *Being with you would be enough.*

Her guilt mounted from never telling Hannah goodbye to not being fully available to Marcus. It was time she put her focus on him. Hence, the car ride.

Which made it more frustrating that Marcus worked on his phone until they reached the office building of *PhotoStyle Magazine*. They needed to get back on track. Once they were on the same page, things would go back to normal.

He opened the door for Kara and walked with her inside. "The driver will go around to the parking garage. I'll wait here in the lobby for you. When you're done, we can go back to my place and celebrate. Champagne on me."

"I don't have the job yet."

He winked. "I have a good feeling about this."

"Miss Carter?" The desk attendant held a hand over the phone receiver. "You may go up now. Fourteenth floor."

"Thank you."

"Good luck."

She turned her head to give him her cheek, but no kiss. He had already spun around, typing on his phone.

Kara inhaled deeply and exhaled slowly to the elevator. The ding and flash of the light pumped her adrenaline as she got in with the awaiting crowd and headed up. It stopped at nearly every level before it reached the fourteenth floor. A small lobby greeted her, with a desk flanked by four chairs, two on each side.

"Well, if it isn't Kara Carter." A short woman with curly hair stared at her with a big grin.

"Suzie? Oh, my goodness. I didn't know—"

"I know. Didn't know I worked here, huh? That's because you never called. Well, to be fair, I never called you either, but I had to sort out a new job, company phone, blah blah blah. Come here."

Kara walked around the desk and hugged her former coworker.

"I'm glad you were able to find a position quickly after *International Ecologic*. Anyone would be lucky to have you."

"Thank you for that. Yes, I'm glad too, and right back at you. Ben and Ethan would be lucky to have you as a principal photographer. Anyway, they're on a conference call at the moment and should be done any minute. Go ahead and make yourself comfortable."

"Thanks." Kara took a seat, and Suzie came around the front of the desk, leaning on it and folding her arms.

"I have to ask...are you still with Marcus?"

It was a simple question with what should've been a simple answer. "Yes. We—well, I—took some time away. But I'm back now, and we are working things out." The inner knot tightened.

"I wondered." Suzie shook her head. "After what he did to you, it takes a lot of love to accept that."

"It's in the past. I'm sure he knows by now if he has big news like that to tell me up-front."

"You guys are too absorbed in each other's cute faces to discuss the bad stuff, aren't you?"

She sat on the chair next to Kara, on the edge of the seat. "To think he was head of the committee to decide who to lay off. If I had a fiancé who did that, he'd have to pamper me for the next year or two to make up for it."

Kara's throat tightened.

The phone at the desk rang, and Suzie answered it. "They're ready for you."

It couldn't be true. Surely, he would've told her that by now? But...he had been acting weird on the phone. As if he had something important to tell her. Their foundation had been weakened, but now she felt it crumbling to dust.

She had to throw it all at the back of her thoughts, because she was walking into the meeting dreams were made of, one she couldn't have even imagined when she first picked up a camera.

"Miss Carter, so nice to see you again." Other than the deeper tan, Ben looked as she remembered from grad school. He stood in a slate suit, jacket folded over the back of his chair. He shook her hand. "This is my colleague, Ethan Odell."

"Nice to meet you, Miss Carter." Ethan stood two or three inches taller. He wore glasses and tucked his hands into his pockets.

"Please...Kara. And likewise."

"What has it been—four, five years?" Ben sat and gestured for her to do the same.

"Something like that." Her brain refused to remember. She was grateful it managed to sit her down without error.

"We're going to make this short and sweet. We know the kind of work you did at *International Ecologic*. Now it's a bit out of scope for what we do here at *PhotoStyle*, but we think you're quite capable to adjust. You'll have the freedom to really explore photography as an art."

Ethan tilted his head. "What would you say photography is to you, as an artist?"

Kara's tongue sat still in her parched mouth. "Do you mind?" She sipped from a bottle of water on the coffee table between them, hoping for an answer to arrive. *Photography. Pictures. Art.* Her heart thumped. This was an easy question, not a trick question.

"You know what, how about you show us what you've been up to," Ben said. "What latest gems do you have for us?"

Kara nodded. "I have some on my laptop, if that's okay."

"Sure."

She started the slideshow. The green succulent punctured the skyline of Waverly Lake with its needles. She had positioned it with the water behind so that it looked as if it organically grew out of the water.

"Interesting," Ethan said, head tilted in examination.

The presentation flipped to the next photo. It focused on a wispy cloud. *Banana cloud*.

Kara gasped, startled. "I'm sorry. That wasn't supposed to be a part of the presentation." That belonged to Hannah. She must've forgotten to preview the selected photos. She clicked to skip to the next.

The presentation carried on. She closed her eyes, seeing the moment Hannah had first touched the camera. On the shore of the lake. Behind Danny's house. Making *ice pictures*.

The memory was warmth, comfort.

It was home.

She bit her lip, willing the tears to stay in her eyes and not escape. What was she doing here?

What I can give you is all of me. Danny's smile. Hannah's squeal on *Kare Bear*. That kiss. It all rushed through her mind, playing like a series of slides in a presentation of the past weeks away —moments she wanted to freeze and make more of.

"Kara?"

She cleared her throat. "Yeah?"

Ben stared at Ethan, then back to Kara. "What we really want to know is, are you willing to give yourself fully to this job?"

I think you already know how you feel. She was ready to give herself fully, but not to this. Fame and prestige didn't compare to family, friends, and making a difference in people's lives.

She folded the laptop closed. "I'm sorry, Ben. Ethan. I am very appreciative for the opportunity, but I don't think *PhotoStyle* and I are the right fit." She stood, laptop in hand. "I think I knew before coming here all along, but part of me thought I was supposed to be here."

Ben nodded and stood up. "Um, okay then. Can't say this was expected, but I appreciate your honesty. It takes some guts to be upfront about it."

Ethan shook her hand. "Sometimes the pursuit of a dream ends up being better than the dream."

Kara smiled. "I think I know what you mean."

She turned to the door, and Ben stopped her. "Let us know if we could help in any way with other positions here in New York."

"I appreciate your offer. But I think my reputation will be enough where I'm going." She walked out into the lobby.

Had she left anything in there? Because her step definitely felt lighter.

"How'd it go?" Suzie stood, shoulders tense.

"It's a no." She stuffed her laptop in the shoulder bag. "From me."

"What? Why? Do you have an offer from someone else?"

Kara laughed, and Suzie stared, perplexed. "Yes. As a matter of fact, I think I do."

"Well, that's great. Will I be seeing you around?"

"I'll give you a call and catch you up. I promise. But I have to go. There's something else I need to take care of."

Suzie hugged her. "You'd better call."

Kara exited to the elevators. The ride down the fourteen floors wasn't long enough to process the last five minutes, or days, or the past month. But she knew what she had to do—what she *wanted* to do. She hadn't felt that in forever.

The doors opened, and Marcus stood in the lobby, buttoning his suit jacket. "That was quick. Must've been an easy choice."

Her smile faded as she looked him in the eyes. "What are you doing here, Marcus?"

"What do you mean?"

"Why did you try so hard to get me this interview?"

"I wanted to help you. You're my fiancée, and I—"

"If you wanted to help me, you wouldn't have had me fired a month ago."

"What are you talking about?" His stare wavered from her face to the door and back.

"You were responsible for it, weren't you? You put my name on the list."

"Kara, it was my job. I had to come up with six names, and trust me, I tried as hard as I could. I couldn't just keep you on there because you're my girlfriend."

"If that's the truth, you should've told me about it. We could've discussed it, prepared me for what was going to happen, and I could've planned for my future. One that, I thought, included you. Instead, you kept it from me. I had to find out from Suzie just before walking into that interview you arranged out of your heaping guilt."

"I did it for you, Kara. I tried to tell you the truth many times this past month over the phone but—"

"You did all of this for yourself. To make you feel better about what you did to me. But it doesn't matter. None of that matters."

Marcus sighed, a smile returning to his face.

"Why are you with me, Marcus?"

The smile washed away as quickly as it had appeared. "What is this?"

"Here's what I think. I think you want someone exactly like you. Someone who is looking for notoriety, to rise to the top with you. Someone who loves structure and schedules and routine as much as you do. At one point in my life, I thought that's what I wanted. But I know for certain that isn't me. It doesn't mean you're a terrible person. It means we are different."

"What are you saying, Kara?" He held her arms, trying to read the answer in her eyes.

"What we have—had—is not enough for me. And honestly, it shouldn't be enough for you either." She slipped the ring off her finger and placed it in his hand. "I'll make sure to get my things out as soon as possible."

"Kara, don't—"

"Goodbye Marcus."

She held onto the straps of her purse and laptop bag over her shoulder and walked out of the building. For a second, she was right back where she was a month ago, on the sidewalk of a busy Manhattan street, the noise of the traffic drowning her emotions. She was jobless and homeless and newly single.

But it wasn't the same as a month ago. She had a plan for a job, a home, and a relationship. For the first time all day, the lingering nausea disappeared.

Chapter Thirty-Nine

Once again, and only two days after leaving, Kara found herself at Bingham Station, waiting for Sheila Carter to pick her up. She could've flown but she wanted to take the bus. It gave her time to think over the details of her plan. This time, she savored the journey.

It had been all wrong with Marcus. It took two years to see that now. It was a courtship of convenience. They both were focused on career. Success. Status. They didn't have to make it work for the longest time. Kara had thought no work meant it was perfect. But now she saw it wasn't so. They had never discussed marriage beyond the wedding or kids or even the next step or next week. Before the layoff they had never really fought. Never argued over an issue. It was because there was no passion in the relationship. They just existed, together. Danny had been right.

The familiar rusty SUV pulled up, and Kara hopped in. Mom gave her the sad eyes.

"It's okay."

"Come here." She stretched her arms over the console and embraced Kara, squeezing her tight and holding her there.

"Really, Mom. I told you I'm not upset."

"You sure?"

"I'm sure. It wasn't right, taking that job. And Marcus and I..."

Mom nodded and put the car in drive. "You know, I didn't want to say anything."

"About?"

"About you and Marcus."

"You only met him once."

"Exactly. I barely knew his name. When he came to visit, I felt like I was talking to a work colleague. Not someone you were going to spend the rest of your life with."

"I get it."

"You hardly ever talked about him, and when you did, you were about as joyful as Eeyore in the rain."

Kara chuckled. "Okay, okay. You're not the first one to tell me, but definitely the most creative in execution."

"I happen to know you better than you think. I have seen that joy in you. With someone else."

Kara closed her eyes. She was tired yet free from a weight she hadn't realized was on her shoulders the last month. But she had screwed it up with Danny. It was wrong how she had treated him, to walk away like she did. If anyone knew how painful it was to the other person, it was Kara. But she had done it anyway, because it was easier on her. Which was probably why Maggie had done the same.

"I messed things up."

"People make mistakes all the time. It's whether or not you correct them that defines the kind of person you are."

She would have to face him. She knew that coming back to Waverly Lake. It wasn't a place to go to avoid problems. It was a place to confront them. But she had other items to tackle first.

They passed Pearson's Wharf and approached the square. Kara tapped Sheila's arm.

"Can you stop here? There's a parking spot right there." She pointed to the empty spot in front of Portside Portrait.

"What is it?"

"There's something I need to do. Did you want to come?"

"You go ahead. I'll call your father and let him know we aren't coming back straight away."

"Okay."

"Oh, Kara?"

"Yeah, Mom?"

"I know it may not be the outcome you foresaw, but I'm glad you're back."

Kara broke a smile. "Honestly, I am too."

She entered Portside Portrait. The paper on the front desk showed her on the second-place podium, next to Danny and Hannah, who actually smiled for the photo.

"Kara? Hello." Mr. Lawson approached the front desk. "I thought you had left town."

"I did." Faster than the speed of light, word traveled. "But I'm back now."

"For good?"

"Maybe. With your help."

"My help? What can I do?"

"You asked me to think about anyone I knew suitable to take over the business after you retire. I'm here to say I've thought about it, and I have found the perfect person."

"Is that so?"

"Yep. Me."

"You're kidding."

"No, I mean it. I'd like to keep this place going."

"Are you sure about this? I kept out hope you would come around, but the missus wasn't so sure."

"You know, I was away in New York, sitting in front of what I thought I wanted. And what I actually wanted was what you had said."

"What I said?"

"Capturing memories. You spoke about how the work here is treasured by everyone who has been a part of it. I want that."

"Stop now. You're about to make this old man cry. I've been

wanting someone to connect with this place and what we do. You get it."

His sincerity choked her up a little too. "Now, I want to be clear. I can't afford to outright buy the business from you straight away—"

"Oh, no, no. I think we can come up with an arrangement in terms of payment. Maybe have a grace period where I hang around for a while and teach you all the workings until you get a handle on it."

"That would be perfect." Cost was the biggest logistical hurdle of her plan, and whether or not she had the knowledge to own a business came in a close second. Of course, she had worked there before, but helping out as a teenager was much different than learning to run the place.

"I'll set a meeting with Steve Albertson, and we can work out the details from there."

"Sounds great. But isn't he a divorce lawyer?"

"If you're a lawyer in Waverly Lake, there is no specializing."

She laughed. There were countless moving parts to the plan, it was overwhelming. And thrilling.

"There's something else I want to discuss with you. Something I think would interest new people in the business and give back to the community."

"Already thinking ahead, huh?" He grinned. "I'd love to hear it. Sounds like we have a lot to discuss then. Why don't you leave me your number and I'll be in touch?"

She wrote down her information and walked out of Portside Portrait the near future owner. It was the first box to check off on her list. Job, check.

She suspected the second one wouldn't be so easy.

Chapter Forty

"NO YOU DIDN'T. YOU KISSED? WHAT WAS IT LIKE? WHAT happened?" Tracy stood in Danny's kitchen. Hannah sat at the table, eating a granola bar and sipping milk. Danny scrubbed the same pot he had been diligently washing the past three minutes.

"I really don't want to talk about it in front of Hannah. This affects her too."

"What affects her? The relationship? You kissing Kara?"

"Tracy, keep it down." He rinsed the pot.

"Just tell me." She approached closer. "And I'll get out of your hair. Unless you want me to ask Sebastian and George."

"You must've already heard about it from them if you know they were there to see it."

"True. They said she definitely kissed you back. Which is something, right?"

"It's nothing, because I told her my true feelings and she rejected me."

"Have you tried—?"

"Look, I've gone over there. She doesn't want to see me—or didn't want to see me. She's gone already. Went back to New York."

"What? You're that bad of a kisser?"

Tracy half-angered and, admittedly, half-amused him. "She had a job interview and took off. She left Sunday."

"What's today? Have I really been gone that long? How did we not talk about this sooner?"

He nudged her in the shoulder.

"For one, it's Thursday. Two, you're always somewhere else. And three, I'm glad we didn't and wished we wouldn't anymore."

Tracy looked at Hannah and back to Danny. "I'm sorry. Seriously now. I really thought you guys had something."

"Me too."

"You really seemed head over heels. And she was fabulous with Hannah. I honestly thought—"

"I know." He put his hand up to stop the words. He was head over heels. Still was. Which was why it hurt so badly. It was fresh. She had come into his life almost instantaneously, a force he couldn't stop. He fell for her all over again, despite the ten years apart. If anything, he loved her more than he ever had. But she left without saying goodbye to him or Hannah, as if the last month meant absolutely nothing to her.

It was bad enough for him. "No matter how she feels about me, it wasn't right to do that to Hannah."

Tracy shook her head. "I don't know what to say." She squeezed his hand, wrinkled from the soapy dishwater.

"I'm just glad you're here. I feel more comfortable with her being around family right now."

"Of course." She sat down next to Hannah at the table. "Her favorite aunt is always here for her."

"I appreciate the sentiment. But you're not *always* going to be here, are you?"

"Hey now."

"I'm just kidding. But not really."

Tracy scrunched her face in a snooty expression. "As a matter of fact, Aunt Dorothy has invited me to help her out at the cabin."

"I'm sure she could use the help, especially moving into fall." Great Aunt Dorothy was pushing ninety. The mountain retreat on the north side of the lake was a popular destination, especially for hikers in passing via the Appalachian Trail. "I'm not sure how much sarcasm and shenanigans she could use though."

"I will ignore your last words."

Tracy's strengths of being adventurous and energetic didn't exactly play out to be the best qualities in someone who dealt with listening to customers and tending to their needs.

"When do you go?"

"End of the month. Before the foliage seekers arrive."

That gave him around three weeks to stop sulking over Kara and stop relying on Tracy's company in the house. Even with all her craziness, and lack of monetary contributions, it was nice having her around. When she did show up.

She was true family. After giving Mom and Dad a piece of his mind, they had backed off on their visits. They had been more like check-ups on him and Hannah anyway. He couldn't even remember the last time they just talked about their days, their lives —trivial things. It was always about his life choices and what Hannah should or should not be doing.

"I want to do my puzzle."

"I have to go to work, honey. Tracy will help you with the puzzle." He nodded to Tracy, who stood up.

"Of course I will. Come on, let's go out back." She touched Hannah's shoulder.

Hannah shrugged her off. "I want Kara to help."

"I'm perfectly capable of doing the puzzle too."

"I want Kara."

Danny turned away. He had let Hannah down, trusting Kara.

Tracy managed to convince Hannah to move to the back porch. Danny sat at the kitchen table, listening in on the conversation.

"How many times have you done this one?" Tracy said.

"Only three times, but I'm getting faster. Kara got it for me. She helped me one time, and it was super-fast."

"That was nice of her to help." Danny caught the pity in Tracy's eyes all the way from the kitchen.

"Can Kara help?"

The moment of silence from Tracy tugged at Danny's heart. Poor Hannah had been through a lot, and she was only seven. It had been tough when her mother abandoned them, but Hannah was so young she didn't remember. What Kara had done was almost worse. She had gotten to know the both of them, more deeply than anyone, in such a short period of time. They let her in, even Hannah. He had fallen in love with her, only to be abandoned yet again.

"Not this time, I'm afraid."

"I want Kara."

"You know, how about you let me show you how good I can be at this."

"I want Kara, I want Kara." She pointed at the screen door.

"What?"

Danny stood up and looked out the window over the sink. No one was in sight. She must've been pointing next door.

"Kara!" Hannah stood up.

"Hannah, what are you talking about?" Danny walked to the back porch. Hannah pointed to the screen door again.

On the other side stood Kara Carter.

Chapter Forty-One

SHE HAD BEEN STANDING AT THE DOOR FOR FIVE
minutes, nervously tracing the edges of the frame in her hand with
her thumb. Eventually, she was going to knock. That was what she
told herself anyway. It was on her to make things right. The last few
days back in Waverly Lake had been busy ones, making sure her idea
could work, then actually putting it into action. All while avoiding
Danny Bennett, which was hard to do, being his neighbor. Plus,
Hannah spent a lot of her time on the back porch, making it doubly
hard to not be seen.

But now he stood on the other side of the screen door. A
window of see-through mesh separating, keeping her sheltered from
dealing with her actions. It was time to see just how deeply she
screwed up.

"Hi Danny."

"What are you doing here?"

Tracy stood behind him. "Hey Hannah, there was something
upstairs I wanted to show you."

"I want to do the puzzle."

Danny turned around. "No, you guys stay. Kara is the one who
should go."

Tracy crept into the kitchen with the puzzle, enticing Hannah to follow. Danny held his ground.

"I came back."

"I can see that."

"I know what I did was wrong."

"You mean what you didn't do. You didn't talk to me. You didn't say goodbye to me. Or Hannah."

"I know, and I'm sorry."

"So I'm just supposed to say okay and go back to the way things were."

"No. I don't want things the way they were."

"Geez, Kara. Could you be more hurtful?"

"I don't mean that like it sounded. Can you please come out and talk? I'll try to be brief."

"No. I'm not just going to leave Hannah."

Tracy poked her head out of the kitchen. "I thought I was watching her while you went to work."

Danny shot her a look and slowly turned back around. "Thank you for that reminder, Tracy."

"Anytime."

"As Tracy said, I have to go to work."

"Danny, please. I know I don't deserve your trust or your time right now. But please. Just this one thing. Then I'll leave you alone if that's what you want."

Danny ran his hand through is hair. "Fine. Let me tell Tr—"

"We'll be fine!" she yelled somewhere from inside the house.

Danny followed Kara down to the shore, his face unreadable. Did he feel nothing for her anymore? It was worse than being upset with her.

"So? What is it?"

"I wanted you to have this. You and Hannah." She handed him the framed photo. "It was a picture she took on her first day with the camera. She called it a banana cloud."

He chuckled. "Does kind of look like a banana." The smile was encouraging, until it weakened. "Why are you giving me this?"

"It's funny, because I went to New York and sat in that interview. They asked a simple question about what photography is to me. I—I couldn't answer. It's like my mouth dried up, my words scattered to the corners of my brain. And then I showed them my work, but this photo—"

She took it back, examining the white nothings in the sky for the millionth time. "This photo brought me back here. It made me think of Hannah, and how introducing her to a camera changed her. It opened her up to me. It made me realize that big city life, a high-profile magazine gig, wasn't what I wanted. I wanted more of this."

She shrugged. "This is where I'm supposed to be."

"Well, I'm happy for you and your new enlightenment. I just think it's best for everyone if you keep me and Hannah out of whatever it is you're doing next."

Rejection had been a possibility. She had known that coming into this. That didn't mean it hurt any less. "I understand if you feel that way. You have every right to. But I can't keep you out of it."

"Kara—"

"Please listen. That night and the way I acted...I left the way I did because I felt the same way for you as you did me. I didn't want to admit it or face it. I thought it was the wrong path for me because that's not what I had set out for myself. But I was wrong. Wrong about Marcus, the job, where I wanted to be. Everything."

Danny lowered his head, staring at his feet.

"I know I hurt you, and you may not want me in your life, and I get that. If I have to continue on without you, I guess I'll have to face that pain."

He looked up, eyes piercing her core. "How do you feel now?"

"What do you mean?"

"You said you *felt* the same way I did. How do you feel right now?"

Was he really doing this to her? Was he really going to make her say it? As hard as it was to put herself out there, it was time. Time for her to let it out, put it out to the world no matter the consequence.

"I feel like we've known each other for a long time. But the funny thing is, we've been apart longer than we've been in each other's lives. I came back here thinking I would avoid my past. But there you were. Right next door. Looking better than I remembered." She shook her head, fighting the flood of emotions trying to spew out. But it was time to free them.

"And you turned out to be this amazing person. This amazing man with a big heart. A great father to Hannah. A great brother to Tracy. You're so sweet to my parents. You have a life filled with love. I came back with my anger and hurt, and all you did was work at mending my brokenness no matter how hard I resisted."

He took two steps closer. "But how do you feel?"

"I didn't feel like I deserved what you were giving. I was a returning failure. In my head, I didn't allow myself to feel anything."

He stepped closer, close enough for her to reach out and touch him, but she didn't.

"Kara."

Her lips quivered, tears clouding her vision. He touched her chin, lifting it gently until her eyes met his. "How do you feel?"

Tears rolled down her cheeks. "I love you. I love you as much as I can love someone. More than I ever thought I could. I'm sorry I screwed everything up."

He stroked her cheek with the back of his hand.

Kara was broken, muscles wilted and heart stopped. The tears flowed freely, no holding back. "But you were wrong about one thing." She blinked enough to be able to focus on his eyes. "You are enough."

His lips met hers, the wet of the honest tears mixing with the touch of his hands, caressing her face and gently pulling her hair back. No hesitation or assessing what she wanted this time. She kissed him back, clinging to his arms, his shoulders, closing the gap between them, making it their space. She was melting into the ground, nearly dropping the photo, but his strong arms and embrace held her up.

He pulled away, and she reluctantly let him. Her eyes focused, and he grew a smile. It was contagious.

"You forgive me?"

"That depends. You're staying here for good? In Waverly Lake?"

"Yes. For good."

"Am I cradling the newest full-time Carter Furniture delivery driver?"

"No." She chuckled and blotted the tears with the back of her hand.

"Because if that's what you want to do, I'm all for it."

He was too sweet for his own good. "I'm actually working things out with Mr. Lawson. I'm going to take over the studio. I wanted to run by an idea with you—I mean, I had planned on running it by if this conversation went well."

"What is it?"

"It goes back to this photograph again. And here, be sure to give it to Hannah."

"Why don't you give it to her yourself?"

"Really?"

"Really." He put his arm over her shoulder, and they headed toward the house.

She walked with him, the relief immeasurable. She heard a chair scrape across the floor and whispering as they approached the porch. Danny swung the door open for her.

"Oh, how'd it go?" Tracy put the upside-down book on her lap.

Kara caught his gray-blue eyes, lakes she could get lost in if she looked too long.

"We're...okay," Danny said.

"Really?" Tracy stood.

"Really." Danny squeezed Kara's shoulder tighter. "Where's Hannah?"

"Grabbing another fruit snack in the—"

"Kara!" Hannah shook her hands up and down in excitement.

"Kara has something for you." Danny urged her forward.

"Another puzzle?" Hannah sat down by the coffee table, at the ready.

"First, actually, I have something to say." Kara sat on the floor, crossing her legs. Hannah pushed edge pieces into a separate pile on the table. "I left the other morning without saying goodbye. I could say I didn't know how to tell you goodbye or that I was scared. But it doesn't matter. It was wrong of me, and I am so sorry. I hope you can forgive me."

Hannah dropped her hands from the table and looked at Kara.

"Is it okay if I give you a hug?"

Hannah sat in silence. What was she thinking? Had Kara damaged their relationship beyond repair?

Hannah unfolded her legs and stood up. She stuck her right arm out, her hand in front of Kara's face.

Kara accepted the handshake, as Danny and Tracy chuckled warmly in the background.

She placed the photo on the coffee table. "I thought this would look good in this room, but you can put it wherever you like."

Hannah touched the glass, tracing the banana cloud with her fingers and humming a tune to herself. "Can I do it again?"

Kara nodded. "Take more pictures? Of course." She stood and backed up a step, addressing Danny. "That brings me to my idea."

"Oh, right. What did you have in mind?"

To her right, Tracy was enraptured with the whole scene, her head on her hands as if she were listening to the juiciest town gossip.

Kara focused on Danny. "I'd like to introduce more children to photography. More neurodiverse children like Hannah. Mr. Lawson said I could start a class at the studio on a trial basis. What do you think?"

He shoved his hands in his pockets. "I think I love that idea."

"Really? Do you think there will be enough interest?"

"Sure. I can ask the local ASD network."

"What? You mean you joined a group?"

"You weren't the only one who made some changes the past few days."

"It took some prodding," Tracy said. Danny rolled his eyes.

"That would be great." Kara wanted to clap and squeal. It was happening fast, but it was beyond exciting. She had a career, a good cause to work toward, and now she had the man of her dreams.

Danny grabbed his orange toolbox and truck keys. "I hate to cut this short, but I do have to head to work."

"I understand."

"Do you mind coming with me?"

"No, I don't mind. I can ride my bike back from Pearson's."

"Great."

"Why do you ask?"

"Can't I want a few minutes more with you?"

"Get out of here, you two." Tracy waved them off.

Danny hoisted Kara's bike in the truck, and they headed east on Dowager Street. Downtown was alive again, not like the morning she had left, with midday strollers and shoppers dotting the square.

"So your dad sold *Kare Bear*? How do you feel about that?"

She sighed. It shouldn't have been surprising. That was the whole reason for racing the regatta. "Honestly, when he told me, I nearly cried."

Danny patted her knee.

"I know he wanted to start a new venture with his business, but still. There was sentimental value to it, you know?"

"I can see that."

They parked and got out. Kara stood by the truck, and Danny made for the wharf.

"Come see me off," he said.

Kara followed, and he held her hand, guiding her past the boathouse and through the boat slips. They stopped at the familiar sloop. *Kare Bear*.

"What's this? The buyer was local?"

"More than you know." He squeezed her hand and shot her that sly grin.

"You bought her?"

"Something about there being sentimental value."

She practically pounced on him, squeezing him in a tight hug.

He pulled away. "That, and Hannah practically begged me to buy it. It's hard to say no to that face."

She laughed. "You mean we could've skipped the race altogether?"

"That's one way to look at it." He chuckled. "But no. I wouldn't have fallen in love with her if we hadn't spent all that time."

He pulled her close and kissed her again, with a stronger press of his mouth, the intensity sending her heart swimming, before following it with a second gentler touch of his lips.

"Like I have fallen in love with you."

Epilogue

"I can't thank you enough, Liz." Kara stood in the back of Portside Portrait, having raced inside to hear Liz better on the cell phone. The open back door provided ample April light and a constant breeze that demanded she put paperweights in the form of coffee mugs and whatever other objects she scrambled to find on the mounting forms and paperwork. Mr. Lawson kept meticulous files, but unfortunately, they existed outside the digital age.

"The computers arrived this morning. It'll be great experience for them to work on digital processing."

"As I said when you first reached out, I am happy to help out with what I can. I may be out here in San Jose, but Waverly Lake will always be home."

Kara got it. If anyone would've asked her this time last year, she would've scoffed at the thought. But after coming back, she understood the meaning of home.

"Have you visited Grandpappy lately?"

"At least once a week." For the first month or two after Kara released Hannah's photos for a cover piece in the paper about the class, Mr. Bingham had been somewhat of a local celebrity, and he ate up every minute of it. "I refuse to get gas anywhere but Bingham Station."

Liz laughed. "I'm sure he appreciates that. I do too. Well, you take care, and let me know if you have any other needs I can help with."

"Thanks again, Liz. You take care too." There were numerous steps she had taken since August. Reconnecting with her best friend from high school was one of the most rewarding.

Sebastian barged into the office, his soiled gloves dropping bits of dirt in the entranceway. "Will you tell George over here that it's a photography class, not a quest for the next Ansel Adams?"

She followed him out the back door. Sebastian stopped at the rectangular plot of land beside the third building—half cafeteria, half class space. George kneeled on the ground, clad in knee pads, gloves, and sunhat.

"What's going on, George?" Kara stood, hands on her hips.

George squinted up at her, then at Sebastian. "You had to go to Mommy and tell on me, huh?"

"You're being unreasonable. The kids wanted more flowers to take pictures of, not a recreation of the Hanging Gardens."

"I know what it is. There's nothing wrong with wanting to make it look aesthetically pleasing. Besides, it advertises our business from the lakeside." He looked back at Kara. The short acreage from the studio down to the lake had been her outdoor classroom. The kids loved exploring the grounds, but after all the mountain and lake and grass shots, it was time to give them more options without changing the routine too drastically.

Sebastian scoffed. "It looks like our back garden has attacked her property."

"Okay, okay." Kara held up her hands. "First off, you two are adorable. Secondly, I'm ecstatic you are volunteering your time and expertise. Lastly, I think in terms of efficient use of space, we should stick to simple."

Sebastian widened his glance in a snarky face at George, who shook his head and rolled his eyes.

"Everything okay over here?" Danny placed his hand on her lower back.

She grinned at the sight of him. "What are you doing here?"

"Thought I'd stop by on my way to pick up Hannah from school." It wasn't until Danny connected with other parents like him that he learned Hannah could attend school two days a week. September had been a struggle, but Hannah adjusted in her own time. She had at least connected with another eight-year-old girl and even had her over one weekend.

"Oh hey, how'd it go with your mom last night at the meeting? I didn't get to talk to you about it this morning."

"I didn't want to wake you when I got back either."

Kara didn't want to presume Danny and Hannah were ready for her to move in, so she set up her things with Mom and Dad. It took her and Danny about a week before they realized they couldn't be apart for more than a few hours, even if she was just next door.

"It went well, I think. The fact that Mom agreed to go to any ASD group meeting means she's come a long way in accepting and empathizing."

"Well, I'm proud of you for being persistent with her, and forgiving."

"One step at a time." He checked his watch. "I'd better get going." He gave her a peck on the cheek.

Kara's mouth curled in a grin.

Danny's face mirrored hers. "What?"

"Is that how it is now?"

He chuckled and scooped her up, Kara letting out a surprise shout. He twirled her in a full circle and kissed her for real, a passionate, embracing, swoon-worthy kiss. "Is that better?"

"That's more like it."

"Good. I do have to go."

"I know. Me too. I have that engagement photo shoot at four, then I promised Dad I would finalize the layout of the Carter Furniture catalog."

"You didn't forget about tonight, did you?"

"Of course not. I'd never miss spaghetti and puzzle night."

He winked and walked up the gentle slope to Portside Portrait's back door.

Kara turned back to the lake, the mid-afternoon sun shimmering along the water's surface, reflecting the budding greenery and white and violet spring flowers. She had more responsibility than she had ever had in her life. And she was happy. She couldn't imagine it being in a more beautiful place.

She was truly home.

***

Thank you for reading! Did you enjoy? Please add your review because nothing helps an author more and encourages readers to take a chance on a book than a review.

And don't miss more in the of the Waverly Lake series with book two, TRUELOVE TRAIL, available now. Turn the page for a sneak peek!

Also be sure to sign up for the City Owl Press newsletter to receive notice of all book releases!

Sneak Peek of...

TRUELOVE TRAIL

Monday, October 3

Some would say October was the most beautiful month in Waverly Lake. The westerly breeze off the Appalachian Mountains vanished any remnants of heat the lake held from the summer sun. The aspens and oaks sprinkled their golden and burnt sienna branches in leaf confetti, threatening to cover the roads traversing the miles of coastline and hills in this nook, North Carolina's Hidden Gem of the West.

Tracy Bennett found herself riding along one such road, winding the western edge of the lake and turning east. She, however, had not taken in the breeze, or continuously changing color palette of autumn. She had been lucky enough to stumble out of bed after the late nights of the weekend, taking in every ounce of fun she could have with her visiting Floridian friends before starting her endeavor.

"Do you at least get weekends off?" Sebastian kept one hand on the steering wheel, the other tucking the free locks behind his ear. His side shave of the summer had grown out considerably, yet he refused to cut the longer half of hair to match it.

"It's not exactly a nine-to-five job," Tracy managed through a yawn. "It's an as-needed kind of thing. There will be times I'm busy and times when I can come into town." *The best kind of job.* Working was something Tracy did to get by—to make enough to cover her next adventure. Unlike her parents, she didn't believe everyone had a single purpose in life, nor should they limit themselves to one single goal to achieve.

They remained on the road closest to the lake, at the lowest elevation along the northern banks. It still put them well above lake level, with Sebastian's driving around bends and turns displacing her organs.

She couldn't complain, though. Her lifestyle didn't afford her a car, nor did she want to deal with one and its upkeep.

"Kind of reminds me of our little road trip." Sebastian grinned, keeping his eyes on the road.

"Little? You mean, thousands of miles to California and back?"

"You weren't the best at winding through the Rockies."

Tracy recalled gripping the steering wheel tightly for hours, a rainstorm slicking the pavement and blurring the windshield.

Sebastian turned his gaze to her. "I'm still glad we did it. Even if it meant you didn't get that internship."

Tracy smiled, though the injury of rejection from Biltmore Estate was still tender. Never mind it was four years ago, when she thought she wanted to be an event planner. The four-week, looping trip across the U.S. proved that she was both excellent at planning and not ready to align herself with a stationary career.

"Here we go." The sign to Woodsman's Lodge had simple brown lettering atop a cream background, with a large brown arrow at the bottom. Sebastian turned onto the access road, at spots a steep decline on the eastward side of the property. He did his best to avoid the growing potholes as they passed raised garden beds and a near-empty woodpile before leveling off around the side of the lodge. He parked perpendicular to a handful of parking spots in front of Woodsman's Lodge. "Gosh, it's been years since I've been here. Tell Aunt Dee hello for me."

"I will." Tracy grabbed her backpack and suitcase out of the backseat. She leaned to the front passenger door for a brief smile at Sebastian. "Thanks for the ride."

"Any time. Come visit when you get a break."

"You know it." She closed the door, and Sebastian circled around the lot, leaves rolling in the car's faint smoky exhaust.

Tracy paused a moment, examining the eight wooden stairs leading to the front porch. The lodge, by no means an architectural dream, conjured warm memories for her—of playing, of not caring about the world outside its realm. Its simple two-story structure, with covered front and back porches, four dormer windows along the metal roof, and never-ending cedar walls still looked reminiscent of the homestead that had stood before it nearly a century and a half ago. She only knew that to be true because of the framed picture Aunt Dee kept in her office.

Tracy walked up the stairs, the second step creaking the same as it did years ago, as if it purposely sounded a greeting to guests. The front door swung open before she landed a foot on the porch.

"Tracy!" Aunt Dee opened her arms, ready to catch Tracy's hug.

"Hello, Aunt Dee." She welcomed her great aunt's embrace. At nearly eighty-two, Aunt Dee was the eldest on either side of Tracy's lineage. She had the wrinkles and gray-streaked hair to show for it, but her physical fitness and go-getter attitude defied her age. Perhaps it had something to do with the fresh mountain air and living away from the busyness of the city. Not that Waverly Lake compared to Charlotte, or even Asheville in its population or bustle.

"It's so good to have you here." Aunt Dee examined Tracy's face as if she counted the summer freckles fading with the diminishing daylight hours of fall. "Oh, and that hair." She ran her hand along the brunette curls spiraling around Tracy's face. "I've always been jealous of that head of hair."

Tracy gave up on trying to tame or style her hair long ago. Instead, she let the curls do their own thing, and she took pride in her hair reflecting her life's philosophy. Aunt Dee was one of the few who truly accepted her for it too.

"Come on in, let's get you settled."

Tracy followed Aunt Dee into the lodge and set down her backpack and suitcase on the floor to the right, by the front desk. "It still looks as I remembered it." Tracy smiled, unbuttoning her sweater, the heat of the fireplace on the east wall warming the first floor. Two worn tufted armchairs sat in the front corner by a bookshelf of aged books, while four rectangular tables sat in the back corner near the fire, ready for the afternoon's coffee and tea break. A mural covered the back wall, a depiction of the forest and yellow-brick road from *The Wizard of Oz*, where the Tinman was found. Aunt Dee was short for Dorothy, a name most people associated with the tale. It was how she came up with the name Woodsman's Lodge.

"I hope that doesn't mean it's looking as old as me," Aunt Dee said.

"One can only hope to age like you." Tracy touched Aunt Dee's wrinkled hand on the desk. Her silvered hair was fashioned in a low ponytail, the tail part not quite all the way pulled through the hair tie. While she could probably outrun people twenty years younger, her frame was more skin and bones than the muscular tone it had once been.

"I take it you're still hiking? Is that your secret to looking great?"

"Oh hush. Yes, I get in my early morning walks. I can't say my knees are what they used to be, though."

"No one can say that about their knees." Tracy winked. "So, what all do you have planned for me here, or can we keep chatting and delay all the business stuff? My vote is on delaying."

Aunt Dee pulled out a binder from the bar-height desk.

Tracy laughed to herself. Of course Aunt Dee's vote was business.

"I've got quite a checklist that needs completing," Aunt Dee said. "Now that the summer vacationers are back at home with kids in school, I usually take this time to prepare for the holiday rush. Fall is usually slower around here, except for the hikers, of course."

"They're still passing through here, huh?"

"You know, not as many backpackers as there used to be.

Everyone's into their campers and trailers these days. But we still get a few. Thank goodness for the AT."

The Appalachian Trail sliced right by Waverly Lake, more specifically, Woodsman's Lodge. In fact, a side trail split off it and cut across the road she had taken to the lodge. It continued onward east along the lake. For those hiking through, it was a good stop to have a night's sleep under a roof and replenish supplies in town before either heading north through The Smoky Mountain National Park, or south to the trail's end in Georgia. Most hikers this time of year came from the north, heading south. Tracy had enjoyed frequenting a mile or two of it in her youth, hoping to meet hikers. She had never come across a through-hiker that didn't have an entertaining story.

"I hear you've had your share of wandering the past year."

Tracy nodded. "You know me. Before coming back this summer, I was in Australia for three months."

"Oh my, what were you doing there?"

"Exploring. A few of my girlfriends and I took a road trip for about half that time, checking out all the states."

"And the other half?"

"Working to afford the road trip." She chuckled, and Aunt Dee shook her head. Tracy wasn't sure if Aunt Dee took her seriously or thought it was a joke. But it was the truth.

"Well, you're here now and can earn some money for wherever it is your mind takes you."

"That's the plan." A trip to New Zealand after Thanksgiving, to be exact. With the earnings from Aunt Dee, plus what she had saved from odd jobs this summer, and if she limited her spending over the next few weeks, she'd be able to afford the flight. She had assimilated into a group of four girlfriends who called themselves the Aussie Posse earlier this year. They wanted to reunite for a three-month excursion across New Zealand, made possible by half of them working remotely, and the other half living off the grid entirely.

Aunt Dee reached behind the desk and set down a plastic bag.

"Now, in here is your key. You'll be in room one with its own bathroom."

"Are you sure?" Tracy asked. "I'm okay using the shared bathroom if you have guests that want rooms with private baths."

"I'm sure. I will be having an influx of guests soon, but for the time being you can stay in room one."

Tracy pocketed the key. "Thank you."

"I'm also giving you a cell phone." She pulled it out of the bag. "Your mother said you didn't have one, at least not one with a permanent number."

"For as much as she and I don't get along sometimes, she is right on that account." In her travels, Tracy had the habit of buying a cheap phone and phone card to dispose of after her journey. No sense in keeping a permanent one and paying for a plan—an international one at that.

"I only ask that you please use it for business purposes only. It's my way of getting in touch with you, and vice versa."

Tracy crossed an X over her heart. "I promise. Business only. Besides, I've given the lodge's number to my friends anyway, if they need to get in touch."

Aunt Dee gave her a glare, but accepted the indiscretion for now. "Go ahead and put your bags in your room, and I'll meet you down here to go over these tasks."

"Will do." Tracy grabbed her bags and stopped before heading to the stairs. "You said there will be an influx of visitors soon? Is there something special going on?"

Aunt Dee's eyes lit up as she single-clapped her hands together. "Oh yes. It's something new I've arranged this year, to break up the fall lull we have. I'm calling it Lovetoberfest." She stretched out her hands, as if displaying a banner in mid-air.

Tracy blinked slowly, the smile fading on her face. "Do I even want to ask?"

"It's going to be spectacular. Five men and five women will be staying for a long weekend in the hopes of finding love."

"How do you plan on doing that?" *Stop asking.*

"They will go out on five dates with each other, all here locally. Don't worry, you can help pick out what they'll do if you want. I'd love to have your input, seeing as you have expertise in the planning department."

That's why you don't ask, Tracy. "Oh...okay." It sounded like torture. Five blind dates, all in Waverly Lake? Crammed into a long weekend? Who in their right mind would volunteer to do such a thing? Not only volunteer, but *pay* to be a part of it and stay at the inn.

Aunt Dee's expectation for Tracy's positive reaction waned via raised eyebrows and disappearing glee in her cheeks.

"Hey, if it brings in more people for you in the slower season, I'm happy for you." It came out overly canned. Hopefully, Aunt Dee couldn't read through her as easily as the worn edition of Robert Frost's *Mountain Interval* that no doubt still graced the bookshelf in the corner. "Whatever you think is best for business."

Aunt Dee stood a little straighter. "I do think it'll be good for business. Not just for the lodge. I have potential dates set up with local business owners who jumped at the chance to showcase their business on a date."

Tracy softened her skepticism. Not so much skepticism as it was her own discomfort at the idea. "You're right. I can see how that would be great for Waverly Lake in general. More tourists means more local spending. And I bet they'll be sold on the lodge and come back. Maybe even with their significant other they had met here."

"That would be wonderful, wouldn't it? Someone's love story could originate right here at the lodge. It's all very romantic, isn't it?"

Tracy opted for a smile and nod. How she longed to walk into room one and stay there for the rest of the morning.

The rest of fall.

But Aunt Dee needed her and was paying her, and Tracy needed the money if she ever wanted to get out of Waverly Lake soon.

Out of here and onward, to her next adventure.

Don't stop now. Keep reading with your copy of TRUELOVE TRAIL

Don't miss TRUELOVE TRAIL, book two of the Waverly Lake series, available now, and find more from Mary Shotwell at www.maryshotwell.com

World traveler Tracy Bennett agrees to extend her stay in Waverly Lake beyond summer in the hopes of affording her girlfriends' trip —a three-month excursion in New Zealand! And well, Aunt Dee could use her help at Woodsman's Lodge, packing away summer items and prepping for the winter holiday crowd. So, she's stuck until Thanksgiving.

Meanwhile, Ben Walker is drawn back to Waverly Lake after the death of the custodian to his parents' estate. He plans to work at Aunt Dee's for his stay and is surprised to learn his childhood best friend Tracy is also working at the lodge. Hesitant to tell anyone else in Waverly Lake who he truly is for fear the town will want him to fill his parents' shoes, he gives a false name and pretends not to know Tracy.

While Tracy's questioning of the mysterious Ben escalates, Aunt Dorothy assigns them to her pet project—Lovetoberfest. The October event is set to match guests on three blind dates around town. Tracy and Ben are forced to test run and narrow down five proposed dates to the best three.

As the two reluctantly go on match-making practice full of apple orchards, corn mazes, and acorn painting, Tracy can't help but be attracted to Ben. Their chemistry makes her question not only her trip overseas but her long-term future; yet she can't shake the feeling he's hiding something. Ben's (re)connection with Tracy is undeniable, and while the dates push them closer, he's running out of time to face his tragic past and tell Tracy they're not, in fact, strangers at all.

Please sign up for the City Owl Press newsletter for chances to win special subscriber-only contests and giveaways as well as receiving information on upcoming releases and special excerpts.

All reviews are **welcome** and **appreciated**. Please consider leaving one on your favorite social media and book buying sites.

Escape Your World. Get Lost in Ours! City Owl Press at www. cityowlpress.com.

Acknowledgments

Thank you to the publishing team at City Owl Press for believing in this series, and packaging such a beautiful book, front cover to back. Gratitude to my editor Tee Tate, who understood how this story was near and dear to my heart. To my agent Amy Brewer at Metamorphosis Literary, who always gives great editorial advice and matched me with the perfect home for this sweet series.

Thanks to my family, Matt, Luke, Evan and Avery, for putting up with Mommy's writing and editing at odd hours.

Finally, a special thanks to parents of neurodivergent children. Gretchen and Abbey, you both are wonderful mothers and fierce advocates for your kids. Thank you for sharing your experiences so openly with others. I hope I've done Danny and Hannah's relationship justice.

About the Author

MARY SHOTWELL is the author of small-town love stories with happily-ever-afters for all seasons. Her debut romance novel *Christmas Catch* (Carina Press, 2018) was a Golden Leaf Finalist and earned a starred review from Library Journal. She loves incorporating her science and nature background into her fiction. When adulting, she's a wife to husband Matt and mother to three children. She currently resides in Tennessee.

Visit her website to her blog about writing, travels and publication news.

www.maryshotwell.com

 facebook.com/AuthorMaryShotwell

 twitter.com/MaryEShotwell

instagram.com/authormaryshotwell

About the Publisher

City Owl Press is a cutting edge indie publishing company, bringing the world of romance and speculative fiction to discerning readers.

Escape Your World. Get Lost in Ours!

www.cityowlpress.com

facebook.com/CityOwlPress

twitter.com/cityowlpress

instagram.com/cityowlbooks

pinterest.com/cityowlpress

tiktok.com/@cityowlpress